*Two stubborn hearts—
under one roof.*

"That's it," he said, at length. *"You're leaving this place the same way you came in."*

He ducked, caught her by the legs, and threw her over his shoulder—with the ease of a man who'd tossed many a woman over his shoulder. This was definitely not his first go at lady-tossing.

But it was definitely Izzy's first time being tossed, and she had no idea how to respond. Beat her fists against his back? Kick and scream? Later, she'd think of a dozen things. Witty retorts and clever rejoinders. Right now, all the blood was rushing to her head and her mind was a hot, throbbing blank.

He bounced her weight, plumping her backside with his forearm. "There's so little to you."

The dismissive words jarred her tongue loose.

"You're wrong," she said. "There's a great deal to me, Your Grace. More than you know. More than anyone supposes. You can carry me outside, if you like. I'll come back in. Again and again. As many times as it takes. Because this is my castle now. And I'm not leaving."

By Tessa Dare

Coming Soon

Tessa Dare

Romancing the Duke

❧ Castles Ever After ❧

A V O N

An Imprint of HarperCollinsPublishers

AVON BOOKS
An Imprint of HarperCollins*Publishers*
10 East 53rd Street
New York, New York 10022-5299

First Avon Books mass market printing: February 2014

Avon Trademark Reg. U.S. Pat. Off. and in Other Countries, Marca Registrada, Hecho en U.S.A.
HarperCollins® is a registered trademark of HarperCollins Publishers.

Printed in the U.S.A.

10 9 8 7 6 5 4 3 2 1

For anyone who's ever been a fan, of anything.
And for Tessa Woodward,
who has no bigger fan than yours truly.

Acknowledgments

Many thanks to Katie Dunneback and Rachael Kelly for helping with research on low vision and the adaptation process. Any mistakes I made were mine alone.

I owe an immense debt of gratitude to my family and friends, and to the good people of HarperCollins, for their patience with me while I wrote this book. Bren, Courtney, Carey, Leigh, Laura, Susan, Kara, and everyone on the unnameable loop . . . You've saved me in so many ways. I love you all.

And lastly, all my thanks and love to Mr. Dare—I love that we'll grow old and geeky together.

Chapter One

The name Isolde Ophelia Goodnight did rather spell a life of tragedy. Izzy could look at her situation and see just that. Motherless at a young age. Fatherless now, as well. Penniless. Friendless.

But she'd never been hopeless.

Not yet.

Not quite.

Because the name Isolde Ophelia Goodnight also suggested romance. Swooning, star-crossed, legendary romance. And for as long as she could remember, Izzy had been waiting—with dwindling faith and increasing impatience—for that part of her life to begin.

Once she'd grown old enough to understand her mother's death, Izzy had consoled herself with the idea that this was all part of her epic tale. The heroines in fairy stories were always motherless.

When Papa overspent their income, and the maid was dismissed, she told herself the drudgery would pay off someday. Everyone knew that Cinderella had to scrub the floors before she could win the handsome prince.

By time she turned fifteen, their finances had improved, thanks to Papa's writing success. Still no prince, but there was time. Izzy told herself she'd grow into her largish nose and that her frizzled hair would eventually tame itself.

She hadn't, and it didn't. No ugly-duckling-turned-swan here, either.

Her seventeenth birthday passed without any pricking of fingers.

At twenty-one, life forced a difficult truth on her somewhere on the road between Maidstone and Rochester. Real highwayman were neither devilishly charming nor roguishly handsome. They wanted money, and they wanted it quickly, and Izzy ought to be very glad they weren't interested in her.

One by one, she'd let go of all those girlish dreams.

Then last year, Papa had died, and all the stories dried up completely. The money was gone soon after that. For the first time in her life, Izzy verged on true desperation.

Her cravings for romance were gone. Now

she'd settle for bread. What fairy tales were left over for a plain, impoverished, twenty-six-year-old woman who'd never even been kissed?

This one.

She clutched the letter in her hand. There it was, in black ink on white paper. Her very last hope. She forced herself not to hold it too tightly, for fear it might crumble to dust.

Dear Miss Goodnight,

It is my duty as executor to inform you that the Earl of Lynforth has died. In his will, he left you—and each of his goddaughters—a bequest. Please meet me at Gostley Castle, near Woolington in the county of Northumberland, on this twenty-first of June to settle the particulars of your inheritance.

Yours,
Frederick Trent, Lord Archer

A bequest. Perhaps it would be as much as a hundred pounds. Even twenty would be a windfall. She was down to shillings and pence.

When Gostley Castle came into view, Izzy gulped.

From a distance, it could have looked romantic. A collection of mismatched turrets and ranging, crenellated walls, studded amid rolling green fields. But the surrounding park had grown so wild and dense from neglect that by the time the castle came into view, she was already cowering in its shadow.

This castle didn't welcome or enchant.

It loomed.

It menaced.

She almost worried it might pounce.

"Here we are, miss." The driver didn't seem to like it any better than Izzy did. He pulled his team to a halt well outside the barbican, a stone gatehouse set some distance from the castle itself.

After helping her down from the carriage, he turned up the collar of his coat and unloaded her baggage—a single, battered valise. He carried it to the stone steps of the ancient gatehouse, strode briskly back, jammed his hands in his pockets, and cleared his throat. Waiting.

Izzy knew what he was after. She'd paid the man in Woolington—he wouldn't agree to transport her without payment in advance—but now he wanted an additional expression of thanks. She fished a sixpence from her purse. So few coins remained, the purse didn't even rattle.

The driver pocketed her offering and touched his cap. "What was yer name again, miss?"

"Goodnight. Miss Izzy Goodnight."

She waited to see if he would recognize it. Most of the literate people in England would, and a great many of their domestic servants, besides.

The driver only grunted. "Jes' wanted to know it, in case someone comes around asking. If you're never heard from again."

Izzy laughed. She waited for him to laugh, too. He didn't.

Soon driver, team, and carriage were nothing more than the fading crunch of wheels on the road.

Izzy picked up her valise and walked through the barbican. A stone bridge carried her over what once had been a moat but now was only a slimy green trickle.

She'd done a bit of research in advance of her journey. There wasn't much to read. Only that Gostley Castle had once been the seat of the Rothbury dukedom, in Norman times.

It didn't look inhabited now. There was no glass in many of the windows. No lights in them, either. There should have been a portcullis that dropped to bar the entrance—but there was nothing there. No door, no gate.

She walked through the archway and into the central, open courtyard.

"Lord Archer?" Her voice died in the air. She tried again. "Lord Archer, are you here?" This time, her call got a respectable echo off the flagstones. But no answer.

She was alone.

Dizzied from her strange surroundings and weak with hunger, Izzy closed her eyes. She coerced air into her lungs.

You cannot faint. Only ninnies and consumptive ladies swoon, and you are neither.

It started to rain. Fat, heavy drops of summer

rain—the kind that always struck her as vaguely lewd and debauched. Little potbellied drunkards, those summer raindrops, chortling on their way to earth and crashing open with glee.

She was getting wet, but the alternative—seeking shelter inside one of the darkened arches—was less appealing by far.

A rustling sound made her jump and wheel. Just a raven taking wing. She watched it fly over the castle wall and away.

She laughed a little. Really. It was too much. A vast, uninhabited castle, rain, and now ravens, too? Someone was playing her a cruel trick.

Then she glimpsed a man across the courtyard, standing in a darkened archway.

And if he was a trick, he wasn't a cruel one.

There were things in nature that took their beauty from delicate structure and intricate symmetry. Flowers. Seashells. Butterfly wings. And then there were things that were beautiful for their wild power and their refusal to be tamed. Snowcapped mountains. Churning thunderclouds. Shaggy, sharp-toothed lions.

This man silhouetted before her? He belonged, quite solidly, in the latter category.

So did the wolf sitting at his heel.

It couldn't be a wolf, she told herself. It had to be some sort of dog. Wolves had long been hunted to extinction. The last one in England died ages ago.

But then . . . she would have thought they'd stopped making men like this, too.

He shifted his weight, and a slant of weak light revealed the bottom half of his face. She glimpsed a wide, sensual slash of a mouth. A squared jaw, dark with whiskers. Overlong hair brushed his collar. Or it would have, if he had a collar. He wore only an open-necked linen shirt beneath his coat. Buckskin breeches hugged him from slim hips to muscled thighs . . . and from there, his legs disappeared into a pair of weathered, dusty Hessians.

Oh, dear. She did have such a weakness for a pair of well-traveled boots. They made her desperate to know everywhere they'd been.

Her heart beat faster. This didn't help with her lightheadedness problem.

"Are you Lord Archer?" she asked.

"No." The word was low, unforgiving.

The beast at his heel growled.

"Oh. I-is Lord Archer here?"

"No."

"Are you the caretaker?" she asked. "Are you expecting him soon?"

"No. And no."

Was that amusement in his voice?

She swallowed hard. "I received a letter. From Lord Archer. He asked me to meet him here on this date regarding some business with the late Earl of Lynforth's estate. Apparently he left me some sort of bequest." She extended the letter with a shaking hand. "Here. Would you care to read it for yourself?"

That wide mouth quirked at one corner. "No."

Izzy retracted the letter as calmly as she could manage and replaced it in her pocket.

He leaned one shoulder against the archway. "Aren't we going to continue?"

"Continue what?"

"This game." His voice was so low it seemed to crawl to her over the flagstones, then shiver up through the soles of her feet. "Am I a Russian prince? No. Is my favorite color yellow? No. Would I object if you were to come inside and remove every stitch of your damp clothing?" His voice did the impossible. It sank lower. "No."

He was just making sport of her now.

Izzy clutched her valise to her chest. She didn't want Snowdrop getting wet. "Do you treat all your visitors this way?"

Idiot. She cursed herself and braced for another low, mocking "no."

He said, "Only the pretty ones."

Oh, Lord. She ought to have guessed it earlier. The fatigue and hunger had done something to her brain. She could almost believe the castle, the ravens, the sudden appearance of a tall, dark, handsome man. But now he was flirting with her?

She had to be hallucinating.

The rain beat down, impatient to get from the clouds to the earth. Izzy watched drops pinging off the flagstones. Each one seemed to chisel a bit more strength from her knees.

The castle walls began to spin. Her vision went dark at the edges.

"I . . . Forgive me, I . . ."

Her valise dropped to the ground.

The beast snarled at it.

The man moved out from the shadows.

And Izzy fainted dead away.

The girl crumpled to the flagstones with a wet *thud*.

Ransom winced at the irony. Despite all that had happened, he still had the ladies swooning. One way or another.

He released Magnus with a low command. Once the dog had completed his wet-nose investigation, Ransom brushed the animal aside and took his turn.

He ran his hands over the limp heap of joints and limbs before him. Damp muslin, worn boots. Small hands, slender wrists. There wasn't much of her. She seemed to be half petticoats, half hair.

And God, what hair. Thick, curly, abundant.

He felt the warm huff of her breath against his hand. He slid his touch lower, searching for the girl's heartbeat.

His palm brushed over a full, rounded breast.

A surge of . . . something . . . passed through him, unbidden. Not lust, just male awareness. Apparently, he should stop thinking of her as "the girl." She was most definitely "the woman."

Ransom cursed. He didn't want visitors. Especially not visitors of the female kind. He had enough of that with the local vicar's daughter,

Miss Pelham. She came around the castle every week or so, offering to read him sermons or some other foolishness. At least when Miss Pelham made her sunny march up the hill, basket of good deeds threaded over one arm, she came *expecting* to find a scarred, unshaven wreck of a man. And she was far too sensible to faint at the sight.

This woman crumpled on the flagstones hadn't been expecting Ransom.

What was it she'd said about a Lord Archer? She had a letter on her somewhere that explained it, but he couldn't bother with that now. He needed to get her inside—warm her up, give her a splash of whisky and milk in her tea.

The sooner she recovered her senses, the sooner she could leave.

He wrestled her sodden, unconscious form into his arms and stood. He adjusted her weight, finding the fulcrum between her hips and her shoulders, then made his way up the stairs to take her inside.

He counted the steps out. *Five . . . six . . . seven . . .*

As he took the eighth step, she shifted in his arms. He froze, bracing for unpleasantness. She'd fainted dead at her first sight of him. If she woke to find him carrying her now, she might expire from the shock. Or split his eardrums with a shriek. Just what he didn't need—an injury to his hearing.

She mumbled faintly but didn't rouse. No, she did something far worse.

She *nuzzled*.

Slid sideways, curling into his embrace, and rubbed her cheek against his chest, seeking warmth. She gave a faint, husky moan.

Another surge of . . . something . . . passed through him. He paused for a moment, absorbing the sharp invasion of it before he continued his climb.

Gods be cursed. The one thing Ransom wanted less right now than a swooning woman? A *nuzzling* woman. Since his injury, he didn't like anyone too close. And he didn't require any nuzzling, thank you. He had a dog.

The dog led the way as he reached the top of the stairs and turned to enter the castle's great hall. This space was his encampment, of sorts. He slept here, he ate here, he drank here, he . . . cursed and brooded here. His manservant, Duncan, was always after him to open more of the castle's rooms, but Ransom didn't see the point.

He settled the girl—the *woman*—on the decrepit horsehair sofa, pushing it nearer the fire. The sofa legs screeched across the stone floor. He waited to see if she'd stir.

Nothing.

He gave her shoulder a mild shake.

Nothing.

"Wake," he said loudly. "Look there. It's Lord Archer."

Nothing.

Ransom drew up a chair and sat nearby. Five

seconds later, he rose again to pace. Twenty-three paces to the leftmost window, then back. He had his strengths, but patience wasn't one of them. Inaction made him a growly, ill-tempered beast.

When Duncan returned, he could send for a doctor. But it could be hours before Duncan returned.

Magnus whined and nosed about his boots.

Ransom sent the dog to its rug by the fire. Then he crouched beside the sofa and placed one hand on the woman's neck. He slid his touch along that sleek, delicate column until he found her pulse with his fingertips. The heartbeat was weaker than he would have liked it to be, and rabbit-fast. Damn.

She turned her head, sliding her soft cheek into his hand. There she went again, nuzzling. The friction released gentle hints of a soft, feminine fragrance.

"Temptress," he muttered bitterly.

If he had to have a swooning, nuzzling woman collapse on his doorstep, why couldn't it be one who smelled of vinegar and old cheese? No, he had to get one scented of rosemary and sweet, powdered skin.

He pressed his thumb to her rain-splashed cheek. "For God's sake, woman. Wake."

Maybe she'd struck her head on the flagstones. He thrust his fingers into her upswept hair, yanking out her hairpins. There were dozens of them, it seemed, and with each one he pulled, the mass of hair seemed to grow wilder. Angrier. The curling locks tangled and knotted between his fingers, obstructing his explorations. By the time he'd satisfied himself that her skull was intact, he could have believed that hair was alive. And hungry.

But her skull *was* in one piece, with no knots or swellings that he could detect. And she still hadn't made a sound.

Perhaps she was injured somewhere else. Or maybe her corset was too tight.

There was only one way to tell.

With a gruff sigh, he shook off his coat and turned up his sleeves. Rolling her onto her side, he brushed her predatory hair away and set his fingers to the task of undoing the buttons down the back of her frock. He was out of practice, but there were some things a man didn't forget. How to undo a woman's buttons was one.

How to unlace a woman's stays was another.

As he yanked the laces from the corset grommets, he felt her rib cage expand beneath his palms. She shifted and released a throaty, sensual sigh.

He froze. Another surge of . . . something . . . pulsed through his veins, and this time he couldn't dismiss it as some tender nonsense.

This was lust, pure and simple. He'd gone a dangerously long time without a woman in his arms.

He pushed the physical response aside. With brisk, businesslike motions, he pulled the sleeves of her frock down her arms, feeling for any broken bones along the way. Then he began working the bodice down to her waist. He couldn't let her just lie there in wet sacking, or she'd catch a chill.

He would deserve a great deal of gratitude for this when she awoke—but somehow he doubted he'd get it.

Izzy came to herself with a jolt.

She was indoors. Inside the castle. Pillars sprouted around her like ancient trees, soaring up to support the vaulted ceiling of a cavernous great hall.

Looking about, she saw scattered furnishings in various states of decay. The near end of the hall featured a massive hearth. If there weren't a roaring fire in it, Izzy had no doubt she could stand inside that fireplace without even crouching. The blaze within fed not on splits of wood, or even logs, but on full tree trunks.

She lay on a dusty, lumpy sofa. A rough, woolen blanket had been drawn over her body. She peeked beneath it and cringed. She'd been divested of her frock, stays, petticoats, and boots. Only her chemise and stockings remained.

"Oh dear heavens."

She put a hand to her unbound hair. Her Aunt Lilith was *right*. She'd always harped on Izzy during those summers in Essex. "It doesn't matter that no one will see them," she'd squawked. "Always—*always*—wear a clean shift and stockings. You never know when you might meet with an accident."

Oh . . . dear . . . *heavens*. It all came back to her now. The rain . . . her swoon . . .

Izzy looked up, and there he was.

The Accident.

"You're awake," he said, without turning to confirm it.

"Yes. Where are my things?"

"Your valise is two paces inside the entry, to the right."

Izzy twisted her neck and glimpsed the valise, right where he'd said it would be. It wasn't moving or open. Snowdrop must still be asleep. That was a relief.

"Your frock is there." He gestured toward where her frock hung over the back of two upright chairs, drying by the fire. "Your petticoats are draped over the far table, and your corset is on the other s—"

"Thank you." Izzy wanted to die. The whole situation was mortifying. Swooning at a handsome stranger's boots was embarrassing enough, but hearing him catalog her underthings? She clutched the blanket to her chest. "You needn't have troubled."

"*You* needed to breathe. And I needed to be sure you weren't bleeding or broken anywhere."

She wasn't certain why that required undressing her to her shift. A quick glance would tell him if she were bleeding.

"Are you ill?" he asked.

"No. At least, I don't think so."

"Are you with child?"

Her burst of laughter startled the dog. "Definitely not. I'm not the sort of woman who faints, I promise you. I just hadn't eaten much today." *Or yesterday, or the day before that.*

Her voice was hoarse and raspy. Perhaps she was catching a cold. That would help explain the fainting, too.

Throughout this conversation, her host remained at the hearth, facing away from her. His coat stretched tight at the shoulders but hung a bit loose about his midsection. Perhaps he'd recently lost some bulk. But there was plenty of him remaining, and all of it was lean and hard. His body was much like this great hall around them. Suffering from a bit of neglect, but impressively made and strong to the bones.

And that voice. Oh, it was dangerous.

She didn't know which upset her more: That this shadowy, handsome stranger had made so free with her person—carrying her in his arms, unlacing her stays, taking down her hair, and stripping her to her thinnest undergarments? Or that she'd somehow slept through the whole thing?

She snuck another glance at him, silhouetted by orange firelight.

The latter. Definitely the latter. The most exciting quarter hour of her life, and she'd spent it completely insensible. *Izzy, you fool.*

But though she had no firm recollection of being carried in from the rain, her body seemed to have a memory of its own. Beneath her clothing, she smoldered with the sensation of strong hands on chilled flesh. As if his touch had been imprinted on her skin.

"Thank you," she said. "It was good of you to carry me inside."

"There's tea. To your left."

A chipped mug of steaming liquid sat on a table nearby—to her left, as he'd said. She took it in both hands, letting its warmth seep into her palms before lifting it for a long, nourishing draught.

Fire raced down her throat.

She coughed. "What's in this?"

"Milk. And a drop of whisky."

Whisky? She sipped again, not in a position to be particular. When approached with the appropriate caution, the brew wasn't so bad. As she swallowed, an earthy, smoky heat curled through her.

On the same table, she found a small loaf of bread and broke into it, famished.

"Who *are* you?" she asked between mouthfuls. Aunt Lilith would *not* be pleased with her manners.

"I'm Rothbury. You're in my castle."

Izzy swallowed hard. This man claimed to be the Duke of Rothbury? It seemed too much to believe. Shouldn't dukes have servants to make their tea and dress them in proper attire?

God help her. Perhaps she was trapped with a madman.

Izzy drew the blanket close. Despite her doubts, she wasn't going to risk provoking him.

"I didn't realize," she said. "Should I address you as 'Your Grace?'"

"I don't see the point of it. Within a few hours, I hope you'll refer to me as 'That ill-mannered wretch you importuned one rainy afternoon and then never pestered again.'"

"I don't mean to be trouble."

"Beautiful women are always trouble. Whether they mean to be or not."

More teasing. Or more lunacy. Izzy wasn't sure which. The only thing she knew for certain was that she was no kind of beauty. It didn't matter how she pinched her cheeks or pinned back her aggressively curly hair. She was plain, and there seemed no getting around it.

This man, however, was anything but ordinary. She watched him as he tossed more wood on the blaze. He added a log as thick as her thigh, but he handled it with all the ease of tinder.

"I'm Miss Isolde Goodnight," she said. "Perhaps you've heard the name."

He poked the fire. "Why would I have heard the name?"

"My father was Sir Henry Goodnight. He was a scholar and historian, but he was most well-known as a writer."

"Then that explains why I don't know him. I am not a reader."

Izzy looked to the arched windows. The afternoon was darkening. The lengthening shadows worried her, as did the fact that she'd yet to make out the entirety of her host's face. She was growing anxious to see him, look into his eyes. She needed to know just what sort of man held her at his mercy.

"It seems Lord Archer might be some time yet," she ventured. "Might we have a candle or two while we wait?"

After a grudging pause, he took a straw, lit it in the fire, and, carefully cupping the flame with one palm, moved it to a taper fixed atop the mantel.

The task seemed to cause him inordinate difficulty. The candlewick caught, but he held the straw in place until it burned down to his fingertips. He cursed under his breath and whipped it with his hand, shaking out the flame.

"I hate to be a bother. It's just that I'm . . ." She didn't know why she was admitting it, except that she felt sorry he'd burned himself to increase her comfort. "I'm not fond of the dark."

He turned to her, bearing the candle. One side of his wide mouth tipped, like a scale weighted with irony. "I haven't made my peace with it either."

The new flame cast golden light on his face. Izzy startled. His sculpted, aristocratic features did much to bolster his claim of being a duke. But something else about his face told a different story.

A dramatic, uneven scar sliced from his brow

to his temple, ending on the crest of his right cheekbone. Though the candle flame flickered and sparked, his eyes didn't narrow or focus.

Of course.

The realization flared within her. At last, something about this day made sense.

It all made sense.

The darkened room, his refusal to read her letter, his manual assessment of her health. His repeated mentions of Izzy's beauty despite what should have been ample evidence to the contrary.

He was blind.

Chapter Two

Ransom remained still, letting the candle illuminate the mangled side of his face. He'd been keeping his distance to spare her this, but she'd requested the light.

So he waited, allowing her a good, long look.

No shrieks, gasps of horror, or soft thuds as she hit the floor. Not this time. She exuded nothing but that same teasing fragrance of rosemary.

"Thank you," she said. "For the candle."

Her voice was even more alluring than her scent. She had the accent of a sheltered English miss—but with an undeniably husky, sensual undertone.

"Has it been a long time since your injury?" she asked. "Were you wounded in battle? A duel? An accident?"

"It's a long story."

"I'm fond of long stories."

He plunked the candlestick on the table with finality. "Not this one."

"I'm sorry. I know it's terribly forward of me to ask. I had decided against it. But then I thought, surely you must *know* that I'm wondering. If I pretended sudden interest in the ceiling or the weather, that would be an insult of sorts, too. And you seem the sort of man who'd prefer honesty—even the uncomfortable kind—to insincerity, so I just"—her voice dropped a half octave—"decided to ask."

She went quiet. At last.

He was irritated with his body's response to her presence. Her femininity was like a lacy blanket taking up his favorite chair. Not something he would have brought into the room, but since she was there . . . he couldn't deny that a scarred, neglected part of him craved that softness.

Hell, he *ached* for it, straight to his bones.

"Very well, I won't press you for the story behind it," she said lightly, "but be forewarned. I shall probably make one up."

"Make up as many stories as you wish. Just don't make me the hero in them."

"When can we expect Lord Archer to arrive?"

Damned if Ransom knew. He hadn't the faintest idea who this Archer might be. "There's been some misunderstanding. Whoever it is you're searching for, he isn't here. My manservant will be returning soon. I'll have him see you back to Woolington."

She hesitated. "Then I suppose I should dress."

"Go on." He waved in invitation. "There's no dressing room. And if you haven't gathered as much by now, you needn't wait for me to avert my eyes."

Just the same, he turned to the wall. He clucked his tongue, calling Magnus to heel.

Behind him, light footsteps padded across the floor. The rustle of petticoats grated on his calm. He reached down to give the dog a light scratch.

"There's quite a mountain of correspondence on your table," she pointed out. "Are you very sure a Lord Archer didn't write to you?"

Ransom considered. True, he couldn't be sure of anything that pertained to his written correspondence lately. Duncan had many useful skills, but none of them could be described as secretarial.

"It's just . . . I'm grateful for the offer of transport to Woolington," she said. "But I don't know where I'd go from there. I see you've emptied my purse onto the table. You must have noticed how little was in it."

He had noticed. She had exactly three shillings, ten pence in her purse. No jewelry of any value. He hadn't searched the valise, but it weighed almost nothing.

"If you force me out tonight, I've nowhere to go."

Ransom heard the slight waver in her voice.

He shut his ears to it.

He couldn't fathom why a young, unaccompanied woman would make the journey alone to the middle of Northumberland by the grace of her last few shillings.

But this Miss Goodnight needed to say goodbye. He wished her no ill, but he had nothing to offer her, either. If she was looking for a rescuer, she'd found the wrong man.

"My manservant can take you to the village church," he said. "Perhaps the vicar's—"

Magnus's ear perked under his touch. The dog's skull vibrated with a low, nearly inaudible growl.

A moment later, Ransom heard the sound, too. Hoofbeats coming up the road. An unfamiliar rhythm. It couldn't be Duncan. "Perhaps this Lord Archer has come for you after all."

She released a breathy sigh. "Thank heaven."

"Indeed."

In a matter of moments, the intruder's steps sounded in the courtyard. "Hullo, there? Miss Goodnight?"

She flew to the window and called down. "Up here, my lord. The great hall."

Once the man entered the hall, his steps arrowed straight toward their place near the hearth. Confident, clipped. Much too fast.

Ransom gritted his teeth. Damn, he hated this. Being at this constant disadvantage, unable to control the situation.

The fireplace poker was close at hand. He lifted it. "Stop there."

The footsteps halted, some ten feet away. He felt the fresh source of scrutiny burning over his scarred face.

"Is that . . . ? But it can't be." The newcomer took one step forward. "Rothbury? Good God. It's like coming face-to-face with a ghost."

"I don't know you," Ransom said.

"No, but I know you." Archer lowered his voice to a whisper. "I was on the guest list, you see. Bride's side."

Ransom steeled his jaw and kept his expression impassive. He wouldn't give this cur the pleasure of a reaction.

"No one's seen you in months," Archer went on. "The rumor about Town is that you're dead."

"Well, the rumor has it wrong."

The truth was even worse.

Ransom gave the poker a meaningful tap against stone. This was his castle. He didn't answer questions here; he asked them. "Explain yourself. What are you doing, luring unsuspecting women to my home?"

"To *your* home?" Archer chuckled in a low, disconcerting way. "Well, this should prove interesting."

Izzy felt as though she'd wandered into the third act of a play. She had no idea what was going on, but it was unbearably dramatic.

Lord Archer did make a fine-looking player. She was comforted by his starched cravat and fitted gloves. Signs that civility still existed some-where in the world.

"If you'll permit me to speak with Miss Good-night," Archer said, unperturbed by the make-shift weapon leveled at his chest, "I think you'll find all your questions answered."

The Duke of Rothbury—for it would seem he *was* the duke, after all—lowered his poker. Grudg-ingly. "Speak."

Lord Archer turned to Izzy. He smiled and rubbed his hands together. "So. I've been most anxious to meet the famous Izzy Goodnight. My nieces will be green with envy." His enthusiasm faded as he looked her over. "I must say, you're not quite what I expected."

Izzy held back a sigh. She never was.

"I always pictured you as a wide-eyed child," he said.

"I was twelve when my father's stories began appearing in the *Gentleman's Review*. But that was almost fourteen years ago. And, in the natural way of things, I've aged one year every year since."

"Yes." He shook his head. "I suppose you would have."

Izzy merely smiled in response. She'd long made a habit of rationing her remarks when speaking with her father's admirers. The Lord Ar-chers of the world didn't want Izzy to be a grown woman with her own set of likes and dislikes, dreams and desires. They wanted her to be the wide-eyed young girl of the stories. That way, they could continue to read and reread their beloved tales, imagining themselves in her place.

For that was the magic spell of *The Goodnight Tales*. When they settled down with each weekly installment, readers felt themselves tucked beneath that warm purple quilt. They saw themselves staring up at a ceiling painted with silver moons and golden stars, their hair fanned across the pillow for a loving father's hand to stroke. They looked forward to that same, familiar promise:

Put out the light, my darling Izzy, and I shall tell you such a tale . . .

The truth of her childhood didn't match what was printed in the magazines. But if she ever let it slip—oh, how people resented her for it. They looked at her as if she'd just ripped the wings off the Last True Fairy in England.

Lord Archer sat on the arm of the sofa, leaning toward her in confidence. "Say, I know you must be asked this all the time. But my nieces would garrote me with their skipping ropes if I didn't try. I don't suppose your father . . ."

"No, my lord." Her smile tightened. "I don't know how Cressida escapes from the tower. And I'm afraid I've no idea of the Shadow Knight's true identity."

"And Ulric's still dangling from that parapet?"

"As far as I know. I'm sorry."

"Never mind it." He gave her a good-natured smile. "It's not your fault. You must be more tortured by the uncertainty than anyone."

You have no idea.

Tortured by the uncertainty, indeed. She was asked these same questions at least three times a week, in person or in letters. When her father died suddenly of an apoplexy, his ongoing saga had been interrupted, too. His beloved characters had been left in all sorts of perilous situations. Locked in towers and dangling from cliffs.

Izzy found herself in the most desperate straits of all. Stripped of all her possessions, cast out of the only home she'd ever known. But no one thought to inquire after *her* well-being. They all worried over Cressida locked in her tower, and her beloved Ulric, hanging by three fingers from the parapet.

"My father would be most gratified that you asked," Izzy told him. "I'm thankful, too." It was the truth. Despite her current circumstances, she was proud of the Goodnight legacy.

Over by the hearth, the duke cleared his throat.

"My lord," she said, "I think our host is eager to have us gone. Might I ask about this bequest my godfather left me?"

"Ah, yes." Lord Archer rummaged in a small portmanteau. "I've brought all the papers with me. We can have it done today. Rothbury can hand over the keys if there are any."

"Keys?" She sat tall. "I don't understand."

"Your inheritance, Miss Goodnight. It's this. The castle."

Her breath left her. *"What?"*

In a dark voice, the duke protested, too. "Impossible."

Lord Archer squinted at the documents. "Here we are. 'To Miss Isolde Ophelia Goodnight, I leave the property known as Gostley Castle.' Is it pronounced like 'Ghostly' or 'Ghastly'? Either one seems accurate."

"I thought the bequest was money," Izzy said, shaking her head. "A hundred pounds, perhaps two."

"There is no money, Miss Goodnight. Just the castle. Lynforth had several goddaughters, and apparently he gifted them with too few ponies or hair ribbons over the years. In the last months of his life, he decided to leave each of them every girl's dream. Her very own castle."

"Now wait," the duke interrupted. "This castle has been in my family for hundreds of years."

Archer looked at the papers. "And apparently it was sold to Lynforth just a few months back." He looked over his papers at Izzy. "I take it you're surprised by this?"

"I'm stunned," Izzy admitted. "The earl was kind to me, but he wasn't even my godfather. Not properly. He was my father's patron at Court."

Izzy had been introduced to Lord Lynforth a few times, most recently when Papa received his knighthood. On that illustrious occasion, the dear old man had slipped Izzy a sweetmeat from his waistcoat pocket and given her a fond pat on the head. Never mind that she'd been mere days from her twenty-second birthday. His intentions were kind.

Now the dear old man had left her a castle?

A castle.

Archer pressed the folio of papers into Izzy's keeping. "It's all there. A copy of the will, the property deed. This castle and everything in it— it's yours now."

She blinked at the folio. "What am I to do with the place?"

"If you don't want to live in it?" Lord Archer looked at the soaring ceiling and shrugged. "I suppose you could clean it up. Try to sell—"

Crash.

Izzy ducked as something exploded against the far wall.

She looked around for the source. She didn't have to search far. In another fearsome explosion of strength, the duke picked up a chair and sent it sailing against the wall, too.

Crash, part second.

Splintered wood cascaded to the floor.

In the aftermath, he stood working for breath, every muscle tensed and coiled with energy. He was a magnificent, volatile, and undeniably *virile* portrait of anger. Izzy was torn between admiration and fear.

"She can't have it," he said. "She can't live in it. She can't clean it up to sell." He pounded one fist against his chest, and the small hairs on Izzy's arms lifted. "I am Ransom William Dacre

Vane, the eleventh Duke of Rothbury. This is *my* castle."

The wolf-dog growled. Tension crackled and filled the great hall, right up to the vaulted ceiling.

Lord Archer shuffled papers at his leisure. As though furniture hadn't recently exploded. "Yes, well. Duke or not . . . Matters don't seem to have gone your way recently. Have they, Rothbury?"

The duke didn't reply. Unless one counted palpable seething as a reply—in which case, he replied quite fiercely.

"I'm afraid the papers are clear," Archer said. "The castle is Miss Goodnight's now."

"It can't be," the duke replied. "Because I didn't sell it."

"When a man drops off the face of England for seven months, I should think his solicitors begin handling matters." Archer cast a glance at the long table heaped with unopened envelopes. "Most likely, the information is somewhere in that postal avalanche."

Izzy stared at the folio in her hand. She'd arrived with an empty purse and a growling belly. She still had an empty purse and a growling belly. But now she had a castle. And there was a duke in it.

"Well, then. That's done. I'll be off." After snapping the portmanteau closed, Lord Archer picked up his case and moved as though he would quit the room.

"Wait." Izzy lunged after him, catching him by

the sleeve. She lowered her voice. "You mean to just leave me here? Alone, in this . . . this ghostly *and* ghastly castle? Surely not."

"Miss Goodnight, much as I'd love to spend more time in this charming locale, I'm a very busy man. Lynforth's estate has me running all over England parceling out these musty heaps of stone to unsuspecting young women. I could offer you a ride back into the village. But surely your driver will come for you soon?"

Her driver?

Of course. Lord Archer would never believe her to be destitute—utterly without funds, a home, or transportation. He assumed that her well-sprung carriage and white ponies were just around the corner.

And unless she meant to sully her father's memory, exposing him as a neglectful spend-thrift, Izzy couldn't correct the assumption.

"Yes, he will come for me soon," she said weakly. "Doubt not."

Lord Archer looked around at the castle, then at her. His brow arched in amusement.

And then he did the most unforgivable of things.

He gave her a patronizing pat on the head. "That's little Izzy Goodnight. You do love an adventure."

Chapter Three

"Well," Izzy ventured to remark, some minutes into the tense silence Lord Archer had left behind, "this is an awkward situation."

"Awkward." The duke paced the floor, swinging his arms at his sides. Then he stopped in his tracks and said it again. *"Awkward."*

The word rang through the great hall, bouncing off the ceiling vaults.

Izzy just stood there. Awkwardly.

"Adolescence," he said, "is awkward. Attending a past lover's wedding is awkward. Making love on horseback is awkward."

She was in agreement, so far as the first part. She'd have to take his word on it when it came to the second and third.

"This situation is not awkward," he declared. "This is treachery."

"Treachery?" She clutched the folio of papers tight. "I'm sure I didn't do anything treacherous, Your Grace. I didn't ask Lord Lynforth to leave me a castle. I didn't know him any better than I know you."

"This castle was never Lynforth's to give." His voice was low and stern. "And you don't know me at all."

Perhaps not. But she wanted to. She couldn't help it. He was just so intriguing.

Now that they were alone again, she took the opportunity to study his face. His scar aside, his facial topography was a proud, noble landscape, with strong cheekbones and a wide, square jaw. His hair was tawny, leonine brown with streaks of gold. But his eyes . . . those were Celtic eyes. Dark, horizontal slashes in his face, wide-set. Guarded.

Those eyes would be difficult to read even if he had perfect eyesight. If not for his trouble with the candle, Izzy might have gone hours without realizing he was blind.

She had a hundred questions she wanted to ask him. Nay, a thousand. And the stupidest questions of all were the ones that clamored loudest to get out.

Have you truly made love on horseback? she wanted to ask. *How does that even work? Was it how you were injured?*

"Your Grace, I don't plan to evict you." She didn't imagine a man like this could be *made* to do anything. "I'm not your enemy. Apparently, I'm now your landlady."

"My *landlady*," he echoed, sounding incredulous.

"Yes. And surely we can reach an understanding."

"An *understanding*."

He strode to the opposite side of the hall, navigating the space and its furnishings with an ease that made Izzy envious. *She* stumbled more often than he did, and she had functioning eyesight.

If he'd been recovering in Gostley Castle ever since the injury, he must have worked tirelessly to chart a map of the place in his head. She began to understand why he would be so loath to leave it. Even if he did have finer estates elsewhere, moving houses would mean starting all over again. She didn't want to be the heartless landowner who forced a blind man from his home.

He lifted her valise from its resting place near the entry—two steps to the right of the door, as he'd told her earlier. Then he strode the same distance back and set it on the table.

"Understand this," he said. "You are leaving."

"What?" Panic gathered in her chest as she stared at the valise. "But I haven't anywhere to go, or any means of getting there."

"I won't believe that. If your father was renowned throughout England—knighted, even—you must have funds. Or if not funds, friends."

At his heel, the wolf-dog snarled.

"What's in this valise?" he asked, frowning.

"It's my . . ." She waved a hand. "It's not important right now. I've told you I won't ask you to leave, Your Grace. But you can't force me out, either."

"Oh, can't I?" He gathered her shawl from its drying place and wadded it into a ball, preparing to stuff it into the valise.

The dog growled and barked.

"What the devil is in this thing?" He opened the valise's latch.

"No, don't," Izzy said, jumping forward. "Be careful. She's sleeping. If you startle her, you'll—"

Too late.

With a primal howl of pain, he jerked his hand from the valise. "Mother of—"

Izzy winced. Just as she feared, his finger had a swoop dangling from it. A swoop of slinky, toothy, brown-and-white predator.

"Snowdrop, *no*."

The dog went mad, jumping and yipping at the snarling creature attacking his master. Ransom cursed and raised his arm, backing in a circle, trying to keep the two animals apart. Snowdrop being Snowdrop, she latched on tighter still.

"Snowdrop!" Izzy chased circles around the knot of tangling beasts. "Snowdrop, let him go!"

Finally, she scrambled atop the table and made a wild grab for the duke's wrist. She latched onto his arm with both of hers, using all her weight to hold him in place.

And then she paused there, trying to ignore the accidental intimacy of their posture. His shoulder was a stone against her belly. His elbow wedged tight between her breasts.

"Hold still, please," she said, breathless. "The more you flail, the harder she bites."

"I'm not *flailing*. I don't flail."

No, he didn't. Clutching his arm this way made her acutely aware of the power in his body. But she was equally aware of another force. His restraint.

If he chose, he could fling both Izzy and Snowdrop against the wall, just as easily as he'd demolished those chairs.

She calmed her trembling hands and reached for Snowdrop. With her fingers, she coaxed the animal's tiny jaws apart. "Let him go, dear. For the sake of us all. Let the duke go."

At last, she succeeded in prying Snowdrop free of his savaged, bleeding finger.

Every living thing in the room exhaled.

"Good God, Goodnight." He shook his hand. "What is that? A rat?"

Izzy descended from the table, clutching Snowdrop close to her chest. "Not a rat. She's an ermine."

He swore. "You carry a weasel in your valise?"

"No. I carry an ermine."

"Ermine, stoat, weasel. They're all the same thing."

"They're not," Izzy objected, giving the agitated Snowdrop a soothing rub along her tiny cheek. "Well, perhaps they are—but *ermine* sounds more dignified."

She cradled Snowdrop in one hand and rubbed her belly with the other, then carried her back to the valise and opened the small door in her ball—a spherical cage fashioned of gilded mesh.

"There you are," she whispered. "Now be good."

The dog growled at Snowdrop. In response, Snowdrop curled her lip, flashing needlelike teeth.

"Be *good*," Izzy whispered, sharply this time. She turned to the duke. "Your Grace, let me see to your wound."

"Never mind it."

Undeterred, she caught him by the wrist and examined his fingertip. "There's a fair amount of blood, I'm afraid. You'll want to clean this. It shouldn't wait. Perhaps we could . . . Ooh."

As she prattled on, he'd picked up his decanter of whisky from the table and poured a liberal stream of the amber spirits right over the oozing bite.

Izzy winced, just watching.

He didn't even flinch.

She pulled a clean handkerchief from her pocket. "Here. Let me see."

As she dabbed at the wound, she studied his hand. Big, strong. Marred with all manner of small cuts and burns—some fresh, others faded. On his third right finger, he wore a gold signet ring. The oval crest was massive. Apparently, dukes did everything writ large.

"The wound is still bleeding," she said. "I don't suppose you have a plaster about?"

"No."

"Then we'll just apply pressure until the bleeding stops. Allow me. I've dealt with this before." She wadded the handkerchief about his fingertip and pinched hard. "There. Now we wait a minute or two."

"I'll hold it." He wrenched away, applying the pressure himself.

Thus began the longest, most sensually charged minute of Izzy's life.

In the past, she'd suffered through many an unrequited infatuation. But she typically lost her wits for pensive scholars in tweed or poets who sported tousled dark curls and woeful airs.

The Duke of Rothbury was unlike any gentleman she'd ever fancied. He was hard, unyielding, and even before his injury, he didn't care to read. What was more, they were engaged in a property dispute, and he'd threatened to turn her out into the cold Northumberland night.

Nevertheless, her stomach was a giddy frolic of crickets and butterflies.

He was just so *near.* And so *tall.* And so *commanding.*

So *male.*

Everything female in her was rallying to the challenge. Perhaps this was how mountaineers felt when they stood at the base of a soaring, snow-crested alp. Exhilarated by possibility; awed by the inherent danger. A bit weak in the knees.

"Snowdrop," he scoffed, leaning his weight against the table edge. "You ought to change her name to Lamprey. Who keeps a weasel for a pet, anyhow?"

"She was a gift."

"Who gives a weasel as a gift?"

"One of my father's admirers."

"I should think it was one of his enemies."

Izzy joined him in sitting on the table's edge, resigned to explaining the whole story. It made a good illustration of how her father's literary success and the public's adoration never translated into much practical benefit.

"My father wrote an ongoing saga of knights, ladies, villains, sorcerers . . . castles. Anything to do with romantic chivalry. And the tales were all framed as bedtime stories told to me. Little Izzy Goodnight."

"That's why Archer was expecting a young girl?"

"Yes. They always expect a young girl," she said. "The heroine of the tales kept an ermine as a pet. A *fictional* ermine, of course. One that was brave and loyal, and every bit as majestic, pale, and slender-necked as her mistress. And this *fictional* ermine managed to accomplish all sorts of clever, fierce, *fictional* deeds, such as chewing her mistress free of bindings when she was kidnapped, for the third time, by the *fictional* Shadow Knight. So a devotee of my father's stories thought it would be a lovely gesture to give real-life Izzy Goodnight a real-life ermine to call her very own."

Wouldn't that be precious? the fool must have thought. *Wouldn't it be marvelous and adorable?*

Well, no. It wasn't, actually. Not for Izzy, not for Snowdrop.

A real-life ermine did not make a cuddly, brave, loyal pet. Snowdrop was sleek and elegant, yes—particularly when winter turned her thick coat white. But though she weighed a mere half pound, she was a vicious predator. Over the years, Izzy had suffered her share of bites and nips.

"A stupid gift," the duke said.

She couldn't argue with his assessment. Nevertheless, it wasn't Snowdrop's fault. She couldn't help being a weasel. She was born that way. And she was ancient now, near nine years old. Izzy couldn't just toss her to the wolves—or to the wolf-dogs.

"I can only imagine," she said, "that Lord Lynforth was following a similar impulse. He thought it would be an enchanting gesture to give little Izzy Goodnight a real-life castle of her own."

"If you don't want his fanciful gift, feel free to refuse it."

"Oh, but this gift isn't the same as an ermine. This is property. Don't you understand how rare that is for a woman? Property always belongs to our fathers, brothers, husbands, sons. We never get to own anything."

"Don't tell me you're one of those women with radical ideas."

"No," she returned. "I'm one of those women with nothing. There are a great many of us."

She turned her gaze to the floor. "When my father died, everything of value passed to my cousin. He inherited my childhood home, all the furnishings in it. Every dish in the cupboard and every book in the library. Even the income from my father's writings. What do I have to my name? I have Snowdrop."

Her hands began to tremble. She couldn't help it; she was still angry with her father. Angry with him for dying and angry with him for dying this way. All those years she'd helped him, forgoing any life she might build for her own, and he'd never found time to revise his will and provide for Izzy should the worst occur. He was too busy *playing* the role of doting, storytelling father.

The duke didn't seem to appreciate the injustice of her situation. "So you *do* have somewhere to go. You have a cousin. He can support you."

"Martin?" She laughed at the suggestion. "He's always despised me, ever since we were children. We're speaking of the same boy who pushed me in a pond when I was eight and stood laughing on the bank while I sputtered and thrashed. He didn't throw me a rope that day, and he won't now. There's only one thing I can do. The same thing I did then."

"What's that?" he asked.

"Learn to swim," she answered. "Quickly."

His wide mouth tugged to one side. She couldn't decide if it was an appreciative half smile or a belittling smirk. Either way, it made her anxious.

"Listen to me, prattling on." She tilted her head and peeked under his makeshift compress. "I think the bleeding has stopped."

With his teeth, he tore a strip of linen from a corner of the handkerchief and wrapped it around his finger, carefully folding under the ends and knotting it tight.

"I know you don't want to leave Gostley Castle," she said. "Perhaps we can agree on a quarterly rent."

Surely the rents on a property this size would be enough to secure her a well-appointed cottage somewhere. Izzy didn't need much. After several months as an itinerant houseguest, she yearned for the smallest comforts. Curtains, candlesticks. Sleeping beneath linens embroidered with her own monogram.

Just something, anything, that she could call her own.

"That's madness," he said. "I'm not paying rent on my own property."

"But this property isn't yours. Not anymore.

The Earl of Lynforth purchased it, and he left it to me."

He shook his head. "Lynforth was gulled. Some swindler must have drawn up false papers just to bilk a dying man out of his money. I employ more than a dozen stewards and solicitors to manage my affairs, and they would not sell property without my consent."

"Are you very sure?" Arching her eyebrow, she surveyed the expanse of unopened letters and envelopes. "How can you know if you haven't gone through the post in months?"

She plucked an envelope from the pile and turned it over in her hands. "I could help you read and answer these, if you like. I served as my father's secretary for years."

"I don't want your help."

He said it so sharply, she dropped the envelope.

"Let me give you a little history lesson, since your father was so fond of those. My ancestors were granted a dukedom because they successfully held the Scottish border. For centuries. And they didn't do that by throwing up their hands and saying, 'Very well, then' whenever someone knocked at the gate and claimed this castle was theirs."

Izzy laughed a little. "But I'm hardly a marauding band of Scotsmen. And we aren't living in the sixteenth century."

"No, we're not. We have laws and courts. So if you mean to stake a claim on this castle, go find a solicitor. Have him look over the papers and write to my solicitors. The two can argue back and forth. Chancery will hear the case eventually. Perhaps as soon as three years from now. That's if you're lucky."

Three *years*?

Izzy didn't have three years. If forced to leave, she wasn't sure how she'd manage for the next three days. And she didn't have money for solicitors—much less solicitors qualified to take on a duke.

She had no choice but to stand her ground. Behave as though the place was hers. If he succeeded in removing her today, she would never get her toe in the door again.

"If your solicitors would care to come here and examine the documents, they are welcome. But I'm not leaving."

"Neither am I." The unscarred half of his brow furrowed. If he could properly glare at her, Izzy surmised, he'd be giving her a glare hard enough to chip diamonds.

"It's no use being stern," she told him. "Glower all you like, but for heaven's sake, you gathered me into your arms and carried me in from the rain. I could swoon all over again just thinking of it."

"Don't mistake that for chivalry."

"Then what was it?"

"Practicality. I couldn't have simply left you there. You would have attracted vermin."

She smiled. "Oh, dear. All this and a sense of humor, too."

Apparently, no one had given him a compliment lately. He looked as though he'd been thrown a grenade. Or a wet kitten.

He might be wealthy, powerful, angry, and big. But on at least one score, Izzy had him outmatched. Buoyancy. She knew how to handle prickly creatures, and she knew how to make the best of a less-than-ideal situation.

When thrown in the pond, she learned how to swim.

"This isn't such a quandary as it seems," she said. "You want to stay. I want to stay. Until the legal matters are settled, we'll share."

"*Share?*"

"Yes, share. This is a vast castle, built to house hundreds of people. I'll just take a spare tower or wing for my own. You won't even notice me."

He leaned close. "Oh, I'd notice you, Miss Goodnight. I'd notice you. There's no castle big enough to keep a man like me from being aware, every moment, of a woman like you. You don't have to speak a word. I can hear the rustle of your petticoats. I can smell the scent of your skin. I can feel your heat."

Heavens. If he could sense her heat, he must feel it right now. She was hot everywhere.

"I'm not Lord Archer," he went on in that low, seductive rumble. "I've never read your father's soppy stories, and you're not some little girl to me.

I've run my hands all over your body. And these hands have an excellent memory."

Oh . . . goodness.

She hadn't known. She *couldn't* have known, sheltered as she'd lived, and he couldn't have guessed. But he'd just articulated everything she'd been wanting for so long. To be noticed. Not merely known as a girl in some precious stories, but *noticed*, as a woman.

"Do you understand what I'm saying to you?" he asked.

"Yes," she breathed. "And you're mad if you think I'll back down from this now."

They stood in tense silence.

"That's it," he said, at length. "You're leaving this place the same way you came in."

He ducked, caught her by the legs, and threw her over his shoulder—with the ease of a man who'd tossed many a woman over his shoulder. This was definitely not his first go at lady-tossing.

But it was definitely Izzy's first time being tossed, and she had no idea how to respond. Beat her fists against his back? Kick and scream? Later, she'd think of a dozen things. Witty retorts and clever rejoinders. Right now, all the blood was rushing to her head, and her mind was a hot, throbbing blank.

He bounced her weight, plumping her backside with his forearm. "There's so little to you."

The dismissive words jarred her tongue loose.

"You're wrong," she said. "There's a great deal to me, Your Grace. More than you know. More than anyone supposes. You can carry me outside, if you like. I'll come back in. Again, and again. As many times as it takes. Because this is my castle now. And I'm not leaving."

Chapter Four

Ransom shook his head. A brave speech, for a tiny scrap of a woman currently slung over his shoulder. Miss Goodnight could say whatever she wished. The truth of it was, she was a defenseless, near-penniless, unmarried woman, and he was a duke. The decisions were his to make.

What remained of his logic—and that smarting finger on his right hand—insisted she was a problem. With his impaired vision, Ransom depended on an elaborate mental map of the place. That map included every room, every stair, every stone. It did not have room for scampering weasels or distracting, tempting women.

She needed to leave.

But now that he had her in his grasp again,

with her breasts pressed against his back and her sweetly rounded bottom resting on his forearm, other parts of him—parts located far from his brain—were making other suggestions. Dangerous suggestions.

Which meant she *really* needed to leave.

Even before his injuries, he didn't allow women close. Oh, he took a great many women to *bed*. But he always paid them handsomely for the indulgence—with pleasure, gold, or both—and then he bid them farewell. He never woke beside them in the morning.

The one—and only—time he'd sought a more lasting arrangement, it hadn't ended well. He'd landed here in this decrepit castle, blinded and broken.

But then, there was a part of him—a withered, neglected corner of his soul—that had grown painfully aware of how small and alone she was. And that for all her brave words, she was trembling.

Good Lord, Goodnight. What do I do with you?

He couldn't let her occupy this castle. Any sort of "sharing" arrangement was out of the question. But was this truly all that was left of him? A cruel, unfeeling brute who would cast a defenseless young woman out into the night?

He didn't want to believe that. Not yet. He didn't surrender anything lightly, and that included what few shards remained of his broken soul.

He set Miss Goodnight back on her feet. As he lowered her to the floor, her body slid down his, like a raindrop easing down the surface of a rock.

Ransom knew he'd regret the words he was about to speak. Because they were the decent thing to do, and if there was one thing he'd learned in his life, it was that every time he did the decent thing, he paid for it later.

"One night. You can stay one night."

He'd been a fool to waste all that time arguing legalities. The castle itself would do the convincing. Once she'd spent a night in Gostley Castle, she wouldn't be able to run away fast enough.

Miss Isolde Goodnight was about to have a Very Bad Night indeed.

You can stay one night.

Izzy could have whooped with triumph, but she restrained herself.

Instead, she stepped back, smoothing her skirts and hair. Her cheeks burned, but at least he couldn't know.

"Just one night," the duke said. "And I'm only agreeing to that much because I expect one night in this place will be enough for you."

It was a small victory, admittedly, but it was a start.

"Come along, then. I'll show you to a room. My manservant will bring your things later."

Izzy followed him out of the great hall and up a

spiraling flight of stairs. The closeness of the stairwell made her shudder. Once darkness fell, these stone stairways and corridors would feel like a tomb.

"You'll want the finest chamber, no doubt. Since you seem to believe it's your castle now."

They emerged into a long corridor. Heavy steps carried him down the center of it. He didn't count aloud, but she could feel him taking the measurements in his head. His mastery of the space was a marvel.

At last he stopped, then made a brisk quarter turn.

"Here you are. I expect this will suit."

When Izzy peered inside, she was surprised to find a richly furnished chamber. A massive bed occupied one half of it, situated on a raised dais with mahogany posts soaring nearly to the ceiling. Velvet and tapestries hung on all sides. The rest of the furniture didn't consist of much—a chair with a caved-in seat, a few abandoned traveling trunks, and a dressing table covered in dust an inch thick. A gallery of arched Gothic windows lined the far wall, but the glass had been broken out of nearly all of them.

"Oh," she said, struggling to take in the room's decrepit state. "My."

"Take it all in," he said wryly. "View the full splendor of your supposed inheritance. Until I arrived some months ago, no one had resided in this place for decades. It's been looted thoroughly.

There are only a few furnished rooms, all of them in states of decay."

"If that's the case, I'm grateful this many furnishings have survived." Izzy moved into the room. A patterned carpet covered the floor. A threadbare one, but to have lasted this long, it must have been well made. "Just look at this bed."

"Eight paces wide. Big enough for a duke and a half dozen women, besides. Makes a man yearn for the medieval ages."

"It wasn't for sleeping," she told him. "At least, it wasn't for . . . *that*. This would have been the castle's great chamber. The medieval lords conducted business from these beds, the way kings sit on thrones. That's why it's raised on a platform and built to such an impressive size."

"Fascinating."

"My father was an expert on these things." Izzy approached the bed, peering at the hangings. She pulled a face. "It looks as though the moths have feasted on these tapestries. What a shame."

"Yes. And the rats have had their way with the mattress."

Rats? Izzy jumped back. She put her hands over her face and peered through her fingers at the bed enclosed by shredded hangings. Yes, the mattress had been disemboweled—its straw and horsehair contents strewn about and arranged into . . .

Oh, goodness, those could be nests.

If she stared hard enough, she could have sworn she saw the rotted straw *moving*.

She forced herself to say, "Snowdrop will be happy. And very well fed." A distant moaning startled her. "What's that noise?"

He shrugged. "Probably one of the ghosts."

"Ghosts?"

"This is a borderlands castle, Miss Goodnight. If you know about castles, you should know what that means."

"I do."

Gostley Castle's original purpose would have been to quell Scottish rebellion. Quelling rebellion meant capturing rebels—and not to keep them as houseguests. There was no telling how many people had been imprisoned in this castle, even tortured and killed, over the centuries. By the duke's own ancestors, no less.

"I don't believe in ghosts," she said.

He smirked. "Give it a night."

Night. It would be nightfall soon. Izzy's stomach twisted in a knot at the thought.

"I take it you're pleased with your accommodations." He leaned one shoulder against the archway.

" 'Pleased' isn't the word."

The word was something more like "horrified." The thought of spending the night in this room reduced her insides to a quivering, whimpering puddle.

But she couldn't let on. That was just the reaction he hoped for. He wanted her to run away.

This would have to be home for tonight. Rats and moths and all.

She forced an enthusiasm she didn't quite feel. "I'm sure this will make an enchanting bedchamber, with a bit of work and imagination. The proportions are majestic. The bed only wants a new mattress and hangings." She walked to the row of windows. "And there's a lovely view of the sunset."

"For those who can view it."

Izzy winced, regretting her insensitive comment. "I could describe it for you."

"Don't bother. I've seen sunsets."

"But you haven't seen *this* sunset."

The prospect from the window was breathtaking. The cloud-covered sky had fragmented into puffs of gray, alternating with swatches of vibrant blue and rosy orange. From this vantage, one could see the castle walls rambling through romantic evening mists that curled all the way from the sea.

"The sun is setting just beyond the tower. But 'setting' is the wrong word for this. Too peaceful. This sun is struggling. Going down like a bloodied fighter in the jaws of a great, stony beast."

Heavy footsteps carried him to stand behind her. "Has it disappeared yet?"

"Almost. One final flash of gold, as it slips into the beyond, and . . ." She released her breath. "There. It's gone."

"There's a rule about sunsets in this castle, Miss Goodnight."

"There is?"

"Yes." He turned her to face him. "And a man and a woman standing in this very place are compelled to heed it. No choice. There's only one thing to be done."

"What's that?"

Her pulse stumbled. Surely he couldn't mean to . . .

He lowered his head and made his voice a seductive whisper. "*Duck.*"

Duck?

She was still blinking at him in confusion when a strange sound tugged her attention aside. It sounded like . . . a great amount of wet laundry, flapping on the line in a stiff breeze.

She turned away from the window.

Oh, Lord.

Before her eyes, the vast bed canopy seemed to come alive. First, it began to shimmer, then to ripple—like a quicksilver cloak caught by the wind.

Then small pieces of it began to break away, one by one, each following the other.

"Oh, no." She stiffened. "Those can't be . . ."

They *were*.

Bats.

An entire colony of them had been roosting in the highest reaches of the canopy. Now they took wing one by one, then ten by ten . . . and then hundreds all at once.

She turned—just in time to see another black, swarming cloud pouring down the chimney. There must have been thousands.

And all of them were flooding straight for the windows.

"*Duck*," he repeated. "Now."

When she didn't immediately react, the duke wrapped his arms about her and hauled her toward the floor.

In seconds, the bats were everywhere, swarming above them in a rolling black cloud. Izzy ducked her head and took the shelter he offered. His chin tucked hard on her head, and she could feel his whiskers rasping against her scalp.

And through it all, his heart pounded, strong and steady. She clutched his shirt in both hands, burying her face in that constant rhythm, until it was all she could hear. No flapping. No screeching. Just *thump-thump-thump*.

At last, he lifted his head.

Izzy did the same. "I thought you said this was the best room."

"Nothing wrong with it," he said. "They're all out. Won't be back until morning. It's safe now."

Oh, it was anything but safe. Now it was nightfall, and she was stuck in this haunted, infested castle. In the arms of this tormenting, intriguing, devious duke. She didn't know what to do with him. She didn't even know what to do with herself.

Flailing her hands and stammering were all that came to mind. Neither idea seemed useful in the least.

And then . . . she felt a little scratching sensation.

Just behind her ear.

And all she could do was shriek.

Ransom was just about to release her when she latched onto him with sudden force.

"Help me." Her whisper trembled. Her body did, too.

"What is it?" he asked.

"B-b-bat."

He almost smiled despite himself. "The b-b-bats are all gone, Miss Goodnight."

"No, they're not. They're not. There's one caught in my hair."

"There's nothing in your hair. That's an old wives' tale. Bats don't get caught in people's hair."

"There. Is. One. In. My. Hair," she pronounced in distinct syllables, each word rising a halftone in inflection. And then, in one frantic high-pitched squeal: "Getitout!"

To be sure, bats didn't normally get caught in people's hair. But he'd forgotten, hers wasn't normal hair. This curly mane of hers could snare a rabbit. Perhaps a horse.

Ransom worried, as he plunged his fingers into her dense, wavy locks, that this hair could possibly ensnare *him.*

It had his curiosity entangled, that was certain. These locks must be dark. She *sounded* dark-haired, with that sultry voice, and most girls with hair this aggressively curly were dark. And if her hair was dark, her eyes were probably dark, too.

Before he could quash it, an image bloomed in his mind's eye. A raven-haired, dark-eyed beauty with plump, red lips.

"Keep still," he said.

That goes for you, too, he told the stirrings in his groin.

He wove his fingers into her roots near the scalp and shook the curls apart. "Did that free it?"

"No. It's still there. I can feel it." A shudder ran through her.

"I see how it is. You're a strong, independent woman of property. Right up to the moment something creeping or crawling comes along. Then it's, 'Oh, dear! Oh, help!'"

She growled.

"It's small," he told her, having found the thing. "No bigger than a titmouse. Far more frightened of you than you are of it."

She sighed. "Why do people always say that? It's never helpful."

"I'd tell you to distract yourself by focusing on my face, but that wouldn't help. You swooned the last time."

"I didn't swoon because of your—"

He made a shushing noise and worked his fingers downward, separating and shaking free the tangled hair. He didn't want to hear her explanations or apologies.

With his free hand, he held her shoulder. He stroked his thumb up and down, soothing.

Just to keep her still, he told himself.

Not because he cared.

He wanted her fearful. He wanted her to run away from this place, and from him. The way any young woman with sense would do.

He most definitely didn't want her to stay in his arms, warm and trusting, with her heart beating faster than a bat's wings.

He felt the moment the bat untangled itself and flapped free. The weight was gone from her hair, and now the unburdened locks filled his hand, soft and wild and sensual.

"There," he said. "It's flown away."

"You *knew* that would happen," she accused. "The sunset. The bats."

He didn't try to deny it. "Consider it repayment for the weasel."

"Oh, you . . . You . . ."

"Cruel bastard?" he suggested. "Heartless rogue? Blackguard? Villain? I've been called all of the above and more. My favorite is 'knave.' Fine word, 'knave.' "

"You ill-mannered wretch I importuned one rainy afternoon and then never pestered again." She pushed away from him and rose to her feet. "You can keep all the bats to yourself. I'm leaving."

Really? She was leaving already?

This was almost too easy.

Ransom followed her out of the room and back down the corridor, to the stairs that led down to the great hall.

"You needn't leave this very moment," he said. "At least wait until my manservant returns. I can give you a bit of money, and he can find you a coach in the village."

"I don't need a coach or money. I'll walk."

"Walk?"

"I know some people in Newcastle. Newcastle can't be that far."

"Oh, not far at all. Just . . . some twenty-five miles or so."

She paused midstep. "Then I'll be walking for some time. I had better get started."

He followed her toward the entryway. Walking to Newcastle, his eye. What the hell was she thinking? Perhaps those fairy tales she'd grown up with had rotted her brain. Was she planning to skip through the woodlands and meadows, plucking mushroom caps for parasols and letting friendly woodland animals guide her way?

"Don't think this is over," she informed him as she gathered up her caged weasel and valise. "You were right, I do have many friends. Influential friends. There are thousands of people scattered all over England who'd love nothing more than to have little Izzy Goodnight as a houseguest. Some of them are surely solicitors." He heard the rustle of papers. "So I will be in contact with Mr. . . . Blaylock and Mr. Riggett, and I'll see you at Chancery in three years. Farewell, Your Grace."

As she breezed past him, his arm shot out. He snagged her by the elbow.

"Not so fast. What do you know of Blaylock and Riggett?"

"Their names are on the deed. I told you, I served as my father's secretary. I do know how to read a legal document. Now, if you'll kindly release me, I will bid you a not-very-fond farewell."

His hand tightened on her arm. "No."

"No?" she echoed.

"No."

Ransom kept a firm grip on Miss Goodnight's arm. After what she'd just said, he wasn't letting her go anywhere. Not tonight.

"I'm confused, Your Grace. You just put a great deal of effort into scaring me off."

Yes, he had. But that was before he heard the names of his own most trusted solicitors fall from his lips. Blaylock and Riggett had been his men of business for years. They had power to manage everything in his absence. But they should never sign away a property without his knowledge and consent.

Something was going on. Ransom didn't know what it was, but he knew he didn't like it.

"Your efforts worked, Your Grace. Congratulations. I'm leaving. I've no desire whatsoever to spend a single night in that horrid room."

"You're not leaving."

She gave a little hiccup of laughter. "Are you conceding your claim of ownership and forfeiting the property?"

"No," he said. "And I'm not offering to host you as a guest in my house, either."

"Well, then I fail to see what—"

"I'm offering you a post. As my secretary."

The silence with which she received this news was stony.

Hell, Ransom wasn't happy about it, either. But with those two words—"Blaylock" and "Riggett"—she'd made it painfully clear that he needed someone to go read his correspondence for him. He had estates and responsibilities. If his solicitors were mismanaging his affairs in his absence, thousands would be affected. He needed to unravel just what was going on.

"I will hire you to read through my correspondence for me," he said. "I know it's hardly the ideal arrangement."

"You're right. It's not."

"Under ordinary circumstances, I would never entrust a woman with the task. But time is of the essence, and there's no one else around."

He heard her inhale slowly.

"I mean to compensate you handsomely," he said. "Fifty pounds."

"Per annum?"

"Per day."

That breath she'd inhaled whooshed out of her.

"Think on it. You seem to have wits, if not the best ideas on how to apply them. Chances are, the answer to our little property dispute is somewhere in that pile of paper. When we confirm that the castle is still mine, you'll have the money to go somewhere else."

He could sense her softening.

Or maybe his senses deceived him.

"One hundred," she said.

"What?"

"I want one hundred a day. I'll use it to fix up the castle once it's confirmed to be mine." A coy note crept into her voice. "And I want you to say please."

He gave her arm a swift tug, drawing her to him.

She collided with his chest.

"Don't be a fool," he said low. "You need money. We both need answers. The arrangement makes sense for us both."

"Then release my arm. And ask nicely."

He lowered his head until he felt a stray curl of her hair against his cheek. "Two hundred. Two hundred pounds per day is a very *nice* sum indeed."

"Saying 'please' costs you nothing."

He kept silent, refusing to relent. If she was going to be his employee, she needed to learn that he alone gave the orders.

"My goodness," she whispered. "Are you truly so afraid of asking for help? It's that terrifying?"

He balked. "I'm not afraid at all."

"I hear you saying that." She pressed a hand to his shirtfront. "But this frantic, pounding thing in your chest is saying otherwise."

Little minx.

There was exactly one reason his blood was pounding, and it had nothing to do with "please." It had to do with "yes" and "God, yes" and "just like that, but harder."

"I beg your pardon." The familiar voice came from the entryway. "I seem to be interrupting."

Duncan

Ransom gave himself a shake. "I didn't hear you come in."

"That's obvious, Your Grace."

Obvious, and worrisome. It was a testament to this woman's effect on him that Ransom hadn't even noticed his valet's return.

"I never thought I would say this, Your Grace, but it's strangely heartening to see you back to your old debauchery. I'll clear out of your way for the evening."

"No," Miss Goodnight jumped to insist. "Please, don't misunderstand. This isn't debauchery. I was just lea—"

"Duncan, this is Miss Isolde Goodnight. My new secretary. Tomorrow, we will find her new lodgings. But tonight, she will stay here. She'll need a clean, comfortable room, a proper bath, and a hot dinner." He gave her wrist a squeeze before releasing it. "Isn't that right?"

Chapter Five

Izzy had always been raised to believe that "please" was a magic word.

She'd been misled.

Apparently, the magic word was "dinner." In addition, the words "bath" and "comfortable room" had their own particular charms. When spoken in quick succession, they had the power of an incantation. Izzy hadn't been able to say no.

"I hope this will do for tonight, Miss Goodnight." Duncan showed her into a small, sparsely furnished chamber. "I know it's meager, but it's the only proper bed in the castle. My own."

"How generous of you to offer it." And how strange, that it would be the only one. "The duke doesn't have a bedchamber?"

"No." Duncan sighed, as if to communicate that

this was a point of frequent contention. "He sleeps in the great hall."

Izzy studied the manservant. He was tall and lean, with dark hair turned silver at the temples. Unlike the duke, he was turned out in a brushed black coat, a crisp neckcloth, and gleaming boots.

"So you are Rothbury's valet?"

"Yes. Though it pains me to say it when his appearance is so willfully slovenly. It's an embarrassment."

"And how long have you been living here?"

"Seven months, miss. Seven long months."

Heavens. Seven months *was* a long time. "What happened?" she asked. "How was the duke injured?"

"Miss Goodnight, I have served the family since before His Grace was even born. I am bound, by duty and honor, to avoid any gossip about my employer."

"Yes, of course. Forgive the liberty. But I had to ask."

Izzy supposed she would have to get the story from the duke herself.

Over the course of several trips, Duncan brought up her valise, a tray of simple, yet hearty food, a ewer of warm water, and a basin.

"It is paining me, Miss Goodnight, that I cannot offer you finer accommodations."

"Please don't worry. This is lovely." Anything was lovely, compared to that chamber of horrors with the bats.

"It's so frustrating. After long months of having my every attempt at proper valet service rebuffed, finally, we have a guest at Gostley Castle. A guest who ought to be cause for a proper guest suite and a seven-course dinner." He dropped his voice to an unnecessary whisper. "You are *the* Miss Izzy Goodnight, am I correct?"

She nodded. "I'm surprised you've heard of me. The duke hadn't. He said he isn't a reader."

"Oh, he isn't. And wasn't. Neither am I, for that matter. I only had one year of schooling. But the housekeeper used to read your father's installments in the servant quarters. The Shadow Knight? Cressida and Ulric? Can you tell me anything?"

She shook her head sadly. "No."

"Forgive *me* the liberty. But I had to ask."

She smiled. Everyone had secrets. "I understand."

He left and closed the door behind him.

Once she was alone, Izzy tried to make herself comfortable.

Snowdrop, of course, might as well have died and gone to heaven. This castle, with its ready supply of rodents, was the little beast's equivalent of a stay at London's finest hotel.

As she went about undressing and plaiting her hair, she recalled the sensation of the duke's hands tangling through it. The prickling tension between their bodies as they'd ducked together, hiding from the bats.

She still felt that tension simmering within her now.

He's not attracted to you, she told herself. He just wanted to intimidate her, and besides—any flirtations he might engage in were predicated on a misunderstanding. He wouldn't be interested if he had his eyesight.

Before climbing into the narrow bed, she lit a stumpy taper with her flint, then fixed it on the floor with a dab of wax.

It was going to be a cold, lonely night. Izzy steeled herself to withstand it.

She'd been given the deed to this castle. Now she had to stake her claim to it, earn her place as its mistress. And she would. Excepting her clothes and a set of seed-pearl earrings left to her by Aunt Lilith, Gostley Castle was the first thing worth more than a pound or two that Izzy had ever owned outright.

She wasn't going to give that up.

Tonight, no bat, rat, ghost, or wounded duke would frighten her.

But she couldn't escape the dark.

It was childish to be afraid of the dark. As a grown woman, Izzy understood this. She knew it with her mind, and she felt it with her soul— but her gut. Oh, her gut could never quite be convinced. Much less her heart, which woke her with the sort of pounding that could drive nails.

She sat bolt upright in her bed, disoriented and sweating, despite the cold. Her candle must have burned itself out. All was black. A thick, oppressive sea of black without so much as a sliver of moonlight to sail by.

Her eyes strained, peering in every direction, unable to settle on any spark or shadow but unable to give up the search. She fumbled about for her flint and came up empty. Where had she left the dratted thing?

How she hated this. Her fear, and how stupid it made her. Yesterday, she'd made a journey to Northumberland by herself, taken possession of a medieval fortress, and held her ground against a scarred, angry duke. She ought to feel like a strong woman, by any measure. But in the dark of the night, she was always—*always*—nine years old and terrified.

Distant memories came clawing back. She swallowed, and her throat felt raw. As if she'd spent hours screaming.

She began to tremble. Drat.

Izzy tucked her knees more tightly to her chest and wrapped her arms around them, curling into a tight ball.

What o'clock was it? She hoped that she'd managed to sleep the majority of the night before waking, but in her bones she felt it was probably only midnight or some short time past. An eternity before dawn. Every heartbeat drawn into a lifetime. She would huddle here for hours and hours, staring into the black and feeling pure agony.

Just this night, she told herself. *You only have to last this one night. And it will never be this bad again.*

Then she heard it.

No ghostly moaning or groaning. Just a light, rhythmic scraping. Back, then forth.

Back . . . then forth. Raising every hair on her arms.

Oh, Lord.

Izzy knew she had a choice. She could hide in her bedchamber and cower for the rest of the night, sleepless and miserable. Or she could go investigate. If she truly meant to stay in this castle, she needed to be its mistress.

She left her room on trembling legs, feeling her way down the spiraling stairs and into the main corridor. The scraping sound continued.

She moved toward it.

Probably just a branch or shutter moving in the wind, she told herself. Definitely not a ghost. Nor snakes. Nor the hanged body of a border rebel, left dangling from a rafter until it wasted and decayed to mere bones, swaying back and forth just enough that the toe bones scraped the floors. Leaving grooves in the stone, after centuries.

She stopped and shook herself. She could hear her father now.

God's blood, Izzy. You have the most gruesome imagination.

Yes, she did. It was a blessing on occasion, but in the dark, it was always a curse.

She moved along the corridor, hastening toward

that faint yet promising red glow from the great hall. There was light and heat there. The fire in the hearth had to be burning still—the duke had placed a small tree on it earlier, plus the remnants of the two splintered chairs.

All she needed was a bit of light. Once Izzy could see a little—just a little—she would feel so much better about everything. That was always the case.

She tiptoed into the great hall and peered hard toward the hearth. She glimpsed an unlit taper in a candlestick, perched atop the mantel.

Perfect.

She padded across the floor, reaching for the candlestick. The thing weighed thirty pounds if it weighed an ounce. Giving up on the brass holder, she wrested the candle loose and lit it in the fire.

Glowing candle in hand, she could breathe easier. She stood in place for a solid minute, doing just that. Breathing.

"Miss Goodnight."

Izzy jumped in her skin. She nearly dropped the candle.

"Making your escape already?" he asked dryly. "Can't even last one night?"

She turned, gathering the open neck of her nightrail with one hand. There the duke stood, not five paces away, still fully dressed. Apparently, he'd been awake. And walking. That must have been the sound she heard—his footsteps, brushing over stone.

"No, I . . . I'm not escaping at all." She tried to sound breezy. "I just couldn't sleep."

"Too scared, I gather." He slid a flask into his coat pocket.

"Too excited," she lied. "I've inherited a whole castle, and I've barely seen any of it yet. I'm keen to explore."

"In the dead of night? Return to your chamber. You can't traipse about the place in the dark. It's not safe for you."

She moved to his side. "Do you mean to join me, then?"

"That's not safe, either," he muttered.

Nevertheless, he put a hand on the small of her back, following close as she left the great hall and began to climb the stairs. At the top of the staircase, she turned down the corridor, retreating toward her chamber. She thought.

"See?" he said. "You've already turned the wrong way."

Izzy stayed quiet, determined not to admit fault. "I'm not lost. I'm exploring."

He made a disbelieving noise.

"I'll be fine. I'm not afraid of rats. The bats are gone for now. And I don't believe ghosts are real."

"Do you believe I'm real?" he asked.

If she were honest, Izzy had her doubts. He seemed so larger-than-life. Even she, with her wild imagination, had never dreamed up anyone quite like the Duke of Rothbury.

As they moved down the corridor, his hand never left her waist. Her skin burned beneath his touch.

She poked her candle into a series of cavernous, mostly empty rooms. "Tomorrow, I'll make a thorough search of these and choose another to make my bedchamber."

"And how would you propose to do that? You'll need fabrics, furnishings, servants. I'm not advancing you any wages. You haven't any funds."

A sad truth. Izzy *had* considered that, of course. "While I'm making my survey tomorrow, I'll catalog any items of value. Surely there's something in this place worth selling."

His denial was swift. "If there were anything worth selling, it would have been looted ages ago. There's nothing of value here. Nothing worth saving."

Nothing of value? Nothing worth saving?

He didn't include himself in that assessment, did he?

Concerned, she turned to look at him. The flickering glow of the candle danced over the handsome planes on the left side of his face. But the scar on his right side defied illumination, shunned the taper's golden warmth. At night, his wound appeared even wider, more dramatic.

It looked unhealed.

"What makes you so sure?" she asked.

"I know every inch of this castle," he said. "From the lowest cellar to the highest tower."

A small, darkened arch beckoned to her left. Her eye was drawn to it, and to the coy whisper of a staircase beyond. A naughty little pigtail of intrigue, spiraling out of view.

"There's an arch to the side," she said. "If you know the castle backward and forward, what's up there?"

"Thirty four stairs and a circular room at the top, some six paces across."

"My," Izzy said, impressed. "That was a very specific answer."

"Count for yourself if you doubt me."

She left his side and followed that small, curling staircase up and up, lighting the way with her candle. The way was narrow, and even as slight-figured as Izzy was, she had to climb at an oblique angle. Broad-shouldered Rothbury fell behind.

"Thirty-one, thirty-two, thirty-three . . ."

He was right. Exactly thirty-four steps later, she emerged into a small, round room. There were no bats. No rats. No ghosts. Just a single slit of a window. She crossed the uneven stone floor in cautious steps and poked her head through the rectangular opening.

Oh.

Oh, her heart.

She had to press a hand to her chest to keep it from jumping out of her body and crashing to the ground below.

How glorious.

The turret was high above the castle, offering

a view unimpeded by trees or hills. A patch of sky had cleared just overhead. She was floating among the stars.

Glowing taper in hand, she could almost imagine she *was* a star. Isolated. Insignificant amid the multitudes. Yet every bit as afire with heat and heart.

Strange, how contemplating the vastness made her feel a little less alone. From far enough away, on some other world, perhaps she would appear to be part of a constellation.

"This is it." She spoke the words aloud, so there could be no taking them back. "This is mine. I don't care about the bats, the rats, the ghosts. This turret is going to be my bedchamber, and this castle will be my home."

The duke joined her, having climbed the thirty-fourth stair. "For the last time, you can't stay here."

"Why?" She looked around the room. "Is the turret structurally unsound?"

"No. The peril isn't from crumbling walls. It's not from rats or bats or even ghosts." Skimming his fingers along the wall, he circled the turret perimeter, until his fingers just grazed her arm. "It comes from me."

He was a large man and a strong one. If he truly wanted to hurt her, there would be little Izzy could do about it.

But in her heart, she just didn't believe he would.

She couldn't say he wouldn't hurt a fly. But he'd

declined to hurt a weasel, and that seemed to say volumes more.

"Miss Goodnight, I'm a man who has spent a great deal of time in solitude. You're a defenseless, tempting woman. Do I have to spell it out for you? You're in D-A-N . . . ger."

She bit back a laugh. "Your spelling *is* a bit scary."

"I could ravish you."

He said it so solemnly. Now she couldn't help but laugh.

His brow furrowed. "You think I'm joking."

"Oh, no," she said. "I'm not laughing at you. Forgive me. I don't doubt your skill at ravishing women. I'm sure you're quite accomplished at . . . at ravishing. Expert, even. I laughed because no one's ever threatened to ravish me."

"I won't believe that. With this hair?" His touch drifted to her neck. "And this softness? You have the voice of a temptress."

What Izzy had was the beginnings of a cold, and she could have told him so. She could have explained that there was a very logical reason she'd never been in danger of ravishment, and it was because she was plain.

But was she truly plain, here and now? With a blind man, in the dark?

If he was tempted . . .

Didn't that make her a temptress?

She'd always envied beautiful women. Not solely for the beauty itself but because when attributes were parceled out by whatever deity assigned them, beauty seemed to come tethered to confidence. She craved that more than anything.

He swept a touch up her spine, and his hand brushed aside her plaited hair to settle on her bare neck.

A rush of power went through her, magnificent and intoxicating.

"Who lets a woman like this go untested?" He caressed her nape. "I won't believe no man's tried."

"Oh, you know how it is," she said lightly. "It must be the stunning degree of my beauty. It puts them off." Surely, he would catch her joking tone. And if he did take her to be serious . . . Whom could it possibly hurt? "I suppose all the gentlemen are intimidated."

His thumb rubbed over her lips. "I'm not intimidated."

Suddenly, she didn't feel quite so bold.

"Goodness, think of the hour," she said. "If I'm going to set about improving this place tomorrow, I suppose tonight I ought to return to my—"

A drop of molten wax rolled downward, singeing her hand. Izzy dropped the candle. The flame was extinguished before it even hit the floor.

The turret was instantly plunged into darkness.

Her heartbeat began to race. Oh, drat. And just when she'd been holding her own with him. So much for being a woman in his eyes. So much for being his temptress. He'd laugh at her if he knew how she felt. How could this little girl hold a claim to any castle? She was a ninny who swooned in the rain and shrieked at bats and quivered helplessly in the dark.

Perhaps he wouldn't notice the quivering part.

His hands went to her shoulders. "You're shaking."

Drat, drat, *drat.*

"I'm fine. I just dropped the candle, that's all. If you'd just be so good as . . ." She swallowed hard. "As to show me back downstairs."

"I don't think so."

Oh, Lord. The bottom dropped out of her stomach. He was going to leave her here. Alone. In this tiny room, up thirty-four steps, in the miserable, moving blackness. And that would teach her, wouldn't it?

But he didn't leave her. Instead, he took her in his arms.

And pulled her close.

Izzy didn't know how to resist. Those strong hands . . . they were her only anchor in the spinning dark. She was reeling with surprise, so very frightened.

Then suddenly . . .

She was so very kissed.

Chapter Six

Ransom kissed her.

Framed her face in his hands, held her still, and claimed her lips with his own. No prelude, no finesse. Just a strong, unyielding press of his lips against hers.

She needed to understand a few things, and he was done trying to explain them with words.

The girl was so damned innocent. She'd grown up on tales of chivalry and romance. She hadn't a clue what danger a man like Ransom could pose.

Very well. No great pain for him to demonstrate. This one uninvited kiss should send her fleeing to her chamber tonight—and then, in the morning, away.

"There," he said, breaking the kiss. "You seem

to have me confused with some innately decent man. I hope that clears matters up for you."

He released her, giving her the space to run away.

Instead, she fisted her hands in his shirt and clung tight. "Do it again."

He couldn't speak for a moment. Nothing made sense.

"Do it again," she whispered. "Quickly. And this time do it right."

"What on earth are you on about?"

"That was my first kiss. Do you know how long I've been dreaming of my first kiss?"

Ransom didn't know. He couldn't care less.

"All my *life*." Her fists pounded his chest for emphasis. "And so help me, Your Grace, I won't let you ruin it."

"You don't seem to understand. Destroying your romantic fancies was rather the point of that little exercise."

"No, *you* don't understand." She drew closer, still clutching tight. "I've always tried to make the best of what life gave me. When I was a girl, I longed for a kitten. Instead, I got a weasel. Not the pet I wanted, but I've done my best to love Snowdrop just the same."

He took a step back.

She moved with him.

"Since my father died, I've been desperate for a place to call home. The humblest cottage would do. Instead, I've inherited a haunted, infested castle in Nowhere, Northumberland. Not the house I wanted, but I'm determined to make it a home."

She tilted her face to his. He could feel her breath against his neck. Soft wisps of heat.

"And ever since I was a girl," she whispered, "I've dreamed of my first kiss. I just knew in my heart that it would be romantic and tender and knee-meltingly sweet."

"Well, now you know you were wrong. By this age, you should be accustomed to disappointment."

"That's where you're mistaken." Her grip tightened on his shirtfront. "I've started fighting against it. You're not going to ruin my first kiss. I won't let you. You're going to kiss me again, right now. And make it better."

He shook his head, incredulous. "It's over. It's already done. Even if I did kiss you again, it wouldn't be your first kiss anymore."

"It counts," she said. "So long as it's part of the same embrace, it all counts as one."

Bloody hell. Where did women come up with these rules? Did they keep them in a book somewhere? Sometimes he wondered if women were all lawyers, with an extensive code of Romantic Law that they kept stubbornly hidden from men.

"Stop dithering," she urged. "Surely, that kiss wasn't the best you could do."

He bristled. "Of course it wasn't."

"I mean, you've made love on horseback enough

times to draw generalizations about it. You must know how to kiss better than that. I'm not leaving this turret until—"

He grabbed her by the shoulders and kissed her again. Harder this time. Mainly just to quiet her prattling, but also to underscore the original meaning. If she wanted tender starlight interludes, Ransom was not her man. When it came to physical pleasure, he was aggressive, bold, and unashamed of it. If he had to make the point twice, so be it.

But as he kissed her, something went horribly, horribly wrong.

This time, she kissed him back. Not with mere curiosity or artless enthusiasm but with a sweet, unfettered passion that made his ribs ache.

His eyes flew open in shock—not that it made a damn bit of difference. He still couldn't see, only feel.

Sweet God above, did he *feel*.

This was . . . This was not supposed to happen.

Her lips were even more tempting than he'd dared suppose. Plump, wide, sensual. He savored each in turn, then swept his tongue between. She matched him kiss for kiss, taste for teasing taste.

He tugged her close with one arm. As he thrust his tongue deep, her mouth shifted and softened under his. Generous. Giving.

This was everything he'd been craving for so damn long. Closeness, warmth, sweetness, surrender.

He might have confined himself to this castle in the months since his injury, but he hadn't stopped moving. He'd walked this place every night, traversing the galleries, climbing the stairs, measuring the rooms in paces and learning the way his steps echoed off the stone. Hour after hour and day after day turned into month after month.

First, he'd walked to rebuild the strength sapped from his limbs. Then he'd walked to master the lay of this castle without his sight. He might be a wreck, he told himself, but he'd be damned if he'd be an invalid.

But there was something else that kept him walking, prowling the corridors and towers of Gostley Castle. Even if he wished to rest, he couldn't. Not without indecent amounts of whisky, anyhow. He just never felt easy. He never knew true peace. He was beginning to think he never would.

And now . . . now, this woman grabbed that tormented, wandering part of him and kissed it. Like a long-lost lover welcoming him home.

Good God. Good God.

She kissed him with *everything*. As if she wanted to. As if she'd *always* wanted to. As if her small, slender body were nothing more than a cunningly crafted decanter of some bewitching potion. An essence of desire, aged and corked and waiting for years. As if in one single kiss, she'd sensed her chance to foist it all on him because she was weary of the burden.

Take this sweetness, her kiss said. *Take this passion. Take all of me.*

He explored her mouth thoroughly, desperate for more.

He should have refused those reckless gifts. But he couldn't bring himself to pull away. His desires had been caged a long time, too. He couldn't evade the longing she kindled. Couldn't deny the hard, hot response of his body—not with his cock throbbing vainly against his buckskin falls.

God, he felt alive. Fully alive, for the first time since . . .

Since dying.

Ransom didn't know if this Beware-My-Dangerous-Kisses ploy was having any effect whatsoever on Izzy Goodnight, but he knew this much.

This kiss had *him* rattled to his boots.

Well, Izzy thought, her first kiss wasn't everything she'd hoped and dreamed it might be.

It was a thousand times more.

Now *this* was a proper kiss.

Not just a harsh press of bruising lips, but a real, true kiss, by a man who knew what he was doing. He was kissing her with not only skill but with *passion*. And *ardor*.

And *tongue*.

Best of all, she was somehow managing to acquit herself in a manner that had him growling against her lips. Pure luck there, she had to imagine. Or maybe he was the kissing equivalent of those London dancing masters—the ones who made a girl look graceful and competent when she was just following his lead.

It didn't matter. She was being kissed, and she was kissing in return, and thus far, it wasn't a humiliating disaster.

This . . . was . . . glorious.

For the second time in a single day, he made her knees go weak.

She threw her arms around his neck for balance. And then she kept them there for the sheer pleasure of lacing her fingers at the nape of his neck and sifting through the heavy locks of his hair.

He smelled so good. So simply, and so masculinely, good. It made no sense to her, how the most humble, unlikely scents could add up to an exotic cologne. If one gathered a flask of whisky, a strop of old leather, and a cake of plain soap, then tied it all together with a few wisps of dog hair—no one would expect the resulting "bouquet" to smell more enticing than an armful of roses. But somehow it *did*.

And then there was his heat. He seemed made of it. The man was a coal-fired furnace. He radiated warmth through his grasping hands, his hard chest, his lips.

Oh, his lips. The whiskers dotting his chin and jaw were abrasive, but his lips were . . . not soft, exactly. Soft meant pillows or petals, but his lips were the perfect blend of resilience and gentleness. Give and take.

When at last he reached her mouth again, his taste was easy to name. Whisky and tea. And when he thrust his tongue deep, whisky and need.

So much need.

That was the most stirring, intoxicating part. Everything about his embrace told her that he needed, and what was truly astonishing—that he sought something he needed in *her*. He twisted his hand in the back of her nightrail and kissed her more deeply, relentless, as if chasing that something. Searching for it.

And part of her wanted nothing more than to surrender. To offer whatever he needed of her, and gladly.

Be careful, Izzy.

"Enough." With that gruff pronouncement, he released her. So quickly, she almost stumbled.

The sounds of labored breathing filled the turret.

At length, he cursed. "That was a disaster."

Izzy put her hand to her temple. She was alone in the dark again, and her head was spinning. This was the moment for a witty, sophisticated retort.

What came out of her mouth instead was, "You kissed me first."

"You kissed me back."

"And then you kissed me more." She sighed. So much for sophisticated banter. "I won't make too much of it if that's your concern. I know you only kissed me to intimidate me. But you should know this. It didn't work."

"I think it did work." He pulled her close again. "I felt your heart pounding."

Well, if a pounding heart was a sign of fear . . .

She flattened one hand against his chest, covering the thumping beat there. The man must be terrified.

Izzy felt a strange pang of sympathy for him. Growing up as Sir Henry Goodnight's daughter had taught her all about male pride. Her father had labored for years in obscurity as a poorly paid, frustrated scholar. Once the stories found success, the adulation of readers was the food that sustained him. He couldn't last a week or more without another meal of fawning praise.

And if pride was that important to a middle-aged scholar, Izzy could only imagine how vital it must be to man like the Duke of Rothbury. How difficult adjusting to blindness must be for a man like him, young and strong and in his prime of life. For the first time, he was forced to rely on others. He must hate that feeling.

So he'd learned Gostley Castle, pace by pace, month after month, building a painstaking map of every room in his head. By now this castle was a fortress to his pride. The one place he still felt in control.

And today . . . thanks to some legal quirk, he'd lost it. To a plain, penniless spinster.

It wasn't any great wonder he despised her.

But just because Izzy understood and sympathized, that didn't mean she would give up. She couldn't surrender her own interests just to soothe his pride. She'd made that mistake before, and it was why she found herself here, penniless and stranded in a crumbling castle with nowhere else to go.

She had to look out for herself. No one else would.

"You needn't be anxious, Your Grace. We will do whatever it takes to sift through the papers and legalities. In the meantime, I promise, I won't be much trouble." She gave his chest a gingerly pat.

His hand closed on her forearm and pushed it away. "What you'll be in the morning, Miss Goodnight, is gone. I will see you back to your bedchamber now. And when morning comes, I *will* find you somewhere else to stay."

Izzy relented, saving her strength for tomorrow. In the morning, he would try to make her leave. He might scare her, shout at her, ply her with threats or kisses.

She would be strong as these castle walls.

She would not give one inch.

Chapter Seven

The next morning, Ransom awoke with a surplus of inches—all of them straining against his breeches falls.

Hazy, dreamlike images lingered in his mind. Images of dark hair spilling through his hands and a lush mouth moving under his. A soft hand splayed against his chest.

He turned on his side and groaned. God, that kiss. That stupid, ill-conceived, arousing, soul-rearranging kiss.

She could not spend her nights in this castle. He had to find her other lodgings. Today.

Sitting up, he pushed both hands through his hair. A bath was in order. Preferably a cold one.

"Duncan," he called.

No answer. No valet-sounding noises, either.

He made his way out to the cistern just off the courtyard and drew a bucket of water. Then he stripped to the waist, lifted the bucket high, and poured its freezing contents straight over his head and torso.

Lust be drowned.

The cold shock of his dousing was just starting to wear off when Magnus joined him by the cistern. Ransom drew some water for the dog and gave him a scratch behind the ears.

"Good morning, Your Grace."

Damn. One day, and he'd know that voice anywhere. Husky. Soft. Much too close. How did this woman keep sneaking up on him?

"Goodnight," he muttered.

Her footsteps crossed the courtyard, destroying his calm beat by beat.

Ransom braced himself for his first sight of her.

No one knew it but Duncan and a few useless surgeons, but his injury hadn't left him *completely* blind.

Oh, he was mostly blind, most of the time—blocky shapes and shadows were the best he could make out. And sometimes, he was fully blind. Everything was a dark, murky gray.

But then there were a precious few hours of the day when he was only *partly* blind.

In those hours, he had the vision of a nonagenarian with no spectacles. He could make out vague contours and a few muted colors. A tree might appear as a fuzzy, irregular patch against the sky, its foliage a gray-green shade, like mold on cheese. If he stared at the page of a book, he could force a dark square of text to separate into lines. But he couldn't make out any words or letters. He could get a vague idea of a face—the most prominent features standing out, like the simple face of a child's rag doll. Two button eyes, a slash of mouth. No subtleties of expression.

That was how much he could see at his best. And for once, that seemed like a blessing. He might have been addled by the feel, scent, and taste of Miss Goodnight last night . . . but at least he wouldn't be overwhelmed by the sight of her. At best, she'd appear to him as an anemic, pale column with dark hair. Bland and uninspiring.

He was counting on it.

But as she entered his view, she had the wretched luck to pause just in front of the castle's eastern archway, which was flooded by morning sun.

His first glimpse of Izzy Goodnight was to see her bathed in gold. The sunlight showed him, in blazing relief, a slender, gracefully curved silhouette and a corona of wild, loose hair that seemed to be afire.

Holy God.

If he'd been standing, he might have dropped to his knees. He was sure he heard a choir singing. This was the kind of beauty that one could rightly call "striking."

As in, he felt struck by a brick.

Move, he silently begged her. *Take two steps to the right. Or the left. No, no. Just leave entirely.*

"I didn't think you were awake," he said.

"Oh, I'm awake." He saw a smile—a wide, reddish curve—bloom across her face.

He ran his gaze down her body, taking in the hazy but quite evident curves of her bosom and hips. He'd hold all that against him last night. And now he couldn't fathom why on earth he'd let it go.

"Believe me," she said, "I've been awake since the batwing crack of dawn. I've been exploring my castle."

Right. That was why.

With a whistle to Magnus, he headed back inside. She followed him, of course. All the way into the great hall.

"Do you know," she said, yawning a sultry yawn, "this place really is lovely in the morning. The way the sunlight comes through the windows, taking all that dust in the air and whirling it into gold. We had a rocky start yesterday, but today . . . Gostley Castle is starting to feel like home."

No, no, no. This was not home. Not for her, and most definitely not for *them.*

"Did you . . . want to put on a shirt, Your Grace?" she suggested.

In reply, he crossed his arms over his bare chest. He wasn't doing anything to make her more comfortable.

"I'll make tea," she said, moving toward the

hearth. "Oh, look. Fresh bread." When next she spoke, she did so with her mouth full of it. "Did Duncan fetch this, or does someone bring it up? I know there was milk yesterday." She poked around, making busy clanging noises. "I don't suppose there are eggs? If I do say it myself, I make a very good pancake."

Oh, no. This just grew worse and worse.

I make a very good pancake.

Appalling.

What was even more appalling was that Ransom found himself suddenly hungry for a very good pancake. Starving. Ravenous. Damn it, he was faint with yearning for a very good pancake.

Any self-respecting rake had two kinds of women in his life: those he took to bed at night and those who made him a pancake in the morning. If he suddenly wanted both from the same woman, it was a warning flag. One big and red enough for even a blind man to see.

Get out now. The threat is coming from inside the castle.

"Keep your breakfast simple," he said. "And quick. Duncan will take you to the village this morning. We'll see about finding you lodging in the inn, or—"

"Oh, I'd love to go into the village," she said. "But only for provisions. What sort of fish do you have hereabouts? I'd wager there are some lovely trout in the river."

Ransom gritted his teeth. There were, indeed,

lovely trout in the river. Miss Goodnight was never going to taste them.

He rose to his feet. "You need to understand. You cannot stay here. Not after what happened between us last night."

"Last night," she repeated. "Yes. Do you mean the part where you tried to frighten me off from a property that's legally mine?"

"No. I mean the part where we kissed like illicit lovers."

"Oh." She drew out the word. "That. But we both know that was nothing."

Nothing? Offended, he pushed a hand through his hair. "That was not nothing."

"It was one kiss. One kiss doesn't change anything."

"Of course one kiss changes things. If it's done right, a kiss changes everything. A kiss is the first step on a long, winding, quite perilous path of sensuality. This morning, Miss Goodnight, is where you turn back."

She was quiet for a moment.

"I promise, Your Grace. I won't fling myself at you again. I wanted a kiss, and you gave me one. You are safe from my curiosity."

God. So that's what this was. The girl was letting him down gently. In his eagerness to get a first glance at her, he'd forgotten that she'd be doing the same—taking her first well-lit look at him, and all his scars. Or her second proper look, if he included the time she'd swooned.

You're not a handsome, swaggering buck anymore, you fool.

She went on, "When we're not at work with your correspondence, the castle will keep me fully occupied. There's a great deal to be done here. Rooms to survey. Vermin to purge. A proper bedchamber to furnish." She dropped into a chair nearby. "Bread?"

She touched his hand with a hunk of bread. He took it, resentfully, and tore off a bite with his teeth.

He was beginning to think he'd have to go back to his first strategy—tossing her over his shoulder and toting her away. The problem was, considering how much he enjoyed tossing her over his shoulder, he wasn't sure they'd get very far.

"But before I can think of anything else"—her head turned, and that mass of unbound curls became a fiery whirlwind—"I must find my hairpins. Do you know where you placed them yesterday?" She reached and prodded the cushions to his side. "Maybe they're in the sofa."

He tried—and failed—to ignore the scent of rosemary.

"Aha." She jumped with discovery, and her arm brushed his. "Here's one of them. And another."

Damn her hairpins. He pushed to his feet. "You're not staying here."

"Your Grace, you've made a valiant effort at scaring me off, but you've thrown your worst at me, and it didn't work. Don't you think it's time to give up?"

"No." He jabbed a finger in his chest. "I don't give up. On anything."

"You don't give up?" She laughed a little. "Forgive me, but from what I can gather, you were injured many months ago, and you haven't left this castle since. People in London think you're dead. Your post has gone unanswered, your servants aren't allowed to serve you, and you haven't done a thing to improve your living conditions in a moldering, decrepit castle. I don't know what definition of 'giving up' you're using, Your Grace, but this looks rather like mine."

Ransom fumed at her. How dare she? She had no idea what he'd been through. She had no notion of how hard he'd had to work in those first few months to regain the simplest of capabilities. The ability to walk without stumbling. To count higher than thirty. Damn, it had taken him ages just to relearn how to whistle for his dog. And he hadn't needed any cosseting, nor any managing female to cheer and goad him on. He'd done it on his own, step by excruciating step. Because the alternative was to sit down and die.

He ground out his words. "I . . . don't . . . give up."

"Then prove it."

Easy, Izzy told her galloping heart. *Go easy now.*

The next few minutes called for extreme caution.

In truth, she needed to watch her every step, move, word, and breath with this man . . . but this was different.

Rothbury stood over her. He was shirtless, wet, wild-haired. Handsome as sin and angry as Lucifer. A duke accustomed to having his way. Now she'd not only defied him, she'd directly challenged him.

His words were low and even, but they smoldered like a fuse burning toward gunpowder. "I don't need to prove anything to you."

He propped his hands on his hips. One of his pectoral muscles twitched angrily. As if registering an indignant *harrumph.* A little rivulet of water slalomed through the golden brown hairs on his chest.

Izzy clutched her hairpins so hard, they bit into the soft flesh of her palm.

She rose to her feet. Because that's what one did when moved to genuine awe.

"Of course not, Your Grace," she replied, speaking as calmly she could to his incensed left nipple. "But there are things that need proving. Such as the validity of the property transfer and the . . . and the . . ."

Oh, heavens. Now her *own* nipples decided to have their say in this conversation. Standing this close to him brought back all the memories of their embrace last night. Distracting sensations coursed through her body. Not to mention all those pent-up emotions she'd poured into their kiss.

She crossed her arms over her chest.

"I have a strong hand, literacy in several languages, only two of which are dead—and an abundance of discretion. I will help you sort through all your affairs, and we'll solve the mystery of just how this castle was sold."

"It *wasn't* sold."

"But I won't be pushed about." Izzy opened her eyes. Good heavens, the man was stubborn.

It must have been the nerves raised by proximity, but she had the uncanny sense that he was looking at her. Or through her. And she suddenly felt very embarrassed for staring at his chest.

She tried gentling her voice. "I know you're apprehensive."

"I'm not apprehensive." He pushed a hand through his hair. His arm muscles bunched and flexed in distracting ways. "Good grief, Goodnight. You are the most vexing woman."

Despite everything, Izzy smiled to herself.

She couldn't help it. He'd called her a woman.

"The two of us residing in this castle . . . it's not possible. If you meant to set up house here, you'd need more than brave words. You'd need furnishings, servants. Most importantly, a companion."

"Why a companion? There's Duncan. And there's you."

He snorted. "I'm no chaperone."

"Is it still that silly kiss that's concerning you? I thought we'd reached an understanding."

"Oh, that kiss gave me plenty of understanding." He moved close and lowered his voice to a growl. The air heated between them, and she could have sworn the beads of water on his chest sizzled and became steam. "I understand how your body feels against mine. I understand how sweet you taste. And I understand—precisely— how good we could be together. In bed. Or atop a table. Or against a wall. The problem with understanding seems to be yours."

The air left Izzy's lungs in a breathy, "Oh."

She stared up him. The poor, confused man. He seemed to believe this sort of growly, lewd declaration would send her running and screaming into the countryside. Instead, his words had the opposite effect. With every carnal suggestion he made, her confidence soared to a new, dizzying pinnacle.

He *wanted* her. He wanted *her*.

And she wanted to do a little dance.

"Your Grace?" A bright, feminine voice trilled up from the courtyard, like birdsong. "Do be calm. I'm on my way. Whatever it is you need, I'm here."

Ransom jerked into motion. Whirling away, he reached for a shirt thrown over the sofa's back. It took him a few seconds of fumbling to lay his hand on it.

"Who is it?" Izzy asked, gathering his coat in advance.

Whoever the visitor was, he wanted to look presentable for *her*.

"It's Miss Pelham." He jerked the shirt over his head, punching in different directions to work his arms through the sleeves, then accepted the coat she offered. "The vicar's daughter. Another interfering woman I can't seem to be rid of."

Good heavens. Even vicar's daughters were throwing themselves at him? Izzy didn't find it hard to believe, but she found it a bit disappointing.

Oh, listen to her. It wasn't as though she had some claim on the man. One kiss in the dark, and she'd become a jealous harpy. She pushed the envy aside.

Then a young woman entered the great hall, and the envy pushed right back.

Izzy had been to Court, many parties, and even a London ball or two. She could honestly say this was the most beautiful woman she'd ever seen. Golden hair, with little ringlets placed artfully about her face. Ribbons streaming from her blue muslin frock. Pleasing figure. Practiced smile. Immaculate lace gloves.

"Your Grace?" The young woman breathed the words as a sigh of relief, pressing a hand to her chest. "You're well. Thank the Lord. I expected to find you prostrate and delirious from fever, after the tale I heard from Mr. Duncan. It simply can't be true. Surely you haven't recently received a visitor by the name of—" Then her eyes landed on Izzy, and she halted abruptly. "Oh it is true. She *is* here."

The basket Miss Pelham carried dropped to the floor, and she clapped both hands to her cheeks. "You're Izzy Goodnight?"

Izzy dropped a slight curtsy.

"*The* Izzy Goodnight?"

"Yes. That's me."

The young woman gave a small cry of excitement. "Forgive me. I just can't believe you're here. Really here, so close to my own home. Oh, please say you'll call at the vicarage."

"I . . . I'm sure I'd like that very much, Miss Pelham."

"What an honor, truly. But I can't imagine what brings you to Northumberland."

"It's this." Izzy gestured about them. "Gostley Castle. I have inherited the property from the late Earl of Lynforth."

"Inherited? This?" The young woman's eyes flew wide. "I can't believe it."

Izzy smiled. "It was a shock to us all, I believe. His Grace and I have been negotiating our landlady-tenant relationship."

Miss Pelham bounced in place, and her heels clicked on the stone floor. "I'm going to be neighbors with Izzy Goodnight."

"Miss Pelham . . ." the duke interrupted.

"I've read all the *Tales*, you know. So many times. When I was younger, I cut each installment from the magazine and pasted the pages into a book. I brought it with me just in case the rumor was true." She reached into her basket and pulled out a large, loosely bound volume. "I'd be ever so honored if you'd sign your name to it."

"Miss Pelham."

"Oh, I can't help but ask," she blurted out. "Can I have a lock of your hair, Miss Goodnight? For the book."

"Miss *Pelham*," he interrupted, jarring them both. "Miss Goodnight is under the mistaken impression that it would be safe for her to reside here at the castle until our property dispute is settled. Kindly help me persuade her that this is not the case."

"Oh," Miss Pelham said, drawing out the sound. "Oh, no."

The young woman laid the folio aside. As she drew near, her scent was overpoweringly sweet. Izzy recognized vanilla and . . . gardenias?

Her white lace glove closed protectively on Izzy's wrist. She whispered, "Miss Goodnight, you can't live here alone with him. I've been visiting for months with no inroads. The man is the worst sort of rogue."

Izzy stared at her with amusement. Did she think the duke couldn't hear her whispers?

Rothbury went on, "Now tell her that most of the castle is barely habitable."

"He's right, Miss Goodnight. I've lived down the hill all my life, and it's a shambles in places. Rotted timber, vermin. Most unsafe."

"Good and good," he said. "Now kindly explain that this is not London or York. This is the country, and people hold to traditional values. An unmarried woman cannot take up residence with an unmarried man."

"It's all true," Miss Pelham confirmed. "There would be vicious gossip. The villagers wouldn't have anything to do with you."

Rothbury crossed his arms. "Well, then. It's settled, Miss Goodnight. You cannot remain here, living alone with me. It simply can't happen. I'm sure Miss Pelham will be glad to—"

"Stay with me?" Izzy interrupted.

"What?" His chin jerked in surprise.

Oh, this was good. She had all the advantage now.

"Miss Pelham could stay with me," she explained. "As my companion, just for a few weeks. If she'd be so kind."

"Stay? As companion to *the* Izzy Goodnight?" Miss Pelham squeezed Izzy's arm to the point of inducing pain. "But I'd love nothing more than to help you with whatever you need."

It was becoming evident that Miss Pelham was a very *helpful* sort of young lady. Even when her help wasn't strictly needed or desired.

"I'd be most grateful, Miss Pelham," Izzy said.

"I'm sure Father can spare me. What an excellent solution for all concerned."

"We should thank the duke. I believe it was his suggestion." He couldn't see it, but just the same—Izzy cast a defiant smile in the direction of his scowl. "Isn't he brilliant?"

Chapter Eight

Within a matter of minutes, it was decided. Miss Pelham was overjoyed at the prospect. Duncan offered to accompany her to the vicarage to help fetch her things.

"There," Izzy said, clapping her hands once the two had left. She turned to the duke. "That's all settled. While they're gone, the two of us can get to work."

"What the devil was that?" the duke asked.

"What do you mean?"

"You. Your behavior, the moment Miss Pelham arrived. It was like you became an entirely different person." He mimicked her girlish lilt. " 'Oh, yes, Miss Pelham.' 'I'd be so grateful, Miss Pelham.' "

She sighed. "There's no need for you to be concerned about it."

"I'm not concerned. I'm envious. Why does *she* get the compliant Miss Goodnight, and I get the weasel-wielding harridan?"

"Because she's a Moranglian."

"A what?"

"A Moranglian. My father's stories took place in a fictional country called Moranglia. His most devoted admirers call themselves Moranglians. They have clubs and gatherings and circular letters. And they expect a certain wide-eyed innocence from Izzy Goodnight. I don't want to disappoint them, that's all."

He tapped his fingers on the back of a chair. "So. If I read these stories of your father's, does that mean you'll be meek and docile with me?"

"*No.*"

She was never going to be meek or docile with him, and she was never going to let him read *The Goodnight Tales*. The possibility was out of the question. In fact, the possibility was so far out of the question, the possibility and the question were on separate continents.

"Even if you did read my father's stories, I doubt you'd enjoy them. They require the reader to possess a certain amount of . . ."

"Gullibility?" he suggested. "Inexperience? Willful stupidity?"

"Heart. They require the reader to possess a heart."

"Then you're right. They're not for me. And I'm certainly never going to style myself a Mordrangler."

"Moranglian."

"Really," he said, clearly annoyed. "Does it matter?"

"It doesn't. Not to you." She moved to the table. "And we don't have time to be reading stories anyhow. Not with all this correspondence to go through."

She surveyed the snowdrifts of letters and packets, debating how best to proceed.

"It looks as though they're somewhat chronological. The older letters are the ones nearest to me, and the newer ones spill toward the far end of the table. Do you want to begin with the old or the new?"

"The old," he said without hesitation. "If I'm going to understand just what's going on here, I need to start at the beginning."

Going through every bit of this correspondence would likely take weeks, but Izzy wasn't going to complain. More work meant more money for her fix-the-castle fund. And if she was being honest, as difficult as the Duke of Rothbury was to live with, she wasn't terribly eager to be left alone in the place. Not until it had a good scrubbing. Perhaps an exorcism.

"Very well," she said. "I'll start here at the beginning. As I read, we'll sort papers into two piles: Significant, to be revisited later, and Insignificant, to be set aside. Does that plan meet with your approval?"

"Yes." He reclined on the sofa, sprawling across

the full length of it. It was a largish sofa, but he was an even more largish man. Magnus curled in a heap nearby.

"So while I read, you're just going to lie there. Like a matron reclining on her chaise longue."

"No. I'm going to lie here like a duke, reposed in his own castle."

Hah. He ought to recline while he still could. This wouldn't be his castle for long.

Making use of a nearby letter opener, Izzy started breaking seals and prying open old envelopes. She opened the first, and fattest, one her fingers could locate.

It would seem she'd chosen well. A long list of lines and figures and sums fell out.

"This one looks promising," she said.

"Then don't tease, Goodnight. Just read it."

" 'May it please Your Grace,' " she began. " 'We were most distressed to hear news of your recent injury. Please accept our wishes for your speedy recovery and a return to good health. Per your request, we will forward all estate-related correspondence to your holding in Northumberland, Gostley Castle, until such time as we are given other notice. Enclosed, please find a list of all bills and payments drawn on estate accounts in the previous—"

The duke interrupted. "Are you aware that you're doing that?"

"Doing what?"

"Reading in voices."

"I'm not doing any such thing." Her cheeks warmed. "Am I?"

"Yes. You are. I never knew my accounting clerk sounded just like Father Christmas."

Very well. She *had* been reading the letter in a puffed, clerkish baritone. What of it? Izzy didn't believe he had any cause for complaint.

"Everything's more amusing when read in voices." With a mild shrug, she carried on. "'Enclosed, please find a list of all bills and payments drawn on estate accounts in the previous fortnight.' And then the list follows. One hundred fifteen pounds paid to the wine merchant. Horseflesh purchased at auction, eight hundred fifty. Monthly credit at the Dark Lion gaming club, three hundred."

Wine, fast horses, gambling . . .

The further she scanned, the less favorable a portrait this list painted.

However, she perked with interest at the next line. "Charitable subscription to support the Ladies 'Campaign for Temperance' . . ." She looked over the page at him. "Ten whole guineas. What generosity."

"Never let it be said I do nothing for charity."

"There are lines for servants' wages, the costermonger . . . Nothing strikes me as out of the ordinary." Izzy squinted at a scribbled line. "Except this. One hundred forty paid to The Hidden Pearl. What's that, a jeweler's shop?"

"No." That now-familiar smirk curved his lips. "But they do have lovely baubles on display."

"Oh."

The meaning behind his sly answer and devilish expression sank in. The Hidden Pearl was a bawdy house, of course. And she was a fool.

"You could *call* it a charitable establishment, if it helps," he said. "Some of those poor women have hardly anything to wear."

Izzy ignored him. She held up the letter. "Significant or Insignificant?"

"Significant," he said. "Anything to do with money is significant."

She set the letter on a clear patch of table, making it the base of what would become a small, yet steadily growing stack.

They worked through the envelopes, one by one. A few invitations for long-ago events went into the Insignificant heap, as did the months-old newspapers and charitable appeals. Estate reports and accounting tables went in the Significant pile.

Izzy pulled a thin envelope from the sea of unread letters. "Here's something that was franked by a member of Parliament. It must be very important."

"If you think every letter bearing an MP's frank is important, you have fairy-tale notions of government, too. But by all means, read."

As she opened the letter, a hint of stale, soured perfume assaulted her senses. The penmanship within was scrawling and florid—very feminine. It would seem the letter was not written by the MP himself. Most likely by his wife.

" 'Rothbury,' " Izzy began aloud.

Well, there was a remarkably familiar salutation. The letter must come from someone who knew him well.

She continued. " 'It will shock you to hear from me. It's been months, and we are not the sort to exchange tender missives. But what is this news of you suffering a mysterious injury? In Northumberland, of all the godforsaken places. I hear a hundred rumors if I hear one. Some report you've lost an eye, your nose, or both. Others insist it was a hand. I, of course, care little which appendages you might lop off, so long as no harm comes to that marvelously wicked tongue of yours, and no inches disappear from your magnificent—'"

Izzy froze, unable to read further.

"Do go on," the duke said. "I was enjoying that one. And I've changed my mind—feel free to be creative with the voices. Something low and sultry would be excellent."

"I don't think it's necessary for me to read on. Clearly this letter belongs in the Insignificant pile."

"Oh, Miss Goodnight." His unmarred eyebrow arched. "Weren't you paying attention? There's nothing insignificant about it."

She burned with embarrassment.

"Don't think you'll shame me with your prim silence. I'm not ashamed in the least. Just because you make friends by acting as though you were found under a turnip leaf and raised by gnomes, it doesn't mean everyone takes pleasure in being prudish."

"Prudish?" she echoed. "I'm not a prude."

"Of course not. The reason you stopped reading that letter had nothing to do with being England's innocent sweetheart."

He laced his hands behind his neck and propped his boots on the opposite arm of the sofa. If an artist were to capture this image, it would have been labeled, *Smugness: A Portrait*. She wanted to shake him.

"Cock." She blurted it out. "There. I said it. Aloud. Here, I'll say it again. Cock. Cock, cock, cock. And not just any cock." She glanced at the paper and dropped her voice to a throaty purr. " 'Your magnificent cock, which I long to feel deep inside me again.' "

He went quiet now.

She released her grip, letting the paper drop from her hand. "Satisfied?"

"Actually, Goodnight . . ." He sat up on the sofa, shifting awkwardly. "I am the furthest thing from satisfied. And heartily sorry I pressed the matter."

"Good."

Izzy huffed a breath, dislodging a stray curl from her forehead. Her whole body was hot and achy, and a low throb had settled between her thighs.

Worst of all, her mind was a buzzing hive of curiosity. When it came to a man's organ, just what constituted "magnificence" anyhow? There were clues in the letter, she supposed. Something about precious inches and the ability to reach depths.

She propped her elbows on the table and extended one index finger into the air. How long was that, she mused? Perhaps four inches, at the most? Four inches didn't strike her as a measurement one associated with magnificence.

She extended both index fingers toward one another, letting them touch at the tips. Their combined length was more impressive. But also a little bit frightening.

"Goodnight."

Oh, Lord.

Her elbow slipped, sending a sheaf of papers cascading to the floor. Thank heaven he couldn't see her. "Yes?"

"Do you intend to carry on with your work?"

"Yes. Yes, Your Grace. Of course. Yes."

Enough with these missives from his former lovers.

Izzy searched through the letters, hoping to choose something dry and boring. A report on the state of his tenants' barley crop. Something with absolutely no evidence of his career as a virile, unapologetic, *magnificent* libertine.

"Here's something that was sent as an express," she said, plucking a battered envelope from the bottom of the heap. "It was addressed to you in London, but your people must have forwarded it here."

He sat up, giving her his full attention. "Read it."

"'Your Grace,'" she began.

But before she could read further, she lowered the letter. "So strange. I must have opened twenty of these now. Not one of them has begun with a warm salutation. Not a 'My dear duke' or 'Dearest Rothbury' in the bunch."

"It's not surprising," he said flatly. "It's the way things are."

She laughed a little. "But not always, surely. Somewhere in these hundreds upon hundreds of letters, there's got to be one that's mildly affectionate."

"Feel free to think so. I wouldn't advise holding your breath."

Truly? Not one?

Izzy bit her lip, feeling like a heel for bringing it up. But if no one dared to address him with warmth, it could only be because he forbade it with that stern demeanor. Surely someone, somewhere found him lovable—or least admirable. Hopefully, for a reason that had nothing to do with his financial or physical endowments.

She went back to the letter at hand. Within a few lines, she realized that this was a very different letter than any of the ones she'd read before.

"'Your Grace. By now, you will know I have gone. Do not think I will have regrets. I am sorry— most heartily sorry—for only one thing, and that is that I lacked the courage to tell you directly.'"

The duke's boots hit the floor with a thud. He rose to his feet. His expression was forbidding. But he didn't tell her not to continue.

"'I realize,'" Izzy read on, clearing her throat, "'forgiveness will be beyond you in this moment, but I feel I must offer some explanation for my actions. The plain truth of it is, I could never lov—'"

The paper was ripped from her hands.

Rothbury crumpled it in one hand and tossed it in the grate. "Insignificant."

Insignificant?

Balderdash.

Izzy knew the contents of that letter had been significant. So significant, he couldn't even bear to confront them, so he'd snatched them from her grip and destroyed the truth.

But there was another significant fact to be dealt with, and it had nothing to do with correspondence at all.

She stared at him. "You deceitful rogue. You're not blind."

Chapter Nine

"Y ou're not blind," she repeated.

The statement took him by surprise, but not in an unwelcome way. He would discuss his wretched eyesight all day long if she forgot ever opening that damned letter. The foolish chit who'd penned it should have saved her ink. If forgiveness had been beyond him then, it was utterly hopeless now.

"I am blind," he informed Miss Goodnight. "Why would I pretend it if I weren't?"

"But you just crossed those five paces and ripped a page directly from my hand, with no hesitation. No fumbling." She paused. "And every so often, the way you look at me . . . I've wondered. Sometimes it seems you're completely blind, and at other times it doesn't."

"That's because sometimes I am completely blind, and other times I'm not."

"I don't understand."

"You, and the entirety of the medical establishment. There's some damage to the nerve, I'm told. Inside. It's variable. At certain hours of the day, I can make out shapes and shadows. A few muted colors. On my left side, particularly. Other times, it's all a dark fog. I'm at my best in the mornings."

She slowly pushed back in her chair and stood. "What do you see when you look at me? Precisely."

He let his eyes flitter over her. "I don't see anything 'precisely.' I can tell you're slender. I can see you're wearing white, or some light color. Your face is pale, your lips are reddish. And there appears to be a dark brown octopus attacking your head."

"That's my hair."

Ransom shrugged. "You asked what I see. I see tentacles."

He could sense her irritation with that answer, and he was glad of it. What was she expecting, compliments? He wasn't about to tell her that her mouth was a splash of wine he wanted to lick. Or that her rounded curves made his hands ache to cup and stroke. Even if those things were the truth.

"Who else knows the full extent of your injuries?" she asked.

"Only a few useless doctors, Duncan, and . . . and now you."

Ransom intended to keep it that way. He'd had enough trouble wrestling his own stupid hope into submission. He couldn't contend with others' expectations, too. If Abigail Pelham knew he could sometimes see, for example, she'd be forever pestering him. She'd write to London specialists for eye-training exercises, and she'd ask him a thousand questions.

Is it getting better yet?

Do you notice some improvement?

Does this make any difference?

How about now?

And now?

And, of course, the answers would be nothing but no, no, no, no.

And no.

"Enough about my eyes. There are only two things you need to know. One, I can navigate this castle better than you can. Two, I can't read those letters on my own." Ransom returned to the sofa and took his seat. "So pick up the next and get on with it."

"Yes, Your Grace."

Happily, this time she selected a dry, boring report from one of his land agents. Timmons, at the Surrey estate. A very thorough man, bless him. There were pages upon pages of sheep-health advisements and crop-rotation plans.

He could have cut her off one page into the

reading. There was nothing he expressly needed to hear about improvements to the old stables. But he couldn't bring himself to stop her.

He liked listening to her read. He liked it far too much. Listening to her voice was like floating along a river. Not a babbling stream, bouncing over rocks and such, but a river of wild honey with depth and a low, sweet melody. To keep afloat, he would have let her read just about anything. Even those soppy stories from Menstrualia, or whatever it was called.

"Here's another from the accountant," she said, after some time had passed.

Excellent. Another long, meaningless list of information for her to read. However, she hadn't progressed very far into it before stopping.

"That's odd," she said.

"What's odd?"

"Your expenses with the costermonger have quadrupled when compared to the previous report."

"What of it? It's the costermonger."

"Well, yes . . . and it's not exactly a great sum. But it's odd that your housekeeper would have suddenly spent four times as much on vegetables. You weren't even in residence by then."

Ransom supposed it *was* a bit odd.

"Never mind," she said. "I only notice because I always paid those sorts of household accounts. The butcher, the costermonger, the laundress. It wouldn't be important to you."

No, it wouldn't. Such an expense would have been completely beneath Ransom's notice. Which suggested one thing: If someone was trying to steal from him, padding the costermonger bill was the perfect way to do it.

"Let's compare the two reports again." He walked over to the table and joined her. "In detail, slowly."

"Give me a moment to find it."

Miss Goodnight wasn't the secretary he would have chosen. But she might have just the critical eye he needed. Considering the amounts of money his solicitors had access to use—and potentially misuse—she could turn out to be a bargain.

But they didn't have a chance to begin their scrutiny of the accounts.

"Miss Goodnight!"

Ransom groaned. Miss Pelham was back.

"Miss Goodnight, doubt not! We have returned. I have all my things from the vicarage, and our cook and housemaid will be coming along shortly to help us get started."

"Wonderful," Miss Goodnight called back, rising from her chair. "I'll be right there." To Ransom she said, "We'll have to continue this tomorrow, Your Grace."

"Hold a moment," Ransom objected. "I'm not waiting until tomorrow."

"I'm afraid there's no choice."

Oh, that's where she was wrong. He was a duke. He always had the choice.

Through gritted teeth, he told her, "You have a post as my secretary. I'm not paying you two hundred pounds a day to rearrange furniture and hang drapes. Now, sit back down and find that list of payments."

"Did I hear a please?" She waited a beat. "No, I didn't think so."

"Damn it, Goodnight."

"Dock my wages for the afternoon, if you like." She began walking away. "The accounting will have to wait for tomorrow. If you don't allow me and Miss Pelham to prepare a warm, comfortable, rat-and-bat-free bedchamber before nightfall, I promise you—there won't be a tomorrow at all."

Miss Pelham called down from the gallery. "Do come along, Miss Goodnight! Let's set about making this castle into a home."

A home.

Those words sent dread spiraling through him.

There was no use fighting it any longer. Miss Goodnight was settling in. Making a home. Just bloody wonderful.

Ransom began to wonder if he'd made such an excellent bargain after all.

As young ladies went, Miss Abigail Pelham was everything that made Izzy despair. From the moment the vicar's daughter had walked—nay, floated—into the great hall, Izzy had known they were creatures of different breeds.

Miss Pelham was the sort of young woman

who had plans, made lists, kept a beauty regimen. The sort who knew, somehow, which straw bonnets in the milliner's shop would suit her and never ended up looking a beribboned scarecrow. The sort who always smelled of vanilla and gardenias, not because she liked baking or working in the garden—but because she'd decided it was her signature scent, and she kept sachets tucked between her stored undergarments.

She was competent in the art that motherless, awkward Izzy had never mastered. The art of being feminine. If she had met Miss Pelham at a party, they would have had less to say to each other than a bright-winged parrot sharing a perch with a common wren.

Luckily, this was not a party. This was a housecleaning, and it became immediately clear that in *this* endeavor, Izzy couldn't have asked for a more enthusiastic partner.

Miss Pelham surveyed the ducal chamber, sniffing at the moth-eaten hangings. "It was horrid of the duke to put you in this chamber. This room isn't without its potential. But it's hardly the place to start, either."

"I agree," Izzy said.

"We'll make a tour of the whole castle this morning." Miss Pelham left the room in a brisk swoop. "This afternoon, we'll choose one room to begin with," she went on. "One that's small and easy to clean. We'll sweep it out, fit it with a proper bed by tonight. Check the chimney, of course. Some of them are clogged with birds' nests and only the good Lord knows what else."

She stopped in her paces, shivered—and squealed.

"I can't tell you how excited I am to be doing this. At last. It's been torture, living down the hill from this wonderful castle all my life and watching it slip further and further into ruin. And, finally, we will have some jobs and custom for the local parishioners."

Izzy followed the relentless ribbon of chatter, amused. If Miss Pelham was at all winded by their pace, she didn't show it.

For her part, Izzy kept her mouth shut and her eyes open. As they moved through the corridors, the daylight revealed most of the chambers to be in a discouraging state. Many of the windows were broken out. Everything that could be chewed by moths or mice, had been. Dust and cobwebs coated the rest, like a blanket of grayish snow.

"We'll have to set reasonable goals," Miss Pelham continued. "This castle wasn't built in a day, and it won't be made livable in one day, either."

"Judging by the architecture, building it took a few hundred years," Izzy said. "I hope making it livable doesn't take *that* long."

Miss Pelham turned at the bottom of the stairs and smiled. "You must know so much about castles. From dear Sir Henry, of course."

Here we go.

"Yes." Izzy pasted a sweet smile on her face. "I always loved hearing my father give his lectures."

"How lucky you were to have him." Miss Pelham looked her over. "And how clever you are today. I'll have to change into my work smock, but here you've had the foresight to wear yours already."

Izzy touched the skirts of her frock—her best morning dress—and tried to smile.

As they turned a corner, she recognized a familiar set of stairs. "Let's go up here."

Miss Pelham followed reluctantly. "There can't be much up here. The stairs are too narrow. We'll have to resist the urge to explore every nook just yet, or we'll never complete our survey of the castle. We'll walk through the main towers today, and by afternoon, we should be able to narrow down the options for your bedroom."

Thirty-two, thirty-three . . .

"This one," Izzy said, emerging into the turret room. "This is the room I've chosen."

The turret room was even more enchanting by day than it had been by night. The vaulted ceiling tapered to a point above, and a golden shaft of sunlight pierced the sole window.

As Izzy went to the window, her heart beat faster. An inspiring green vista of rolling hills and castle walls spread below. Oh, there was even ivy climbing the walls, with songbirds nesting in it.

"This one?" Miss Pelham didn't sound as though she saw the room's charms. "This would be terribly impractical, what with all those stairs. Drafty, too, I'm sure. There isn't even a hearth."

"No hearth means we wouldn't have to clean out a chimney." *No hearth means no bats.* "And it's summer. I can make do with blankets." Izzy circled the room. "This must be my chamber."

"You truly are little Izzy Goodnight, aren't you?" Miss Pelham smiled broadly. "Oh! Shall we paint the ceiling with silver moons and golden stars?"

She referred to Izzy's bedroom in *The Goodnight Tales*—the one with a purple counterpane and the starry heavens painted on the ceiling. The room that had never even existed.

"No need to do that," she said. "At night, I can see the real stars."

She didn't want to feel like a little girl in this room. In this room, she was a woman. A temptress. This was where she'd had her first *true* kiss.

A kiss from a roguish, impossible duke, who'd only kissed her under duress. But it was a kiss nonetheless, and one she still felt at the corners of her whisker-rasped lips.

"Well," Miss Pelham said, "eventually, on the floor below we should make you a proper suite, with a sitting room and quarters for your lady's maid. But I suppose this room will do for a start."

"I'm glad you like it."

"Like it?" She linked arms with Izzy and squeezed tight. "I'm so pleased, I could squeal."

Please. Please don't.

"We have a hard day's work ahead of us," Miss Pelham said. "But tonight, we'll have a proper bedchamber. We'll plait each other's hair. Dive beneath the coverlet and tell tales until an ungodly hour. Oh, this will be such fun."

And it *was* fun, for an hour or two.

But in the end, that night was just like every other night of Izzy's life.

Once again, she woke to darkness, her heart pounding with terror and her throat scraped raw.

Strange noises assailed her from all sides.

I am not alone, she told herself, struggling to master her breath. I have Miss Pelham here with me.

But she would feel much better if Miss Pelham were awake, too. Izzy tossed back and forth on the bed, hoping her movements would wake her companion.

When Miss Pelham didn't stir, she moved on to direct methods. She laid a hand on the young woman's shoulder and gave it a brisk shake.

Nothing.

"Miss Pelham. Miss Pelham, I'm sorry to disturb you. Please wake."

The vicar's daughter snored, once. Loudly.

But she did not wake.

Good heavens. Just before bed, she'd opined that she wasn't afraid of ghosts. That good Christians had no reason not to sleep soundly. She hadn't been joking about that sleeping soundly bit. The woman slept like a rock.

Which now struck Izzy as highly unjust. Had she been a bad Christian all her life? She didn't attend church so often as she likely should, but she wasn't precisely a heathen.

Although, to be fair, in the past twenty-four hours, she'd shamelessly kissed a duke and spent a great deal of time pondering the idea of . . . magnificence.

A distant wailing rattled her to the bones.

That was it. She was getting out of bed. That noise was definitely not her imagination.

Izzy shook Miss Pelham's shoulder. "Miss Pelham. Miss Pelham, wake."

"What is it, Miss Goodnight?" The young woman turned over lazily, hair mussed from sleep. It gave Izzy a small sense of satisfaction to see Miss Pelham with her hair mussed.

Then the moaning began again, and she lost all interest in coiffures.

"Did you hear that?" Izzy asked.

"I'm sure it's nothing."

"It's a very loud nothing. Hush. There it is again."

Miss Pelham frowned and listened. "Yes, I see what you mean."

Thank God. I'm not going mad.

"What could it be? I've heard that there are wild cattle in the park, but that noise sounds much too close."

They listened to it again—that low, broken howl.

Miss Pelham sat up. "A shepherd blowing his horn?"

"At this time of night? Over and over?" Izzy shuddered.

"Well, it's not a ghost. I don't believe in ghosts."

"Neither did I until I moved in here."

Miss Pelham sighed. "There's only one way to find out. We'll investigate."

"Must we?" Izzy asked. "On second thought, I can live without knowing. Let's just go back to bed."

"You are the one who woke me, Miss Goodnight. I don't think you'll sleep well until we've put the mystery to rest."

Izzy was afraid she'd say that. "Perhaps someone is just playing tricks on us."

"It's certainly possible." Miss Pelham reached for her dressing gown. "I wouldn't put it past the duke. No doubt he wants to lure us out of our bedchambers in our shifts. Be sure to close your dressing gown with a very tight knot."

"He's blind. How would he be able to tell?"

"He'd be able to tell."

Yes, Izzy supposed he would.

Though Izzy wasn't thrilled at the prospect of skulking through the castle at midnight again, she felt more confident knowing that Miss Pelham would be joining the sally.

Once they'd each knotted their dressing robes and donned boots, they lit candles. Izzy patted her pocket. Empty. Snowdrop must be out hunting or curled in her nest.

Lucky Snowdrop.

They took the stairs together, proceeding slowly in the dark. One after the other. Sometimes Miss Pelham would speed up and turn the corner before Izzy, and her figure and candlelight would drift from view. Then Izzy would hasten to catch up, sure she could feel ghostly fingers on the back of her neck.

"Do you see anything that way?" Miss Pelham asked, once they emerged into the corridor.

Izzy held the candlestick high with her right hand and peeked through the fingers of her left. "No."

"Nothing to this side, either."

The noise came again.

"Not to worry, Miss Goodnight. Old buildings like these make all sorts of strange sounds. No doubt it's just timbers settling, or a door creaking back and forth on rusted hinges."

Both those explanations sounded reassuringly plausible.

They emerged into the courtyard, and were nearly across it when an immense figure emerged from the shadows, stopping them in their path.

"Duncan," Izzy gasped, pressing a hand to her thumping heart. "You scared us."

The valet held his lamp aloft, illuminating the stark lines of his face. "What are you ladies doing out of bed?"

Once again, a keening howl rose up into the night, lifting every hair on Izzy's arms with it.

"That's what we're doing out of bed," she said.

"What can it be?" Miss Pelham asked.

Duncan shook his head. "Likely cats wailing or foxes having a fight. Whatever it is, I'll scare it off. You ladies should return to your chamber."

"We're coming with you," Izzy said.

They'd ventured this far. She'd rather face whatever it was with Duncan present than make that walk back to their chamber alone.

"Really, Miss Goodnight. It's not—"

Before he could finish his warnings, Miss Pelham shrieked and pointed. "A ghost!"

A white, filmy apparition came streaking out of the tower. It writhed and howled, twisting its way across the courtyard like a wraith.

It wasn't a ghost.

It was Magnus.

Poor wolf-dog Magnus, caught in a Holland cloth they'd hung up with the washing. He was moving so swiftly, it took Izzy a few moments to discern the reason for his distress.

But she ought to have guessed at the cause.

Snowdrop.

The ermine had gone hunting, all right— hunting for big game.

She was attached to the end of Magnus's tail, holding on by the strength of her vicious teeth. The dog caromed around the courtyard, whipping and howling in an effort to shake her off.

"Oh, the poor thing." Laughing, Izzy set off in pursuit. "Duncan, can you catch him?"

It took some doing, but eventually they managed to corner the beasts. Duncan held the dog still while Izzy pried Snowdrop's jaws from his tail.

"There. You little menace."

Miss Pelham winced as she studied the bite wound on the dog's tail. "I'll see to bandaging the poor dear. It's a deep wound. In my kit, there's some salve that will help. It's in the great hall. Duncan, we'll need bandages."

Duncan started off before she even finished. "Of course, Miss Pelham."

Izzy cradled the ermine in her hands. "I'll take Snowdrop back up to the turret and make sure she can't escape, and then I'll join you."

The plan established, they parted and went their separate ways.

Izzy mounted the stairs, Snowdrop tucked securely in the pocket of her dressing gown. The ermine seemed to have tired from the chase, and she went to sleep at once.

"The duke will be most put out with you," Izzy chided, locking the animal into her gilded ball. "And put out with me, no doubt."

Where *was* Rothbury, anyhow? He couldn't possibly have slept through all that howling. And even if he could, he ought have noticed that the commotion involved his own dog.

Despite her questions, Izzy's steps were light

and carefree as she made her way back down to the great hall. Now that their keening, wailing ghost had been unmasked and proved to be something so benign, she felt a new sense of bravery welling in her chest.

She truly could do this. She could make this place her home.

And then . . .

While breezing down the corridor, Izzy caught a glimpse of something in one of the vacant rooms.

A glimpse of something pale and writhing.

And moaning.

Her heart made an impulsive attempt to escape her body by way of her throat. But she didn't run away. She inched closer, holding the candle tight.

Slowly, the ghostly apparition came into focus.

Izzy blinked. "Your Grace?"

Chapter Ten

Damn, damn, damn.

Ransom winced as her familiar voice sliced through his throbbing skull.

She *would* have to find him here, see him like this. Down on the ground, his knees cut out from under him. Crippled by searing pain.

Why had he ever agreed to a duel with swords? He should have insisted on pistols. He'd be dead now, of course. But in times like this, dying seemed preferable to one more minute of this burning, shooting pain.

"What is it?" she asked. "Are you unwell?"

She padded across the floor and crouched at his side.

"Go away. Leave me." He rolled onto his side,

curling his knees to his stomach and pressing his skull against the cool, smooth stone.

"Are you having some sort of attack?"

"Just . . ." He flinched as a fresh burst of pain ripped from his eye socket to the back of his skull. "Just a headache."

It wasn't just a headache. It was a headagony. The pain ripped from the back of his skull, curving around one side of his scalp to stab him just behind the eye.

Again and again and again.

"How can I help?" she asked.

"By leaving."

"I won't do that. You didn't leave me when I swooned."

"Different," he muttered. "Wasn't—"

"It wasn't kindness. I know, I know. Something about vermin. If you don't want me, shall I fetch Duncan?"

"No." He managed to pronounce the word with gunshot force, but it had a wicked recoil. White streaks of pain flared behind his eyelids.

She didn't leave him. "Do you need water? Whisky? Some sort of powder?"

He gritted his teeth and gave a tight shake of his head. "Nothing works. Have to wait it out."

"How long?"

"An hour, perhaps."

An hour that would feel like a lifetime. A lifetime of being stabbed through the base of his skull with a spike. Repeatedly.

"I'll stay with you," she said.

Her hand settled on his shoulder, and the touch sent a shiver through him.

Ransom was accustomed to dealing with pain on his own. In his early life, he hadn't been given a choice. His mother had died less than an hour after his birth. His father had showed no patience with tears he might shed over stubbed toes and scraped knees. If he hurt himself or fell ill, the old duke thought he should overcome the pain on his own. The nursemaids and house staff were forbidden to give him so much as a hug. No coddling. No small mercies. His father had insisted on it.

And his father had been right. By learning to recover on his own, Ransom had grown into a strong, independent man. Untouchable. Invincible.

Right up until the moment a short sword caught him across the face.

Her fingers brushed over his ruined brow.

"I don't need you here," he said.

"Of course you don't. You're a big, strong, manly duke, and you don't need anyone, I know. I'm not here for you. I'm here for me. Because I need to stay."

With a sigh, he gave in. He hadn't the strength to argue it further.

She settled beside him and drew his head into her lap. "There, now. Be easy. Be calm."

Her fingers drifted through his hair, tracing delicious furrows on his scalp. Each caress seemed to stroke away a bit of the pain.

Her touch was like magic—or the closest thing to a miracle a man like him could ever credit. She found the sharp edge of his pain and dulled it with gentle sweeps of her fingertips.

And her voice. That deep, sweet river of her voice, carrying him away from the pain.

It was so foreign to him, this unsolicited tenderness. Incomprehensible. And much as he craved it, it scared him like hell. With every caress he permitted, he was piling up debts he could never repay.

You don't deserve it, came that dark, unforgiving echo. He'd heard the words so many times, they were part of him now. They lived in his blood, resounding with each hollow beat of his heart. *You don't deserve this. You never could.*

Her thumb found a knot at the base of his skull and pressed. He moaned.

She immediately stilled. "Am I distressing you?"

"No. Yes." He turned so that his head lay in the cradle of her lap, and he stretched one arm about her waist, shameless. "Just . . ."

"Yes?"

"Don't stop." He sucked in his breath as a fresh wave of pain nearly knocked him cold. "Don't stop."

"I won't stop," she promised.

Izzy's heart twisted. There was something so moving about seeing a man so big, so powerful, curled up like a puppy on the floor, damp with perspiration and writhing in evident pain.

His arms laced tight about her waist.

She'd been alone for a long time. In some ways, since well before her father died. And she was well-enough acquainted with loneliness to understand that the worst part wasn't having nobody caring for you—it was having nobody to care for.

Izzy didn't know if these gentle sweeps of her fingertips could erase his pain—but they were dismantling the safeguards around her heart.

She soothed her touch over his brow and scalp, making shushing noises and whispering what she hoped were comforting words.

What happened? she longed to ask. *What happened tonight? What happened all those months ago?*

"Speak," he said.

"What shall I speak of?"

"Anything."

How strange. Izzy found herself on the receiving end of questions daily, but she was never asked to talk about . . . anything on her mind. Now that he'd requested it, she didn't even know what to say.

She stroked his hair again.

"Talk of anything," he said. "Tell me a story, if you must. One from Mudpuddlia."

She smiled. "I'd rather not. My life's work was helping my father. But that doesn't mean I'm a little girl living in his tales. To be sure, I enjoy a romantic story, but I also like newspapers and sporting magazines."

She dropped her touch to his neck and began

to work loose the knots of muscle there, working in gentle circles.

He groaned.

She stilled her fingers. "Shall I stop?"

"No. Just keep talking. Which sport?"

"When I was a girl, I followed all of it. My father was just a tutor then, and I was a girl who read anything she could lay hands on. One of his pupils passed along stacks of magazines. Boxing, wrestling. Horseracing was my favorite. I would read every article, study every race. I'd pick horses, and my father would place the bets. We could always use the extra money."

She reclined her weight on one outstretched arm and settled in to tell him all about the year she picked the winners in both the Ascot and Derby, sparing no detail of her bloodline research and odds calculations. He just wanted her to keep talking, and so she did.

"Anyhow," she finished, minutes later, "we did well with it."

"It sounds as though *you* did well with it." He released a long, heavy sigh and turned onto his back, so that he faced her.

"Is the pain any better, Your Gr—" She cut herself short, unable to complete the proper form of address. She held his head in her lap, and she'd just babbled on about her boring life. This was the least ducal or graceful moment imaginable. What point was there in formality?

She thought of all those letters she'd pored over

that morning. How they all began with "Your Grace" or "May it please the duke" or something similarly cold.

He needed someone to treat him like a *person*. Not an untouchable duke but a man worth caring for. And as she could imagine Duncan would prefer to swallow bootblack before breaking with his traditional role, Izzy decided that person would have to be her.

"Ransom," she whispered.

He didn't object, so she tried it again.

"Ransom, are you better?"

He nodded, putting one hand over his eyes and massaging his temples. "Better. Somewhat."

"Do you have these headaches often?" she asked.

"Not so often anymore. They're just . . . sudden. And vengeful. This one cut my legs out from under me. At least when it's over, the pain leaves as swiftly as it arrived."

He began struggling to a sitting position. "Don't tell Duncan," he said. "He'll insist on sending for a doctor."

"Maybe a doctor would be a good idea," Izzy replied.

Ransom shook his head, wincing as he did. "No. There's nothing they can do."

He pushed to a standing position. Izzy stood, too. And then watched, cringing, as the six-foot-tall column of duke slowly pitched to the right.

"Oh, dear." She lunged into action, using both

hands and all her body weight to prop him back up. "You should rest, Your Grace."

"So should you." His hand stroked up and down her arm. "What are you doing out of bed anyhow?"

"I . . . er . . ." She hesitated, not knowing how to explain the "ghost hunt," and not wanting to tell him her weasel had nearly bitten off his poor dog's tail.

But he didn't appear ready to comprehend the story anyhow. "Are you certain you're well?"

"It's always this way." He steadied himself with one hand on her shoulder. "Even after the pain is gone, my mind doesn't work properly for an hour or two. It's like being drunk."

She smiled at the heavy weight of his hand on her shoulder. At last, he was accepting a small measure of assistance from her, unforced and unprompted.

"Well, at least you're a friendly drunk," she said. "There's that. In fact, I think I might like you much better this way."

"I like you too much." His slurred, mumbled words were almost too low to hear.

They were too ludicrous to be trusted.

I like you too much.

Izzy flushed with heat. He couldn't really mean that. He wasn't himself right now. That was all.

"You really should rest," she said. "Let me take you down to the great hall so you can sleep." She started to drape his arm over her shoulders like a yoke.

He turned to face her. Instead of draping over her shoulders, his arm slid around her back. "At least kiss me good night."

Heavens. He truly *was* behaving as if he were drunk. He probably wouldn't even remember this encounter in the morning.

In which case . . . Why not?

Stretching up on her toes, she kissed his unshaven cheek. "Good night, Ransom."

"No, no." He drew her close, and together they wobbled back and forth. "Not what I meant. Isolde Ophelia Goodnight, kiss me. With every ounce of passion in your soul."

"I . . ." Flustered, she swallowed hard. "I'm not sure I even know how."

The quirk of his lips was shameless. "Use your imagination."

Now *that* was an invitation she'd been waiting a lifetime to hear.

She pressed her lips to his, softly. He remained still, letting her do the kissing. She laced her arms around his neck, leaning close. She brushed lingering kisses over his upper lip, then the bottom. Just lightly, tenderly. Again and again.

These kisses . . . they were confessions. Tastes of everything she had stored inside her. Everything she could give a man if he was brave enough to accept. Kiss by kiss, she was baring herself to the soul.

Here is my soft caress.
Here is my patience.
Here is my understanding.
Here is my tender, beating heart.

He whispered her name, and the raw emotion in his voice undid her. His hands cinched the fabric at the small of her back. As though he needed her. Not only to remain standing, but to go on existing at all. "*Izzy.*"

Light footsteps sounded from the far end of the corridor.

"Miss Goodnight?" Miss Pelham's voice.

Izzy pulled away from the kiss. His brow rested against hers. This was madness.

"I have to go," she whispered.

They couldn't be discovered like this. It would require too many explanations that would embarrass them both.

"Miss Goodnight, are you there?" Miss Pelham was closer now.

"Your Grace. I must go."

He held her tight, forbidding her to move. His breathing was still labored.

And then, suddenly, he lifted his head. His eyes, unseeing as they were, seemed to narrow.

He'd jolted back to himself, she could tell. A sudden lightning bolt had filled him with realizations: who he was, and who she was, and every reason he shouldn't be holding her.

With familiar brusqueness, he released her. "Go."

Chapter Eleven

That night, Ransom dreamed of dark hair and a lush, red mouth. And heat. Tight, wet heat moving over him, under him.

Yes.

No.

No, no, no. He was waking.

Don't wake, he told his mind. Not all the way. Not yet.

He rolled onto his side. Keeping his eyes shut tight, he unbuttoned his breeches and curled a grip around the rigid column of his cock. He rarely felt like a frig anymore, despite how long he'd gone without a woman.

Maybe release wouldn't elude him this time.

He stroked his hand up, then down. Slowly, at first. Then faster.

In his half-dream trance, he felt it as *her* grip. And then as her *mouth*. And then as her sweet, wet, tight . . .

"Fascinating."

Ransom jolted fully awake. Damn him to hell. He knew that husky voice.

"Goodnight?"

"Good morning." Her tone was distracted.

What was she doing down here at this hour? Hopefully not watching with schoolgirl curiosity as he tugged away at his cock. He wasn't ashamed, precisely, but he wasn't eager to explain himself, either.

"I didn't mean to wake you," she said. "It's just that your family's history is so fascinating."

He heard the flip of a page.

She'd been reading a book. Not watching him.

He stretched back on his pallet and released a string of profanity. "Good grief, Goodnight. It's too damn early."

"It's morning. Almost. And I'm reading this book Miss Pelham gave me about the history of the area. The Rothbury story is just marvelous."

"I'm glad my family's centuries of bloodshed, tyranny, and conniving amuse you."

He blinked, trying to make some sense of her. Visually, if not rationally.

She sat in profile, silhouetted by firelight, tucked into an armchair not five feet away. Her whole body made one pale, sensuous, spiraling curve. He glimpsed a bare foot dangling just over the seat's edge, twisting idly to and fro.

Her foot stopped. Stretched forward, with tantalizing slowness.

She turned another page. "I've only read through the fifth duke's imprisonment for treason. What happens next?"

"He was held in the Tower of London for years. Queen Mary held the throne just long enough to remove the charges."

"Ah," she said. "A stroke of luck there. I suppose they had to recover the castle by purchasing it back. That must be why the property was no longer entailed?"

Ransom struggled to a sitting position, his loins still pulsing with unspent lust. He reached for his boots and began tugging them on. Judging by the faint gray cast of his vision, it had to be damned early. Barely daybreak. And if she'd been sitting there reading for some time, as her cozy posture indicated, that must mean she'd come down while it was still night.

"Are you feeling well this morning?" Her question was cautious.

"Yes." His answer was curt. Ransom left no room for further discussion. He couldn't abide thinking about last night—couldn't begin to even make sense of it.

She set aside her book. "Just so you know, I'll only work until noon today. Miss Pelham is hiring housemaids in the village this morning, and we have plans to clear a dressing room in the afternoon. You're welcome to help."

"Goodnight," he said in a low, warning tone. "You're not going to waste more time cleaning house."

She set the book aside. "You're not the only one with a goal here, Your Grace. You want to find out what's happened to your business affairs? Well, I want a home. Mornings will be correspondence, afternoons will be castle. If we do this my way, we both get what we want."

Ransom pushed a hand through his hair. He wanted about a thousand things he wasn't getting, and approximately nine hundred of them involved her lips.

If she was so interested in a cozy home, why wasn't she up in her room?

"Is something wrong with your turret?"

"No. Not at all. I woke and . . . I suppose I was just a little cold. I came down to sit by the fire."

Then she made a strange, small sound.

"*Tsh.*"

"What was that?" he asked.

"What was what?"

"That noise you made. It sounded like a flea in the throes of passion."

"Oh, that. It was nothing. Just a sneeze."

He stopped. "That wasn't a sneeze. No one sneezes like that."

"I do, apparently." She sniffed. "Oh, dear. I'm going to do it again."

Another muffled, high-pitched paroxysm, like a mouse shushing a vole. Then another.

"*Tsh. Tsh.*"

Ransom winced at each one. "Good God, that's disturbing."

She sniffed. "It's not *meant* to be."

"That can't be healthy. If you need to sneeze, sneeze properly."

She did it again. Three of them this time. Little twitchy sounds.

"*Tsh! Tsh! Tsh!* This is just how I sneeze," she moaned. "I can't help it. This castle is dusty. And the turret has a draft."

Now this was a problem. She couldn't do any secretarial work if she fell ill. And Ransom couldn't survive this cohabitation much longer unless she stayed in her room the whole night.

Very well. He would permit her a few afternoons of housecleaning. And tonight, he vowed, she would be warm and comfortable in her bed, and, most importantly, far away.

He made a mental note.

Procure some blankets. Thick ones.

He did procure blankets. Thick ones.

But the next morning, there she was again. "Good morning."

And once again, Ransom jolted awake, with an aching cockstand and furious temper. He swore for a minute straight.

"Reading more history books?" he muttered.

"Writing a letter." Her pen scratched across the page. "I do have correspondence of my own, you know. Would you rather fight one hundred rat-sized elephants or one elephant-sized rat?"

He shook his head, trying to clear it. "What?"

"It's a question. If you had the choice, which would you rather do battle against? A hundred elephants the size of rats, or one rat the size of an elephant?"

"You seem to be under the impression that you're making sense. You're not."

"It's not a practical question, of course," she said. "It's just for discussion. Lord Peregrine and I have been corresponding for years. In his letters, he always poses these silly conundrums, and we debate them back and forth."

"Wait, wait. There's some lecherous old stick who writes you these letters directly? Why don't you tell the presumptuous rogue to go to the devil?"

"It's not like that. He's bedridden, poor thing. And he doesn't think of me as a woman, I assure you."

So this Lord Peregrine fellow had the imagination to picture battles with elephant-sized rats and rat-sized elephants, but he couldn't possibly think of Izzy Goodnight as a woman? On that point, Ransom was skeptical. Even if a man was bedridden, he was still a man.

With his injuries, there were many who'd consider Ransom an invalid. He was still a man. Every morning that he woke to the husky softness of her voice, his cock went granite-hard in response.

"So which would it be?" she went on. "The plague of tiny elephants or one giant rat? And as a corollary, what weapons would you choose?" She tapped her pen nib against the table. "I'm torn, myself. The giant rat would seem easier to kill *if* I could thrust a sword straight in its heart. But then, what if I missed? Then I'd be facing an enraged, wounded, giant rat."

Ransom had to give this Lord Peregrine one thing. His letters were excellent at withering lust.

"Tiny elephants would seem less lethal," she went on. "How much damage could two hundred miniature tusks wreak on a person, anyhow? Perhaps they'd tire themselves out if I had good shin-plates. What do you think?"

"I think you're debating what sort of armor to wear to a miniature-elephant attack. I think that's madness."

"What you call madness, I call . . . creative thinking. You could benefit from some of that, Your Grace."

He speared both hands through his hair. "Why are you down here at all? Write your letters upstairs."

"I don't have a writing desk upstairs."

Today's task: Procure a writing desk.

"Are you awake?" she whispered.

Not *again*.

Ransom rubbed his face. "I am now."

Jesus Christ. This had to stop.

It had been almost a week now. Every day since she'd arrived, he woke to the sounds of Izzy Goodnight all too near.

He didn't know what time of night she was sneaking down here. He didn't *want* to know. He'd taken up drinking himself into a nightly stupor to avoid knowing.

In the past few days, he'd arranged for her to have a companion, blankets, a brazier, a writing desk. What more would it take to get her to stay in her damned room until a decent hour of morning?

A lock and chain, perhaps.

"I thought of something," she said excitedly. "It came to me last night, in bed. R-A-N-S-O-M."

He stretched a knot from his neck. "What?"

"That first night, you said, 'Do I have to spell out the danger?' But then halfway through, you forgot how to spell danger."

"I didn't forget how to spell the word," he objected. "I just got bored with the spelling of it."

The truth was, he wasn't as quick with words as he'd once been. Especially when he grew fatigued.

These predawn conversations with Izzy Goodnight were extremely fatiguing.

"Well, anyway. That's what you *should* have said." She lowered her voice to mimic his. "'Do I have to spell out the danger for you? R-A-N-S-O-M.'"

He scrubbed the sleep from his face with both hands. "That's ridiculous. I'd never say that."

"Why not? It's perfect. Your name is the one word you can't forget how to spell."

He shook his head, frowning. "This argument was days ago now. It's over. And you've been thinking about this spelling nonsense ever since?"

"I know, I know. It's absurd. But that's always the way for me. I never think of the right thing to say until days later." She drifted closer to where he sat on his pallet. "I know it's hard to get back in the spirit of the moment now. But believe me, 'R-A-N-S-O-M' would have been the perfect retort."

He couldn't begin to decide how to answer that. So he didn't.

"I made tea," she said.

She drew very near him. Too near. His whole body went on alert, and his blood pounded in his ears.

Then she bent down and set the mug of tea on the table. "Just to the right of your elbow."

He could feel heat. Probably the tea, but maybe her. He was vibrating between the desire to clutch her close and the instinct to push her away. A muscle quivered in his arm.

"You have a bit of fluff just here." Her fingers teased through his hair, sending ripples of sensation down his spine. When he flinched, she said softly, "Hold still. I'll get it."

No, you won't.

He caught her wrist. And then he caught her in his arms, tugging her down to his lap.

"What are you doing?" she asked, breathless.

"What am *I* doing? What the devil are *you* doing?"

Her hips wriggled, taunting him.

He held her tighter still, immobile. "You come down here and torment me at the crack of every dawn. Now you're making me tea. And flicking fluff. Is this some kind of coddling? I don't want any coddling."

"It's not coddling. It's not meant to be tormenting, either. I just . . . enjoy greeting you in the morning."

"That's impossible."

Ransom would have believed just about any other excuse. But she couldn't expect him to credit that she stole down here in the misty, early dawn for the pleasure of his company.

"It's true. Every time you wake up, you let fly the most marvelous string of curses. It's never the same twice, do you know that? It's so intriguing. You're like a rooster that crows blasphemy."

"Oh, there's a cock crowing, all right," he muttered.

She smiled, and he *heard* it. Or felt it, somehow. The warmth was inside him before he could shut it out.

She said, "But that's what I like most, you see. No one ever talks that way to me. You're so crude and profane. I . . . I know it's absurd, but I can't help it. I find it perversely delightful."

She *liked* crude? She *wanted* profane?

Very well, then. Crude and profane he could give her.

"Listen to me. When a man wakes, he wakes wanting. He wakes hard and rude and aching with need." He shifted, pressing his massive erection against her hip. "Do you feel that?"

She gasped. "Yes."

"It wants in you," he said.

"In . . . in *me*."

"Yes. In you. Hard, deep, fast, and completely. Now don't wake me at this hour again unless you've found the perfect retort to that."

She didn't answer.

Good.

He hoped this time she was well and truly alarmed. Because *he* was alarmed. The pent-up need in his body felt near some kind of breaking point, and he had enough broken parts already.

The most frightening part of all?

He couldn't seem to let her go.

In all his years of bedding women by night, Ransom made certain he never woke up with them in the morning. Now he was waking up to *this* woman—this strange, eccentric, tempting woman—every morning, and he wasn't even getting the pleasure of bedding her first.

It was intolerable. Unjust. And very worrisome. Because he was starting to grow accustomed to her.

Damn, he was starting to *like* her. It felt so easy,

sitting here, wreathed in the aromas of tea and morning mist. One arm about her slender waist, whilst with the other hand he teased her—

Bloody hell.

Somehow, he'd wound a lock of her hair about his finger. There it was. Right This Moment. And he had no recollection of doing it, either.

What was he coming to, when a woman sat in his lap, he gave her a stern what-for . . . and then ten seconds later, oopsy-daisy and la-di-dah, he went and *twirled a finger in her hair*?

That was not ducal behavior. It certainly wasn't normal behavior for him.

He tried to nonchalantly withdraw his finger from its embarrassing predicament, but he recoiled too quickly. The curling strand of hair tightened around his knuckle like a slipknot.

He tried again, pulling harder. Panic began to build in his chest.

Dear God, it wouldn't let him go.

"Stop," she whispered, shushing him. "Do you feel that?"

He felt a lot of things. Far too many things.

"It almost seems as if the ground is trembling."

Oh. That. Yes, now that she mentioned it, he did feel the shiver in the soles of his feet. The ground *was* trembling. Someone was approaching in the drive.

Not just someone, but many someones.

He discerned not only hoofbeats but the smoother clack of carriage wheels.

Ransom shut his eyes and quickly reviewed England's recent military history. The Danes, Napoleon, the Americans . . . all those conflicts had been settled, last he knew. But then, he had been living in isolation.

He asked, "In the past seven months, has England entered any new wars?"

"Not that I'm aware of," she answered. "Why?"

Because by now the vibration had become so intense, he could have believed the castle was under siege.

She clutched his arm. "Goodness. What is that?"

"Am I going mad, or . . . ?" He trained his ear. "Was that a trumpet?"

"It was," she breathed. "Oh, no."

He didn't miss the ominous note in her voice. "What is it? What's wrong?"

She leapt from his embrace and began pacing the floor. "I knew it. I knew it would happen eventually, but I didn't think it would be so soon."

He stood and took her by the shoulders, holding her in one place. He might be blinded, weakened, and on the verge of madness—but while there was still life in him, no harm would come to a woman living under his roof.

"Be calm," he said. "Just tell me what you're on about. At once."

"It's them. They've found me."

Chapter Twelve

"Who's found you?" he asked.

Izzy winced at the prospect of spilling the truth. Within minutes, there wouldn't be any hiding it. But the duke wasn't going to like this. Not at all.

She was preparing to explain when Ransom took her by the shoulders.

His brow was stern. "Now listen to me. I don't know who they are or what they want from you. But while there's breath in my lungs and strength in my body, I swear this much: I won't let you come to harm."

Oh.

There he went again, making her knees go weak. Never in her life had Izzy been on the receiving end of such a pledge. At least, not one made spontaneously, and most certainly not delivered by such a man as this.

Words were momentarily beyond her. His protective promises had left her feeling rather dizzy. And a little bit guilty for worrying him so.

But only a little bit.

"It is an invasion," she said, "but a friendly one. We're getting a visit from the Moranglian Army. Come see, if you can."

She brought him to the gallery of windows that looked out onto the courtyard.

There, visible through the archway, were approximately a score of mounted riders, followed by three coaches drawn by teams. The armored riders dismounted in unison, and the carriage doors opened, spilling forth about a dozen young ladies in medieval dress. Banners waved briskly in the morning breeze. Izzy couldn't make out the words emblazoned on them, but she didn't need to. She knew what they said.

Doubt not.

"Who are these people?" Ransom asked, as the riders and ladies walked through the archway and into the courtyard. "What the hell do they want?"

"I told you, my father's more enthusiastic readers call themselves Moranglians. They have clubs and circular letters to share their news. And the particularly dedicated Moranglians . . . well, some of them take it a bit further. They enjoy dressing as the characters, acting out battles and scenes.

They're very well organized. There's an oath they take, and badges."

"What's that god-awful clanking I hear?"

"It's . . ." She sighed. "It's armor."

She risked a glance at the duke's face.

As expected, he looked revolted. "Armor?"

"I know it makes no sense to you." She reached for her embroidered shawl. "You don't have to approve of it. Just don't disparage them."

Wrapping her shawl about her shoulders, Izzy leaned out the window and waved. "Good people of Moranglia!"

All the young men and women assembled in the courtyard turned and looked up at her. The knights, with their makeshift armor, fell into a formation.

One stepped forward and performed a deep genuflection. "My lady. I am Sir Wendell Butterfield, first knight of the West Yorkshire Riding Knights of Moranglia, also representing our sisters, the local chapter of Cressida's Handmaidens."

"You and your party have traveled far, Sir Wendell."

"We have. Do I have the honor of addressing Miss Izzy Goodnight?"

"Yes, it's I," she called down, smiling. "Miss Izzy Goodnight. Your knights and ladies are most welcome here."

While the crowd below cheered, Ransom made a gagging noise. "There you are with that treacly voice again."

"Stop," she chided, speaking out of the corner of her mouth. "I can't spoil it for them. They mean well."

"How do they mean well, showing up unannounced this early in the morning? What on earth can they want of you?"

"Just a visit, most likely. Perhaps a quick tour of the castle. But I won't know for certain until I go ask, will I?"

She called down to Sir Wendell. "Good Sir Wendell, please be at ease. I'll come thither anon."

He reached for her. "Wait. You can't let all those fancy-dress fools tromp through my castle. Thithering and anon-ing. I'm not having it, Goodnight."

"It's my castle. And I'm not inviting them for a house party, but I will show a modicum of hospitality toward my guests."

"These are not guests. They're uninvited intruders. Don't *ask* them anything. *Tell* them to go." He gestured in the direction of the dwindling, yet still-massive, heap of correspondence. "If you mean to claim this as your castle, there's a great deal of work to be done."

"Work will have to wait." She shrugged away from him, moving toward the front entrance. "They've come all this distance. I can't turn them away."

"Certainly you can. It's bad enough that they pester you with letters and questions. Draw a line, Goodnight. Go out there and tell them you're a grown woman who can sling about the word 'cock' with the ease of a courtesan, and you don't appreciate unannounced visits. Then invite them to sod off, the bunch of clanking idiots. If you won't, I'll do it."

"No." Panicked, Izzy put a hand to his chest, stopping him in his paces. "Your Grace, please. I won't invite them inside the castle if you don't like. I'll send them away as quickly as I can. Just promise me you'll stay upstairs, out of sight. Let me deal with this. Trust me when I tell you, you don't want these people to see your face."

Ransom clenched his jaw.

So. His wrecked face wasn't as disgusting as he'd been thinking all these months.

It was worse.

Apparently, he was such a horrifying monster, he needed to be locked away in the tower, lest he frighten the tenderhearted fools currently filling his courtyard.

Well. At least now he knew.

And today, his terrifying looks would be put to some use. He was going to clear out these intruders himself.

He pushed past her and exited the great hall, heading for the exterior stairs.

"Wait. Ransom, please."

He ignored her, striding forward to stand on the topmost step. The crowd hushed at once. He heard a few gasps, and not all of them feminine, either.

Good.

"This is my castle." His voice rang from the stones. "Rouse yourselves and begone."

He swept his vision over the assembled inanity. The young ladies at the edges were a colorful assortment of blurs. Their gowns trailed behind them on the ground. The "knights" were a clash of metallic glints and silver flares.

Any moment now, they'd all run away. Exit through the archway like a rainbow pouring through a sieve. Any moment now.

Moments later, he was still waiting. They didn't run away.

At last, the one called Sir Wendell found his voice. "All knights, salute!"

A *bang* echoed through the courtyard, as if they'd all thumped their fists against their armored chests in unison.

"All knights, kneel."

With a wince-inducing clanking, the knights went down on one knee.

"Our liege. We are honored."

What . . . the . . . devil.

They were supposed to run away screaming. Instead, they were kneeling and saluting. Ransom couldn't understand it. Just what was going on here?

Miss Goodnight joined him, but she didn't offer any explanation. "Sir Wendell, how can we be of help this morn?"

"We are on our way to the annual North Regional tournament, Miss Goodnight. Someone informed us of your presence in the neighborhood, and we couldn't resist stopping by. We had . . . no idea."

No idea of what, Ransom wondered. No idea of decorum? No idea of common sense?

"We'll be on our way," Sir Wendell promised. "But might we trouble you for so long as it takes to rest and water our horses?"

"Oh, please do visit the village!" Miss Pelham joined them on the step, breathless. She must have thrown on her frock and dashed down the stairs. As usual, she wouldn't miss any chance to promote the goods and services of the parish.

"It's just a half mile down the road," she said. "That way. The stables here at the castle are small, but the inn in Woolington can offer you fresh water, hay. There's a smith, if you need him. And a pub that serves a fine breakfast. The village would be most happy for your custom."

Sir Wendell bowed. "An excellent suggestion. Thank you, Miss . . ."

"Pelham. Miss Abigail Pelham. My father is the local vicar."

Yes, indeed, Ransom silently concurred. Thank you, Miss Pelham. By this point, he didn't care who convinced these people to go. Just so long as they went.

As the knights gathered and made plans to depart, one of the young ladies approached them on the stairs. "Miss Goodnight, please. While the men take the horses to the village, might we stay here? We would so love to have a visit with you. Perhaps a chance to see your castle?"

"I'm afraid the castle isn't fit for visitors just yet," Miss Goodnight answered quickly, and sweetly. "But perhaps you'd be so good as to join me for a walk in the castle park? There are some romantic-looking ruins I've been yearning to explore."

"Oh! That sounds divine." The girl motioned to her friends, and all dozen of them rushed up the stairs.

A girl in some shade of blue or violet sidled up on Ransom's right. "You will walk with us, won't you?"

"Yes, you must join us." A young woman in white took his left side, boldly threading her arm through his.

Before he knew what was happening, Ransom was swept along as they set out on a walk through the castle park. Magnus trotted along at his heel.

Damn his eyes. Why was he taking a walk? He didn't want to take a walk. But no one left him a choice. He was surrounded. And very confused.

He'd never had difficulty attracting female attention before his injury. But those attracted to him were women—worldly and self-possessed. Not impressionable, silly girls. And was he going mad, or had they simply not noticed the scar mangling one side of his face?

Good Lord. One of them pinched his *arse*. Then all of them giggled.

"Won't you say it for us?" the girl in blue urged him.

"Say what?" he asked.

"You know," she whispered coyly. "Say 'Doubt not.' Won't you, please? We've been dreaming of it since we were little girls."

Their group drew to a halt in the overgrown garden. The whole gaggle of ladies went breathless with anticipation.

"Doubt not," he echoed, hardly understanding why.

A chorus of feminine sighs rose up.

"Oh," swooned one. "That voice. Be still my heart. It's so romantic."

God above. This couldn't be real. It had to be some kind of nightmare.

"Handmaidens," Miss Goodnight called out in that childish, innocent voice, "do you see it there in the distance? The ruined folly. Do dash ahead, if you will. I'm so keen to see who can pick the largest posy of briar roses by the time I meet you there."

With a little squeal, the dozen young ladies picked up their skirts and dashed ahead, racing one another toward the horizon.

"There," Miss Goodnight said. "They're occupied for a few minutes, at least. Now I can explain."

"You had better explain. What the hell is going on? What's this 'doubt not' nonsense?"

She took his arm, and they began walking toward the folly. Slowly.

"It's a famous speech from *The Goodnight Tales*. Ulric recites it to Cressida just before he leaves on a quest. 'Doubt not, my lady, I shall return.' It goes on and on. Doubt not my steel, my strength, my heart . . ."

"Why do they want *me* to say it?"

"I'm afraid you won't like to hear this," she said, sounding doleful. "But you bear a certain resemblance to him."

"Me? I look like Ulric?"

"Yes. Just uncannily so. Broad shoulders, longish golden brown hair, unshaven . . . You're a near-perfect match, straight down to the weathered boots."

"But . . ." Ransom frowned. So this was why she wanted him to hide upstairs. "Surely this Ulric character doesn't have a scar."

"He does, as a matter of fact. Ever since episode thirty-four, when he battled the Shadow Knight in the forest of Banterwick."

He inhaled slowly. This was all starting to make sense to him. Sick, stomach-turning sense.

He pulled her to a halt, turning her to face him.

His eyes were good this morning. As good as they ever were now. He could avoid the stump in his path and make out the vague shapes of the trees and ruined archways, if not the color or form of the birds winging through them.

It was the cruelest of temptations, seeing this much of her and knowing he'd never see more.

He could make out the wide, reddish curve of

her mouth and that aura of dark hair, set against the pale . . . was it yellow? . . . of her frock. But he couldn't see well enough to judge her emotions.

"I don't believe this," he said. "This is all a little story in your mind. Since the day you arrived, you've been living out some bizarre fantasy. Your own little castle, and your own scarred, tortured Ulric. That's why you won't leave this place and why you won't let me be. Why you come down every morning and watch me *sleep*. I'm like a plaything."

"No," she protested. He could see her head shake vigorously. "No, no, no. *I'm* not living in a fantasy."

"Get one thing clear, Miss Goodnight. You had better not be forming expectations."

"Expectations of what?"

"Of me. Of us. Of romance. Just because you grew up on all those fanciful stories, don't think this is one of them. I won't be a party to any of this. I'm not the shining hero in disguise."

She exhaled audibly. "I know. I *know*. You're a dangerous ravisher, with brothel bills as long as my arm. Really, I can't imagine you have any remaining ways to communicate the message, short of stitching 'A WARNING TO WOMEN' on your breeches placket. I'm not a ninny. It's understood. I have not cast you in any chivalric fantasy."

"Oh, no? Then why did you kiss me like that the first night?"

Her reply was slow in coming. "Just . . . how *did* I kiss you the first night?"

"Like you wanted to," he accused. "Like you'd always wanted to. Like you'd spent years waiting for just that kiss. From me."

She covered her face with one hand and moaned. "Why must this be so mortifying? Oh, that's right. Because it's my life."

Ransom kept silent, waiting for an explanation.

She lowered her hand. "Believe me, Your Grace. You will never meet another woman with fewer expectations of romance. You've seen how Lord Archer and Miss Pelham and all these people treat me—like a naïve little girl. Everyone's always treated me that way. I've never had even one suitor. So yes, I kissed you like I'd been waiting to kiss you all my life. Because I'd been waiting to kiss *someone* all my life. Yours just happened to be the lips that met mine."

He shook his head. "You didn't kiss me like that was your first kiss."

"Of course not." She turned and resumed walking. "I kissed you like it would be my last."

Her *last*?

The words kept tumbling through his mind as they walked toward the ruined folly. He could scarcely fathom the absurdity of them.

"That's ridiculous. It's like you've crammed your brain so full of fairy tales, you've squeezed out all the common sense. You're clever, quick, attractive. Men should be clamoring for you."

She took his arm and nudged him to the side, around an obstacle in their path. "My life thus far has featured a distinct lack of any such clamoring."

"That's only because you're stuck living in your father's soppy stories."

"It's not only that." She started to drift away.

He tightened his arm, keeping her close at his side. "Wait."

Somehow, she had to be made to understand. He couldn't let her go walking about the world, believing that no more kisses were waiting for her. Or worse—that she shouldn't go searching them out. She didn't belong in this castle, hiding away for the rest of her life until she withered to dust. That was his fate, not hers.

"Ransom," she whispered, "don't you understand? It doesn't matter what these girls suggest or giggle about. I don't see you as Ulric. Ulric is honorable and decent, and you're—"

"Not." With an impatient wave of his hand, he batted her words away. "We've established that."

She tried again. "In the *stories*, which every reasonable person knows are just *stories*, Ulric loves Cressida with a pure, gallant, ridiculously chaste heart. They trade longing glances from opposite turrets. They send little notes back and forth through their servants. In twelve years, they've kissed exactly *twice*. If I wanted a man who was anything like Ulric, I wouldn't have thrown myself at you that first night. I wouldn't sit pondering the exact measurements that make up 'magnificence.' And I surely as anything wouldn't spend hours staring into the darkness every night, dreaming of how your hands would feel against my bare skin."

What? Her confessions bounced right off his defensive bluster.

"You're not making sense."

She growled in frustration. "I know I'm not. It makes no sense at all. I'm not a silly little girl who dreams of knights. I'm a woman. A woman who's inconveniently, completely, and for the first time in her life, in lust. Just burning with desire for the worst possible man. A profane, bitter, wounded duke who refuses to leave her house. Oh, you are dreadful."

"And you want my hands on your body."

A faint whimper escaped her throat. "Everywhere."

Desire pounded through his veins. He was seized by the urge to tumble her into the grass, right then and there, and strip her of every scrap of clothing. She wanted to be touched. He wanted to touch her. There was nothing holding them back.

Nothing, that was, save for a dozen giggling, foolish handmaidens who wanted to sprinkle them with wild-rose petals.

How did one get rid of these girls? They were like fanned-away horseflies. They just kept coming back.

He raised his voice. "Handmaidens, gather round."

Once they'd assembled in a loose, giggling

circle, he clapped his hands. "Let's have a game, shall we? We'll call it 'Rescue the Maiden.' Miss Goodnight will count to one hundred. All of you, go run and hide—and wait for your dashing Ulric to save you. No cheating, now. You mustn't peek."

The handmaidens disappeared before he could have counted three, laughing and tripping over their hems as they darted through archways and ducked around hedges.

Izzy shook her head. "Very well. You win this point. I will concede, these *particular* girls may be just a little bit stupid."

Ransom wasn't interested in scoring points on silly girls. The moment all the handmaidens were gone, he caught Izzy in his arms and dragged her inside the ruined folly.

"We have until one hundred. Start counting."

"One. Two. Thr—"

He drew her close and claimed her mouth with his. He gave her no chance to demur but boldly swept his tongue between her lips, stealing her breath. He tilted his head, pushing deeper.

And once again, she kissed him back. If he'd been standing, his knees would have buckled.

She was so instinctively passionate. So unbearably sweet.

This was madness. He knew it. She knew it, too. If he gave her a moment to reply, she would likely tell him so.

But nothing needed to make rational sense. There were no minds in this, only bodies and heat.

This was something both of them wanted. Hell, it was something he needed. To touch, to tease, to taste. To explore her with his mouth and hands. Kiss her breathless. Feel powerful and alive.

Because there'd been a time, not so long ago, when he thought he'd never get back to this place: A woman's body soft and yielding against his, and the warm summer sun beating down on them both.

This was life.

Bright, brilliant life amid the ruins.

Chapter Thirteen

This was some kind of miracle.

Here they were, in this ruined folly, where so many couples before them must have kissed and embraced. She was surrounded by true romantic legacy—and for once, Izzy wasn't left out of it.

Not anymore.

She relaxed, letting her weight rest against the mossy stones as Ransom trailed hot kisses along her neck.

He drew his hand along her body, sweeping a possessive touch over her waist and hip before settling his palm over her breast.

He paused there, as though he expected her to flinch or pull away.

She wasn't about to do either. His touch awakened all her senses to anticipation, possibility.

Around them, birds whistled and chirped. All sorts of mosses, ferns, and ivies had sunk their green teeth into the stones, sprouting life from the smallest, most inhospitable places. Flowers poured their perfume into the air.

Izzy seemed to be blossoming, too. Her whole body felt flushed and pink. Ripe for his touch.

This was her summer, after years and years of spring.

She went on counting in a fevered, insensate whisper. "Sixteen, seventeen, eightee—"

When he kissed her again, she tilted her head and slid her tongue forward to toy with his.

He moaned. And his fingers curled around her breast, gently kneading her softness through the fabric.

As he touched her, Izzy did some touching of her own. She explored the muscled contours of his forearm, all roped strength and corded sinew. She slid her hand higher, feeling the massive biceps beneath his coat sleeve. He flexed the muscle on instinct. Or on purpose. Who could tell with this man? Either way, Izzy found it ridiculously thrilling. All that power in his body, and the way he could use it to explore and pleasure her.

A soft, surprised laugh escaped her. "I'd given up on this."

"Given up on what?"

"This. All of this. Surprise benefactors, mysterious castles, romantic ruins, forbidden kisses."

He kissed her neck. "What else have you given up on, Izzy Goodnight? This?" He flicked her earlobe with his tongue. "Maybe this?" He nipped with his teeth. "Make a list, and we'll go through it line by line."

She let her head fall to the side, offering him more of her neck to kiss. "What haven't I given up on? Marriage, children, lasting love, manageable hair. Being truly understood by anyone."

Oh, the poor man. He recoiled, his face ashen.

Izzy was utterly convinced. Never mind Arabian horses, African cheetahs. No creature in the world could bolt so quickly as a rake confronted with the word "marriage." They ought to shout it out at footraces rather than using starting pistols.

Ready, steady . . . matrimony!

"I was joking," she assured him.

"I knew that."

"I don't intend to ever marry. I certainly wouldn't think you'd ever—" Gads, now she was making him sound unlovable. "Not with me."

"Right. Exactly. And I don't know a damned thing about ladies' hair." He cleared his throat. "Goodnight, this isn't . . ."

"I know."

"It's only . . ."

"This. It's only this. I know." She put her arms around his neck. "No expectations. Just go back to touching me?"

He exhaled with relief. "That I can do."

Yes. That he could do very well indeed.

His thumb found her nipple, and he teased it through the muslin, drawing the peak to a taut, aching nub. The sensations coursing through Izzy's body were unlike anything she'd ever known. How was it possible, that his thumb could idly slide back and forth across that one tiny part of her, and she could feel it in the roots of her hair and the backs of her knees?

When his thumb abandoned the peak, and she wanted to weep.

But then he slid his touch to the other side, and the sweet torture began all over again. She was afraid her knees would buckle with it, so she clung tight to his neck, weaving her fingers into his hair.

He was driving all thoughts from her head, leaving her with the intellect of a pudding. She was just a quivering mound of sensation, capped by that red, ripe berry of a nipple that he rolled beneath his thumb. Again and again and again.

Yes.

Just when she thought she'd dissolve into a puddle at his boots, his hands slid to her waist. With a low, thrilling growl, he pressed her against the stone wall, pinning her there with his body.

Izzy was breathless. Trapped. This should have made her wild to get free. But she loved the feeling, bracketed by such intoxicating strength. The stones at her back had stood in place for centuries, and the man before her had survived unknown trials. She could melt with fear or bliss, and they would hold her together—this wall, this man.

He groaned, clutching her hips. A hard, heated _something_ pressed against her middle.

Her eyes flew open. Her knowledge of lovemaking was rather like a sieve. She caught the general idea, even if detail and nuance slipped through. Still, she understood this much. That a man's organ grew . . . emboldened . . . when he wished to make love.

This firm, long ridge of heat against her belly . . .

It meant he wanted her. Magnificently.

He pushed her shawl from her shoulders. It fell to the ground. He slid his fingers along her collarbone, dipping under the edge of her sleeve and slipping it down her bare shoulder.

"You stopped counting," he whispered.

"How can I count when you're—" She gasped as he scooped her breast straight out of her stays. Cool air rushed over her exposed nipple. "How can I count when you're doing that?"

"It's easy. I'll help." He bent his head, trailing kisses down her chest until he reached her bared breast. His tongue flickered over her nipple. "Thirty-one." Another lick. "Thirty-two." _Lick_. "Thirty-three."

The alternating heat of his mouth and the coolness of the air . . . She must have gooseflesh everywhere, including the soles of her feet. If he'd continued on in such a manner, Izzy might have incinerated before she reached the count of forty-five.

But he didn't continue. Instead, he drew her nipple into his mouth and suckled hard.

After that, numbers had no meaning.

How many counts were in forever? That's how long she wanted this to last. His tongue made lazy, delicious circles around her nipple, driving her mindless with pleasure. Oh, he was good at this. Very good indeed.

Then he sank to his knees, sending one hand to delve under her skirts.

When he grasped her leg, Izzy panicked.

She clutched at his shoulders, holding him off. "Ninety-nine, one hundred."

He paused, one hand frozen in the act of rucking up her petticoats and the other encircling her ankle.

"You said everywhere," he reminded her, in a low, wicked voice.

"I did say everywhere."

Her heart thundered in her chest. He was giving her the chance to refuse, and everything in her upbringing screamed at her to take it.

But she only had this one life. And so far, in this one life, she had only had this one man show the least bit of interest in tossing her petticoats to her waist.

This could be her one and only chance.

It was just a bit of touching, she told herself.

Harmless. It wasn't as though he could deflower her here, with a dozen handmaidens hiding nearby.

"Have you changed your mind?" he asked.

Oh Lord oh Lord oh Lord. "No."

He muttered something that sounded like, "Thank God." He gathered her skirts in one hand and hiked them to her waist with a single, expert motion.

Izzy reclined against the wall and stretched her arms overhead, feeling wanton and daring. As he ran his hands over her stockinged calf and up her thigh, she let her legs fall just slightly apart.

"Yes," he groaned. "Open for me. Just like that. Lovely, lovely."

Impossible, impossible.

That's what Izzy would have thought about this entire scene just a fortnight ago. She felt like a pagan goddess in an ancient temple. Reclining against the ivy-covered wall of a ruined folly, being ravished in full morning light by a scarred, sensual duke.

This was beyond anything she'd ever dreamed. And Izzy had a vivid imagination. She reeled from the sheer joy of his touch and the exquisite wickedess of . . . of everything.

A new, throbbing pulse started to thrum between her legs. Hurry, it beat. Hurry, hurry.

His hand slid up her thigh, skipping over the garter and proceeding on to the smooth slope of her inner thigh.

"So soft." He kissed her just above the knee. "Like satin."

As his touch swept closer to her sex, the building crescendo of pleasure was unbearable.

Higher . . . higher . . . and a little higher still.

Until his thumb grazed her *there*.

"*Oh.*"

A rocket of bliss shot through her, racking her from toes to scalp. She clenched her fists, tugging on the ivy branches for support lest her quivering thighs give away.

A dusting of white grit showered down on them both.

Ransom looked up. "What was that?"

"Oh, dear. I think a bit of the wall is crumbling." She released her grip on the ivy, but another few pebbles shook loose.

"Then come away from there." He rose to his feet, letting her skirts fall back to the ground, and tucked her close to his chest.

Thunk. An apple-sized chunk of wall tumbled loose and hit him square on the head.

"Oh, goodness! Ransom!"

He cursed and recoiled, pressing the heel of his hand to the wound as he staggered backward to sit in the grass. Magnus circled him, whining.

Izzy rushed to kneel by his side. A fresh bump was already swelling, and a small patch of his skin was scraped raw. It was on the unscarred side of his brow. She didn't know whether that made things better or worse.

It was almost funny when she considered it. She'd been rescued from ruination by . . . ruins.

She picked up her forgotten shawl and pressed the folded edge to his brow. "Are you all right? Are you dizzy? Look at me, and tell me how many—"

She bit off the absurd question. Of course he couldn't tell how many fingers she was holding up.

Unless . . .

Unless he'd experienced some sudden cure. She'd heard it could happen. Soldiers blinded in battle, having their vision returned to them after one good knock on the head.

"Do you have all your usual faculties?" she asked cautiously.

He clenched his jaw. "My ears are ringing, and my head is a throbbing knot of pain. But I can't see any more or less than I could ten minutes ago. If that's your question."

"Oh. Good. I mean, not good, of course. I just hope you're not too hurt, that's all."

Izzy sighed. She was a horrible, horrible person. He told her he hadn't experienced a miraculous restoration of his vision, and her first, instinctive reaction was relief? What kind of person would actually *wish* for a man's continued blindness?

A plain kind of person. One who was enjoying feeling attractive for the first time in her life.

But that was no excuse.

In an attempt to atone for her selfishness, she brushed aside his overlong hair and began dabbing at the bloody scrape on his head.

He shied away. "You're always fussing over me."

"I'm not fussing," she said. "I'm blotting. If you like, I can disparage you while I do it. How about this: Ungrateful man."

"Bewitching she-devil."

She smiled wryly. It would seem his personality was intact, and she was glad of it. No member of the Moranglian Army would ever call her "temptress" or "bewitching." And coming from lips so finely formed, she didn't even mind "she-devil."

He took the wadded shawl from her grasp and applied to his own head. "First weasels, now stoning. Are you working from a list of archaic torture methods?"

"I must admit, you are bleeding through my supply of clean linen at an alarming rate."

"My face is already a wreck. Another lump can only improve it." He lowered the cloth. "How bad is it?"

She tested his bruise with her fingertips. "There's a bit of a bump, but the swelling isn't too awful."

"No, not that." He turned his head, giving her his profile—and a full view of his twisting scar. "The rest. How bad is it? Tell me honestly."

Izzy fell quiet, stunned by his sudden earnestness. *He* was anxious about his looks?

"I can't see it for myself," he said. "I've wondered where I rank in the spectrum between flawed Adonis and ghastly horror. Clearly, I can't judge by these silly chits' reactions, addled as they are by your father's writing. It will have to be you."

Her heart twisted in her chest. How could he doubt himself? In full daylight, he was magnificent. His skin seemed to be bronzing by the moment, soaking up every bit of the day's warmth. The sunlight caught the golden streaks in his hair—hair that was overlong, sprawling over his brow in a rakish fashion. She wondered now at the reason. Was it that he simply couldn't be bothered to let Duncan cut it, or did he purposely grow it long to obscure his scarred face?

Reaching forward, she brushed the sweep of tawny hair from his brow. "Will you tell me how it happened?"

"I was struck. With something big and sharp."

Izzy supposed that was what she deserved. Ask a straightforward question, receive a straightforward answer.

She traced the scar with her fingertip, all the way from his brow to his cheekbone, then let her touch linger on his unshaven cheek. How ironic that the blow had just missed his right eye but taken the sight from both.

"Well?" he prompted.

"Well," she said, "it's plain to see that you were once a devastatingly handsome man."

"And now?"

"Now . . ." She sighed. "I really hate to say it. Don't make me say it."

His hand caught her wrist. "Just say it."

"Now you are a devastatingly handsome man

with an impressive scar. That is the unhappy truth. I wish I could tell you otherwise. You will be impossible now."

"But . . ." He released her, looking bewildered. "But that first day. When you saw me, you swooned."

She laughed a little. "Your face did not make me swoon. I was already feeling faint. I hadn't eaten anything but a few crusts of bread for days."

"So the scars don't frighten you?"

"Not at all."

The words were a lie. The truth was, his scars did frighten her—but only a little, and only because they tempted her to care. Even now, her heart was softening in her chest, faster than a lump of butter left in the sun.

She couldn't let this happen. It was all well and good to say "no expectations," but Izzy knew how her affection-starved heart worked. She was so desperate to love and be loved, she could sprout tender feelings toward a rock. And rocks didn't call her "bewitching" or "temptress." Rocks didn't have touchable golden brown hair.

But rocks and Ransom did have something in common.

Neither one would love her back.

"We should go," she said. "It's been at least one hundred counts, and the girls are waiting."

He stood and brushed dust from his breeches and coat. "I'll make my own way back."

"By yourself?" The moment the words left her

lips, Izzy cringed, regretting how they sounded. Of course he was able to walk back on his own. "It's just that the handmaidens are waiting for their hero to find them."

"Then they'd best keep waiting for some other man." He moved past her. "I'm no one's hero, Miss Goodnight. You'd do well to remember it."

Chapter Fourteen

"Miss Goodnight. Is that you?"

Izzy froze, perched on tiptoe.

Drat.

After several hours of walking, talking, counting wild roses, and fending off questions about *two* Ulrics, Izzy had finally bid a warm farewell to the handmaidens and the Knights of Moranglia. She'd been hoping to sneak back into the castle unnoticed. So much for that plan.

At least it wasn't the duke who'd caught her.

"Yes, Duncan?"

"What is that in your hands, Miss Goodnight?"

Izzy glanced down at her wadded, soiled shawl. She'd been carrying it around ever since her interlude with Ransom that morning.

Embarrassed, she thrust the thing behind her back. "Oh, it's nothing."

"Is that your shawl?"

The man had a marksman's eye when it came to laundry.

She sighed, drawing it out again. "Yes. I . . . You see, there was a bit of a mishap."

Lord, how did she begin to describe what had happened to the thing? She ought to have pitched it in the moat. It wasn't as though it could be salvaged.

"Give it here." The valet took it from her hand. He shook out the frail, tissue-thin fabric and examined it, clucking his tongue. "Dirt . . . grass . . . My word. Are these bloodstains? On silk embroidery?"

She bit her lip, praying that he wouldn't be angry with her for the duke's recent injury. Or worse, demand a full explanation of how it had occurred.

"Miss Goodnight, I don't know what to say. This . . ." He shook his head. "This is marvelous."

"Marvelous?"

"Yes." He gripped the fabric in both hands. "This is what a valet lives for. Removing stubborn stains from quality fabric. It's been months since I had a challenge like this one. I must away to the laundry, at once. If the stains have any longer to set, I'll never get them out."

Amused, Izzy followed him down to the room

designated as a laundry. He stoked the fire, put a kettle on to boil, and gathered soap, an iron, and pressing cloths.

"These grass stains will be the most stubborn." He laid the shawl out on the worktable, assessing every little spot and stain. "Lemon juice and a cool rinse first. If that doesn't work, we'll try a paste of soda."

"Can I help at all?"

"No, Miss Goodnight." He looked faintly horrified. "You'd spoil my amusement. But you'd be most welcome to keep me company."

Izzy took a seat and watched, quite amused herself by his careful campaign to attack the stains. He scraped them first with a knife. Then rubbed them with a soft-bristled brush. Only then did he reach for his small, brown-glass bottles of spirits and salts. She felt as though she were watching a surgeon at work.

"Duncan, how did it happen? The duke's accident."

The valet paused in the act of dabbing vinegar on a grass stain. "Miss Goodnight," he said slowly, "I know we discussed this. A good manservant does not gossip about his employer."

"I know. I know, and I'm sorry to pry, but . . . now I work for him, too. Isn't this what employed people do? Gossip about their employer?"

He arched one brow in silent censure.

She hated seeming so petty, and she didn't

want to break her word to Ransom and disclose his headache the other night. Or mention the letter he'd crumpled and tossed in the grate.

"I'm just concerned, that's all. The duke's so . . ." *Stubborn. Wounded. Maddeningly attractive.* "So angry. At the world, it seems, but especially at me. He's so determined to interpret everything in the worst possible way, and I don't think it's only his injury. I wish I understood it."

Duncan took a break from his scrubbing to attend the whistling kettle. "Miss Goodnight, it wouldn't be fitting for a valet to tell tales about his employer."

Izzy nodded. She was disappointed, but she wouldn't press him further. He *was* saving her best shawl, after all.

"But," the silver-haired man continued, "seeing as you are Miss Izzy Goodnight, and so fond of a story, perhaps I could tell you a tale about . . . an entirely different man."

"Oh, yes." She straightened in her chair, trying not to betray her excitement. "A fictional man. One who isn't Rothbury at all. I would so *love* to hear a story like that."

The valet cast a wary glance around the room.

"I won't tell anyone, I swear it," she whispered. "Here, I'll even start. Once there was a young nobleman named . . . Bransom Fayne, the Duke of Mothfairy."

"Mothfairy?"

She shrugged. "Did you have something better?"

He set the kettle on the hob. "He can never hear of this."

"Of course not," she said. "How could he? This man we're discussing doesn't exist. But this is the tale of his tragic past. In his youth, the nonexistent Duke of Mothfairy . . ."

"Was alone. A great deal. His mother died in childbirth."

She nodded. This much, she'd learned from the man himself.

"And his father might as well have died the same day. The old duke shut himself off from the world to grieve, and he treated his son very coldly. Once this 'Bransom' was old enough, he frequently sought out . . . company." The valet's face contorted as he searched for words. "The female kind of company."

"He sewed his wild oats, you mean."

"Entire plantations of them. Good heavens. He made oat-sewing an industry."

Izzy could believe it. She'd seen the accounts.

"But at the age of thirty, he finally settled down to the principal obligation of his title. Which was, of course, to produce the next Duke of . . ."

"Mothfairy," she supplied.

"Yes." Duncan cleared his throat. "He singled out the most sought-after debutante of the London season and declared his intentions to court her. The two were engaged soon thereafter."

Izzy's jaw dropped. "Ransom was engaged?"

Now she understood why he'd panicked at her foolish utterance of the word "marriage" earlier.

"No." Duncan threw her a stern look. "*Bransom* was engaged. The Duke Who Doesn't Exist. He was engaged to a young lady by the name of Lady Emi-" A distressed look crossed his face. "Lady Shemily."

"Lady Shemily?" Izzy smiled to herself. He was getting into the spirit now.

"Yes. Lady Shemily Liverpail. Daughter of an earl." The valet returned to his work. He uncapped a small bottle of something that scented strongly of lemon. "When the engagement was announced, the duke's long-suffering servants were delighted. Some of the house staff had served the family for thirty years without a duchess. They were eager for a new lady of the house."

"Including his trusty and distinguished valet?" she guessed. "Who went by the name of . . . Dinkins?"

"*Especially* his trusty and distinguished valet. Dinkins was looking forward to removing fewer remnants of rouge from the duke's garments. Devilish tricky to remove, rouge."

"I can imagine." Izzy wondered what kind of woman could tempt the duke away from all that debauchery. "This Lady Shemily Liverpail . . . What was she like?"

"What you'd imagine a successful debutante to be. Beautiful, accomplished, well connected. And young. Just nineteen years old."

Izzy suppressed a plaintive sigh. Of course. Of course Lady Shemily would be all those things.

"What went wrong?" she asked.

He hesitated.

"Fictionally. In this completely fabricated story that you're only concocting to amuse me because you know how I love a tale of star-crossed love."

"Everything was arranged," he said. "Wedding, honeymoon, a well-appointed suite for the new duchess. And then, less than a fortnight before the wedding date, the bride-to-be vanished."

"Vanished?"

"Yes. She disappeared from her bedchamber in the middle of the night."

Izzy leaned forward, propping her chin on her hand. This story was getting rather exciting. And it seemed Duncan was relishing the chance to tell it at last. Poor man, confined here for months with all this melodrama and no one to talk to. And very few stains.

"Lady Shemily," he said, his voice oozing dramatic tension, "had eloped."

"Eloped? But with whom?"

"A tenant farmer from the Liverpail country estate. Apparently the two had been concealing their affections for years."

"What a scandal. What did Ro—" She shook herself. "What did Mothfairy do?"

"Nothing prudent. He should have let the silly chit run off and ruin herself. Loudly disdain her upbringing to all who asked, joke cleverly about his close escape. And then next season, find a new bride. But his pride wouldn't allow it. He rode off in furious pursuit."

"Without his trusty and distinguished valet?"

He sighed testily. "Dinkins followed in the coach. And Dinkins fell, sadly, more than a day behind. Too late to stop the tragedy unfolding."

She bit her lip, already cringing. "Did the duke fall from his horse?"

"Oh, no. Some twenty miles south of the Scottish border, Mothfairy came upon his would-be bride and her lover in a coaching inn. A confrontation ensued, blades were drawn . . ."

She winced, as though she could feel the full length of Ransom's scar burning from her scalp to her cheekbone. "I think I can imagine the rest."

"You will have to imagine it. I can't tell you precisely what occurred. I wasn't there." Duncan dropped all pretense of storytelling. He braced his hands flat against the worktable. "When I found him, he'd spent two nights in a closet at that damned coaching inn. No surgeon had been called. The innkeeper was simply waiting for him to die. I had to stitch him myself."

"Unconscionable," Izzy said. "What about his intended bride?"

"Already gone. Little flibbertigibbet." He shook his head. "He wasn't well enough to risk traveling back to London, so I brought him here. It's been more than seven months. He refuses to leave. He refuses to even let me perform my duties as a valet. His appearance is an embarrassment."

Izzy hedged. "I don't know that I'd say *that*." She rather liked the duke's rugged, unkempt appearance. And a dozen sighing handmaidens couldn't be wrong.

"Half the time, he refuses to wear a cravat. It's shameful."

"Shameful indeed," she echoed. She could agree on that point. The duke's open collars gave her quite shameful thoughts.

Duncan set the iron aside and held up her pristine shawl for examination. "This little task has preserved my sanity for another day," he said. "Thank you. You can't know how unbearable it is to spend your life on one profession and then be forced to abandon it."

Izzy didn't reply. But she could understand that feeling better than he might think. When her father died, her work had died, too.

He folded the shawl and handed it to her. "I've been so out of sorts, it's driven me to . . ."

"To what?"

"I don't even know. That's the problem, Miss Goodnight. I've tried a half dozen different vices, and none of them satisfy. Cheroots are revolting. Snuff isn't much better. I can't abide the taste of strong spirits, and I don't like to drink alone. What's left? Gambling? With whom?"

She shrugged. "I suppose there's always women."

"Unoriginal," he declared. "In this house, that particular vice is taken."

An idea came to her. She dug into her pockets and handed him a clutch of paper-wrapped sweets. "Here. Sweetmeats."

He looked at the sweets in her hand.

"Go on," she urged. "You'd be doing me a favor. People foist the things on me in handfuls. After my morning with the handmaidens, I have more than I could possibly want." She pointed to one. "I think this one's a honeyed apricot."

He took the sweet, unwrapped it, and popped it into his mouth. As he chewed, his shoulders relaxed.

"Better?" she asked.

"Better. Thank you, Miss Goodnight."

"It's the least I can do." She left the remaining sweetmeats on his worktable. "Thank you for rescuing my shawl and for telling me the truth. I mean, not the truth. A fascinating *story*."

Everything made more sense to her now. Naturally, a man who'd been jilted so callously and nearly died in the bargain would take a dim view of love and romance. But was his pride the true casualty, or had his heart been broken, too?

"Duncan?"

"Mm?" he murmured, unwrapping a second sweetmeat.

"Did . . . ?" She screwed up her courage and asked. "Did he love her?"

No answer.

Oh, drat. That would teach her to ask a delicate question just as someone stuffed a sweetmeat in his mouth. Duncan made a wait-a-moment gesture, working his jaw. Meanwhile, Izzy's gut twisted itself into knots.

Worse, she had time to question herself.

Why did it even matter whether the duke had loved his intended or not? Why did she care so much? It wasn't as though he was ever going to marry *her*.

An eternity later, Duncan swallowed the morsel. But apparently she'd waited all that time for nothing.

He said simply, "I don't know."

Chapter Fifteen

Astonishing. In the morning, when she sat working at that table of correspondence, silhouetted by sunlight . . .

Her hair truly did look like an octopus.

It was the way she wore it, he thought. Or maybe the way it wore *her*. It all sat perched atop her head in that big, inky blob. And no matter how strenuously she pinned it, dark, heavy curls worked loose on all sides, like tentacles.

Of course, it was an entrancing, strangely *erotic* octopus. Ransom worried this might be how fetishes developed.

"You've been avoiding me, Goodnight."

Her dark head lifted from her work. "I have?"

"Yes. You have."

She paused. "Your Grace, my presence in this room right now—and this very conversation we're having—would seem to argue against it."

"I'm not saying I blame you." He reclined on the sofa and propped his laced hands behind his neck. "If it were in any way physically possible, I would avoid myself, too."

She picked up the next envelope and cleaved the seal with a savage slice of the letter opener. "I'm not avoiding you, Your Grace. I don't know what you mean."

Little liar. She knew very well what he meant.

Ever since the Invasion of the Idiots, and that sublime, stolen embrace in the folly, Ransom had noted a marked change in Izzy Goodnight's demeanor.

There hadn't been any more surprise visitors, and as many hours as Ransom walked the castle at night, he never bumped into her again. She was always waiting nearby when he awoke, but there were no more queer conversations on elephant-sized rats or rat-sized elephants.

And, queerly enough, Ransom found himself missing them.

Or perhaps just missing her.

"I have a question," he said, interrupting her reading of an assessment regarding some new finance scheme with steam engines. "Are there dragons in Merlinia?"

"Moranglia."

"Right."

"If there are, why do you care?" she asked, sounding wary.

He shrugged. "Just wondering what further madness to expect, that's all. Whether I'll have a herd of unicorns visiting some morning, or discover trolls camping under my bridge."

"No. No, Your Grace. No dragons, unicorns, or trolls."

"Good," he said. She hadn't made it through another paragraph before he interrupted again. "What news do you have from Lord Bedridden?"

"Nothing that would interest you, I'm sure." The flat side of her fist met the tabletop. "Your Grace, you've hired me to read your correspondence. Not discuss my own."

He held up his hands in surrender. "Fine."

Ransom could see what was happening. She was putting distance between them. Which meant she was a sensible, clever woman. Which made her even more attractive. Damn it all.

"I don't mean to be churlish," she said. "It's just . . . I discuss my father's stories with everyone. And I don't mind it, but I rather look forward to speaking of something—anything—else when I'm with you. Even if it's the financial prospects in steam-powered farm machinery."

He supposed that made sense. He was beginning to understand how those ridiculous tales had made her a prisoner of others' expectations.

She would need to break free of that prison soon. Because they were halfway through the formidable heap of letters and packets, and Ransom was certain he knew what was happening.

Someone was stealing from him. And that someone had been getting bolder. The amounts of the discrepancies had been small at first, but they were growing into the tens and hundreds.

He had a theory developing. The culprit must be some clerk in his solicitors' offices, he surmised. Or even one of the solicitors. Whoever the thief was, he has a gaming habit—cards or horses, maybe. Perhaps an expensive mistress. Or maybe he'd decided he deserved better than whatever measly salary his employers paid. So he began by pilfering small amounts, where no one was likely to suspect it. When those went unnoticed, he progressed to larger sums.

And then, one day, he saw his chance to rake in something bigger.

The old Earl of Lynforth's men must have inquired about purchasing Gostley Castle for his goddaughter. Of course, any such offer would have been summarily refused. Everyone knew Ransom would never agree to sell an ancestral property. But if the thief drew up false papers and took them directly to Lynforth's bedside—he could bilk a dying man out of a tremendous sum.

So far, it was merely a theory, but it made more sense than any of the alternatives. And if Ransom's guesses were right, that would mean the sale was invalid.

Soon, Izzy Goodnight would find herself without a home. Again.

"We'll be finished here in a matter of weeks," he said. "Have you given any thought to where you'll go?"

"I ought to ask you that," she said. "I don't believe I'll be going anywhere."

"But you should. That's the thing, Goodnight. You should go places." He sat up and leaned forward, bracing his forearms on his knees. "The wars are over. Those who have money are beginning to travel again. Find some naughty old relic who wants to do the Grand Tour. One who needs a companion to read aloud in voices on tedious ship crossings, make sketches of nude sculptures for her keepsake box, and walk her lapdog twice a day. You could visit Paris, Vienna, Athens, Rome."

Even from his seat on the sofa, he could see her wide, claret-red mouth curve in a smile. It was the first smile he'd seen from her in days.

"Unfortunately, I don't know any wealthy, naughty old ladies with lapdogs," she said. "But that does sound like a lovely adventure."

It was settled then. He didn't know any old women who met the description, either. But he'd find one. If need be, he'd hire a Drury Lane actress past her prime to play the part of Aunt What's-her-face, and he'd foot the bill for the entire journey.

It was time for Izzy Goodnight to stop living

in other people's storybooks. She needed to see more of the world than dusty castles and quaint English villages. Ransom couldn't offer her everything she needed or deserved. But he could do this much.

The decision eased his conscience as he watched her pluck another letter from the heap, reducing her time remaining in this castle by a few minutes more. One more grain of sand slipping through the hourglass.

Sometime later, she put her work aside. "That will have to do for today." Her voice brightened as she said, "I'm going upstairs to dress for dinner."

"You're dressing for dinner?"

This was new. There was never any formal dinner. She and Miss Pelham took their meals in the kitchen with Duncan, or so he assumed. Ransom never joined them.

"We finished the dining room yesterday. Duncan, Miss Pelham, and I. So we decided to take a holiday from dusting and celebrate with a formal dinner tonight." She rose from her chair. "Miss Pelham has been working on the menu all day."

He scratched the thick growth of whiskers on his chin. "No one mentioned it."

"I . . ." Her voice softened to that soothing, wild-honey tone. "Oh, I'm sorry. I should have thought to tell you. Are your feelings hurt?"

"What?" He crossed his arms over his chest.

"Don't be absurd. My feelings—not that I'm admitting to possessing any, mind you—are not hurt."

"We didn't mean for you to feel left out. You're welcome to join us, of course. It's just . . . you never do. You never take dinner with us at all."

It was late in the day, and his vision had faded. She was just a roving patch of darker gray in a sea of light gray mist. He couldn't tell whether her invitation was sincere or pitying.

But then, it didn't matter. She was right; he never dined with their group. For good reason.

He rose to his feet. "Goodnight, I do appreciate your generous invitation to attend this dinner that *my* money paid for, in *my* own home, but—"

"Oh, please do come."

The words rushed from her, impulsive—but they were no more reckless than her concurrent gesture.

She took his *hand.*

She took his hand in hers and squeezed it. Sweetly. As if he were a reluctant child who needed a bit of compassion and encouragement.

At least, that's what he assumed those gestures felt like. His own childhood had been utterly devoid of compassion or encouragement.

"I'd be very glad if you joined us for dinner, Ransom. If only because it means one person at the table who couldn't care less about the true identity of the Shadow Knight."

He frowned. "What's a Shadow Knight?"

"Exactly." She squeezed his hand again. "That's

the best thing anyone's said to me in ages. Do come to dinner and be your ill-tempered, unromantic self. Please."

"I told the duke about our dinner this evening." Izzy sucked in her breath as Miss Pelham gave her corset laces a firm tug. "I invited him to join us."

"Oh, that's wonderful." Miss Pelham tugged again.

"He declined."

Another tug. "Oh. Too bad."

Izzy wondered how many more times she could muster the courage to reach out to him. He was so obstinate and determined to isolate himself. Ever since Duncan's story, she didn't know what to think. Was he heartbroken over his lost intended? Angry about the loss of his sight and independence? Or was he merely a jilted man licking the wounds to his pride?

In any case, he needed to make his way into the world again—and soon.

She'd read through more than half his correspondence now, and Izzy was forming suspicions. Without conclusive proof, she didn't dare mention the idea. But she was almost certain the duke's solicitors were conspiring against him. For what reason, she couldn't imagine. But he stood to lose far more than this castle if he didn't rejoin the England of the living soon.

Tonight's dinner could have been a step in the right direction.

If only.

Miss Pelham gave the corset laces another yank. When Izzy winced, she apologized. "Sorry, Miss Goodnight. But I have to cinch it tight, or the gown won't fit you."

She helped Izzy into a gown of poppy red silk. It was Miss Pelham's gown, of course. Izzy's wardrobe offered nothing appropriate for a dinner like this one.

"Oh, that color does look well on you. Even if the fit is too tight up top."

The bodice *was* tight. Her breasts were pale, quivering scoops overflowing the neckline. Rather scandalous attire, for little Izzy Goodnight. But she had a shawl, and it was only Miss Pelham and Duncan.

"I promise not to overeat." Izzy smoothed her palms over the luscious red silk. "Thank you so much for the loan of it."

"It's nothing. I'm glad to help." Miss Pelham pulled on the first of her elbow-length gloves, then held it out for Izzy to button. "It is taking a dreadfully long time for your belongings to arrive, isn't it?"

"Yes, it is." As Izzy worked the tiny buttons, a pang of guilt twisted in her chest.

"Is something wrong, Miss Goodnight?"

"Only that I wish . . ."

Only that I wish I didn't have to lie to you. Only that I'm wickedly envious of your golden hair and blushing cheeks and confidence. And I wish I could make you the tiniest bit envious of me by confessing everything I've done with the duke.

"Only that I wish you'd call me Izzy."

Miss Pelham's fan clattered to the floor. Her face lit with a radiant, sunbeam smile. "Truly?"

"Yes, of course."

"Then you must call me Abigail."

"I'd like that."

Miss Pelham—Abigail—caught her in a tight hug. "Oh, I knew it. I knew we would be best of friends."

Friends.

So strange. Izzy would have never believed she could be close friends with a woman like Abigail. The Abigail Pelhams of her youth had treated shy, awkward Izzy with disdain, even cruelty. They called her Frizzy Izzy, Witch's Broom, Mop Head, Funny Face . . . the list went on and on.

. But this wasn't her youth, she reminded herself. She and Abigail were grown women, and perhaps it had been unfair of Izzy not to give their friendship a chance.

Abigail pulled back from the hug. "Now that we're friends, will you let me do your hair?" She took one of Izzy's wayward curls and regarded it pityingly. "I have a recipe for an egg-yolk and rosewater preparation that will have this smooth as pressed satin."

Izzy started to protest that it wouldn't work. She'd tried every preparation known to womankind, and none of them had worked.

But Abigail would hear none of it.

She turned Izzy toward the mirror. "You'll see. With the right coiffure and a bright new ribbon . . . this could be almost pretty."

Almost.

Izzy reached for her shawl, trying to ignore the unintended slight. "Let's go down to dinner, shall we?"

Abigail took her arm. "Yes, let's. I have some questions I've been saving for tonight."

Oh, dear.

To her credit, Abigail made it almost through the soup course before beginning the interrogation.

An apologetic smile tipped her mouth. "You must know what I'm going to ask."

I have a feeling I do.

"Forgive me. I can't help it." Abigail lowered her voice to a whisper. "The Shadow Knight. Who is he, really? Don't worry, I won't ever tell a soul."

Izzy allowed the suspense to build while she swallowed her mouthful of creamy parsnip soup and took a moment to enjoy the splendor.

They'd worked for two full days on this dining room, washing down the walls, beating the carpet, polishing the furniture, and recovering the chairs. By day, one could still see the faded patches on the carpet and the nicks on the paneling.

But by candlelight . . . ? Oh, it looked magical. The whole room glittered. The table was laid with crisp, pressed white linen, and every object—from the tiniest spoon to the largest candlestick—had been polished until it gleamed. It could not have been more beautiful if it had been laid with diamonds. The crystal was borrowed from the vicarage, but everything else belonged here. Duncan had found a chest of silver and two crates of straw-packed china that had escaped looting, having been stashed under boards in the cellar.

The soaring ceilings overhead gave the impression of grandeur, but the general aura was one of warmth and welcome, and the scent of roasted lamb curled through the air.

It felt like a home.

"Well?" Abigail prompted.

Yes, yes. The Shadow Knight.

"I'm afraid I don't know," Izzy said. "My father never told me. I don't know any more than was printed in the magazine."

"Not Cressida and Ulric, either? Oh, I can't stand it that they haven't reunited. Do they marry and have babies, the way I always hoped and dreamed?"

"If you hoped and dreamed it, then perhaps they did. I know readers were disappointed that the stories are unfinished. But to me, there's a certain beauty to the fact that Ulric was left hanging, literally. This way, the characters can have as many happy endings as readers can imagine."

Hopefully, that would put the matter to rest.

"Oh, but it's just not enough." Miss Pelham

sighed. "What about that eunuch? I had suspicions about him. I don't suppose Sir Henry ever—"

"For the love of God. Leave her be."

This irritable outburst took everyone by surprise.

Because it came from the duke.

Ransom stood in the doorway. And Izzy regretted using up the words "grandeur" and "splendor" on the dining room because now she was all out of words to describe how he looked.

Well, perhaps there was one word left.

Magnificent.

Clean-shaven, freshly bathed, and turned out in a black tailcoat that fit him snug as poured ink. And he must have done it all unaided, judging by the shocked expression Duncan wore as he rose to his feet. Poor fellow probably worried he'd been replaced in his duties.

But Izzy didn't believe that was the case, judging by the inadvisable color of the duke's waistcoat and the fresh, paper-thin scrape along his jaw.

It was silly, perhaps. But Izzy found that thin red line even more brave and endearing than the scar slashed across his brow.

"It's him," Abigail whispered across the table. "The duke."

"I know," Izzy murmured back.

"Why did he come down? Do you think he fancies you?"

Izzy pinched the bridge of her nose. Goodness.

Why didn't this girl understand that Ransom could hear everything she said?

"He must fancy you," Abigail whispered on. "Wouldn't that be exciting? You could make him believe in romance and lo—"

The duke cleared his throat.

"Your Grace," Duncan said. "Forgive me. We weren't expecting—"

"Sit down." Ransom found the chair at the head of the table and drew it out. "I'm not here to make you work."

"Would you like some soup?" Abigail motioned to the serving maid, one of the newly hired servants.

"Just wine. I'm not here to eat, either."

Silence fell as they all pondered the question no one dared to ask aloud. If he wasn't here to eat or be served . . . why was he here at all?

"Give Miss Goodnight a rest about Morbidia." He took a seat. "Surely there's something else to talk about."

"It's all right," Izzy said, trying to contain the damage to the evening's pleasant atmosphere. "Really. I don't mind."

"I mind on your behalf."

Ah. So that's why he'd come to dinner. To stand up for her. To be her surly, ill-mannered champion. If it wouldn't have spoiled her lovely soup, Izzy could have burst into tears.

He tapped his fork against the plate. "I thought tonight's dinner was meant to be a holiday."

"It is a holiday, Your Grace," Abigail answered.

"Then I would like a holiday from fairy stories. Unless the knights and maidens tumble into bed and do carnal things to each other, I couldn't care less."

Abigail's cheeks turned a subtle shade of pink. "Your Grace. They do nothing of the sort."

"Then I'm not interested."

"There you have it, Miss Pelham," Izzy said. "The duke is not interested."

"That's because the duke doesn't know what he's missing. He needs to experience the stories themselves. We can read from them after dinner."

The serving maid removed the soup and placed a platter in front of the duke. She whisked away a silver dome to reveal a beautifully browned rack of lamb.

Ransom sipped his wine. "I hope you're not waiting for me to carve it."

Chastened, Duncan reached for the carving knife and began to saw the chops apart, offering a serving to each of the ladies before taking his own portion. Ransom refused to take any for himself.

Izzy couldn't help feeling awkward for him. So this was why he never joined them for meals. As the gentleman of rank at any given table, it was his task to carve the game and roasts—something that would be difficult for him to do well. Especially toward the end of the day, when she knew his vision waned dramatically.

She looked down at the lamb chops before her.

Even a plate of food must feel like a test he was set up to fail. She briefly closed her eyes and tried to imagine going about cutting her meat into pieces without the benefit of sight. She might be able to manage it, with practice. But manage it with grace and ducal manners? That was less certain.

The passing and consuming of various dishes occupied them for some time. Ransom just kept drinking, which Izzy feared didn't bode well.

As the dessert course—a lovely fresh berry tart—was served, Abigail rose from the table and returned shortly, carrying her giant bound folio. Evidently she hadn't forgotten her promise to read.

"Here we are," she announced. *"The Goodnight Tales.* We'll start at the beginning tonight."

Ransom muttered a curse. "Is there no escaping this?"

"Please don't read them," Izzy said. "He needn't hear them at all. But if you do read, spare him the beginning, at least. My father was always embarrassed by those installments from the first few years. He didn't consider them his best work."

"But they're the beginning. One must begin at the beginning. Mark my words, Your Grace. Soon, you'll be swept up in the story of Cressida and Ulric."

As Miss Pelham opened the cover of the book, Izzy was struck by the powerful urge to sweep herself under the carpet. Perhaps live there for the next several years. She could reign in beneficence as the almost-pretty Queen of the Dust Mites.

"'Part the first,'" Miss Pelham read aloud. "'Night has fallen over England. In a small village in the countryside, there is a cottage. A cottage with a slate roof and a candle in every window. And in that cottage is a room. A room with silver moons and golden stars painted on the ceiling. And in that room is a bed. A bed with a quilted purple counterpane. And in that bed is a girl. A girl named Izzy Goodnight, who will not go to sleep.'"

Cringing, Izzy glanced toward Ransom at the head of the table. Perhaps it was for the best that he hadn't eaten anything. He looked as though he would be struggling to keep his meal down.

Miss Pelham read on, adding voices. "'Papa, won't you tell me a story,' the little girl pleads. 'The hour is late, my Izzy,' I reply. 'Please, Papa. The dark frightens me. But your tales give me such happy dreams.'"

Oh, God. Now he groaned. It was a faint groan, but a definite groan nonetheless. Izzy groaned, too.

And the whole mortifying experience was about to get worse. Much worse.

"'Very well,'" Abigail continued. "'Put out the light, my darling Izzy, and I will tell you such a tale. Once, in the time of brave knights and fair ladies, there lived an elegant and intrepid young lady by the name of Cressida. She had emerald green eyes and amber hair, sleek as silk.'"

Izzy braced herself. Here it came. Her three-word, lifelong curse. She mouthed the words as Miss Pelham read them aloud:

" 'Just like yours.' "

Miss Pelham looked up from the book and made eye contact with Izzy. "Isn't that curious? I must admit, I've wondered about it ever since we met. Didn't you wonder, too, Duncan?"

Duncan nodded. "If I'm honest, Miss Pelham, I did."

"Izzy, this is a question you can surely answer. Why did your father write you as having emerald eyes and sleek amber hair?"

"I . . ."

Oh, Lord. Izzy never knew how to explain this. Shouldn't the answer be obvious? The Izzy of the stories had to be different. Because no one wanted to read a story about a funny looking girl with a mop of dark, tangled hair and pale blue eyes. Much less imagine themselves in her place. Because she, the real Izzy Goodnight, could only ever hope to be, at best, *almost* pretty.

Because she wasn't good enough.

"Because her father was a jackass," Ransom said. "Obviously."

Abigail and Duncan gasped in unison.

"No," Abigail said. "You're so very wrong, Your Grace. Sir Henry was . . . well, he was the most gentle, loving father a girl could hope to have. Wasn't he, Izzy?"

Once again, Ransom spared her the awkwardness of a reply. "Very well, I revise my statement.

He was a shrewd jackass. Had everyone fooled. But if good Sir Henry was such an amiable fellow and doting father, why couldn't he be bothered to leave his daughter the security of an income and a comfortable home?"

"Your Grace, his death was so unexpected," Duncan said. "A tragedy."

"It *was* sudden," Izzy put in.

Abigail reached across the table to take Izzy's hand. "It must have been devastating. The whole country was in mourning with you."

Ransom shook his head. "That's no excuse. There are few true eventualities in life, but death is one of them." He waved for more wine. "If you ask me, this Sir Henry Goodnight was no better than a cut-rate gin peddler or opium trader. He hooked people on his soppy stories, then just kept shoveling them more, not caring how many people drowned their powers of reason in that treacly swamp."

Izzy thought that was going a bit too far.

"You don't have to admire my father's stories," she said. "But don't disparage the readers, or the notion of romance. Cressida and Ulric are just characters. Moranglia is entirely made up. But love does exist. It's all around us."

He put down his wineglass and turned his head, as if to survey the room. "Where?"

She didn't know how to answer. "Am I supposed to point it out like an architectural feature? There it is, framed and hanging on the wall?"

"You said love is all around us. Well, where is it? There are four of us at this table, all grown adults. Not one romance. Not one instance of love."

"But—"

"But what? Everyone knows your situation, Miss Goodnight. Doomed to spinsterhood by your father's stories." He gestured at his valet. "Duncan here spent ten years pining for one of the London housemaids. Irish girl with bouncy curls and a bouncier bosom. She never took a second look at him."

Duncan made a halfhearted attempt at protest, but Ransom ignored it.

He turned to Abigail. "What about you, Miss Pelham? You seem lively, and by all accounts, pretty enough. Your father is a gentleman. Where are your suitors?"

Abigail stared at her half-eaten tart. "There was someone."

"Ah. And where's the someone now?"

"He left for the navy," she answered. "My dowry is slight, and he was a second son with no fortune of his own. Matters never progressed beyond friendship." She gave a little smile. "I suppose it wasn't meant to be."

Ransom propped his boot on the chair leg. "There. You see? Once again, cold reality trumps feeling." He waved from Izzy to Abigail to Duncan. "Overlooked, unwanted, rejected. Not a happy ending in the lot."

"That's not fair," Izzy protested. "Our own stories haven't ended. And even so, we are but four souls in a vast world. I receive letters from my father's readers every day. People from all walks of life who—"

"Who are desperate and deluded?"

"Who believe in *love*."

He leaned back in his chair, nonchalant. "Same thing."

"It isn't the same thing at all."

Izzy stared at him. She didn't know why arguing this point had become so important to her. If he wanted to live out the remainder of his life bitter and alone, she supposed he had that right. But his smugness made her so prickly all over. And he wasn't merely insulting love and romance. He was insulting her friends and acquaintances. Her own hard work.

The innermost yearnings of her heart.

This wasn't an academic argument. It was personal. If she didn't defend the idea of lasting happiness, how could she hold out any hope for her own?

She tried again. "Everyone . . . well, almost everyone . . . understands that my father's stories are merely stories. But love is not a delusion." To his disbelieving snort, she insisted, "It's *not*."

An idea came to her.

"Wait." She rose from the table and began walking backward, toward the corridor. "Wait right there one moment, and I will prove it to you."

She hurried up to the next floor, then down the

corridor, and tapped her way up all thirty-four stairs to the turret. There, she rummaged through her saved correspondence until she found the envelope she wanted, and clutching it, raced back down.

She arrived breathless and triumphant.

"Here," she said, clutching the weathered envelope. "Right here in my hand, I have proof that my father's stories made a difference in people's lives. Proof that true love will always triumph."

"I shall brace myself." The duke lifted his wineglass and drained it in one swallow. "Carry on."

Izzy unfolded the letter and began to read.

My dear Miss Goodnight,

We have never met, and yet I think of you as a close friend. Perhaps even as a sister. My governess began reading me your father's stories when I was but a girl of six, and for as long as I can remember, the good people of Moranglia have populated my dreams—just as I imagine they have populated yours. When I learned of Sir Henry's untimely death, I wept tears for you every night for months.

I am grown now, as you must be. This year, my father engaged me to a suitor not of my choosing. He is not a cruel or violent man, but he is unfeeling and cold. I am sure he does not love me and probably never could. He intends to acquire me, and he has gone about his goal with less feeling and atten-

tion than other men display when buying a horse. I dread the prospect of a life with him.

This will all sound so familiar to you. Am I not just like Cressida in the thirty-fifth installment, when her father betrothed her to that horrid Lord Darkskull? Excepting the windowless tower and the helpful mice, of course.

And, in the same way as Cressida, my heart has belonged to another for years. Oh, Miss Goodnight. I wish you could know him. Like Ulric, he comes from humble circumstances. But he has proved his worth time and again, displaying such understanding and devotion as I have never known from my closest friends and family. I love him with everything in my soul.

I face a fearsome choice. But I have sought the counsel of my heart and come to a brave decision.

I will follow Cressida's example and escape. With or without the helpful mice.

Doubt not. Tomorrow I shall be with my true love, and together we will embark on our life's adventure. All thanks are due to you, Miss Goodnight, and to your dear father, who lives on in his tales and in a nation's hearts.

A tear burned at the corner of Izzy's eye as she lifted her head. "And it's signed, 'Yours in boundless gratitude, Lady Emily Riverdale.'"

She lowered the letter on a note of victory. There, now. He couldn't possibly listen to that letter and be unmoved.

He was moved, indeed.

Without a word, Ransom rose from his chair. He loomed at the head of the table, big and dark and ominous as a human thundercloud. His hands were clenched in fists. She expected at any moment he would start launching lightning bolts.

The hairs on the back of Izzy's neck prickled.

Ever-proper Duncan was waving both arms in a frenzy, gesturing for Izzy's attention.

"What is it?" she whispered to the valet. "What's wrong?"

Duncan's eyes widened as he pointed at the letter in her hand and mouthed, *That.*

This?

As the duke stormed from the room, she searched the letter again, trying to find the words that would cause such dramatic offense. Nothing, until . . .

Until her eye landed on the sender's name. Her heart and her stomach switched places.

Oh, no. *No.*

Emily Riverdale.

Lady Shemily Liverpail.

Chapter Sixteen

*L*ord, but she was an idiot.

The letter in Izzy's hand was from Ransom's own intended. The flibbertigibbet. The same woman who'd run off with a farmer, leading to the duke's disfigurement and brush with death. And she'd just read this letter aloud to him as proof of everlasting love.

Izzy gave the letter to Duncan in passing. Then she picked up a candlestick in one hand and her silk skirts in the other.

"I must go after him."

Moving as fast as she could in her sausage casing of a gown and corset, she chased him down the corridor. "Ransom, wait."

He didn't break stride, firing a warning over his shoulder. "Not now."

The words hit her square in the sternum, stopping her in place. His wasn't a tone one could easily ignore. Eleven generations of ducal authority rang out in that command.

He was angry, hurt, and on a very short fuse to explosion.

Izzy gathered her nerve and followed anyway.

She struggled to keep pace with him. He knew these rooms and corridors so well, having walked them every night in the dark.

At last, he turned into a room, and Izzy knew she would have him cornered.

He'd ducked into the library.

Ironically enough, the library was one room Izzy had avoided thus far. Though the vastness of the space and the floor-to-ceiling mahogany bookshelves were grand, for a true lover of books, the scene was unbearably sad. A cursory glance on the first day had revealed that any books of interest or value had been removed or looted. The only volumes remaining were dry agricultural treatises or outdated almanacs, and even those had been mildewed or chewed to the point of being unreadable.

Someday, Izzy had told herself, she would find the money to clean this out and fill it with lovely books again. Books bound in every available shade of rich, buttery leather: green, blue, red, brown. Someday, she would pass a rainy day sitting by that massive stone hearth, cuddled up in an overstuffed armchair and caught in the grips of a thrilling gothic novel.

Tonight, she would have to settle for living in one.

She stopped in the center of the room and placed the candlestick on a forgotten, dusty table. "Ransom, I—"

He held her off with an outstretched hand. "I'm warning you, Goodnight. Don't push me right now."

"Please. I don't want to argue. Just allow me to apologize. I'm so, so sorry. It was terribly thoughtless of me to read that. I've had the letter for ages now, and I never drew the connection. I had no idea she was *your* Lady Emily."

Rage flared from him. "So you *know*."

"Yes. I know."

He took two confrontational steps in her direction. The candlelight sent fearsome shadows playing over his scarred face. "You've been gossiping about me. Or maybe it was somewhere in my stack of correspondence. Have you been snooping through my letters on your own?"

"No," she hastened to say. "Nothing like it. I learned about it from Duncan."

"*Duncan.* He told you." He cursed violently as he turned away. "That's it, then. There's not a soul remaining on this earth I can trust."

"No, no. Please don't take it that way." As she talked, she drifted closer, erasing the gap between them step by cautious step. "Duncan worries over you so much. He didn't want to gossip, I promise. And he didn't, exactly. He told me about a Duke

of Mothfairy and a Lady Shemily, and I had to ex-
trapolate the rest."

"Moth-*what*?"

Izzy slapped a hand to her brow. "Never mind.
Please forget I said anything about that part."

Before she knew what was happening, he was
upon her. He caught her by the waist and pressed
her up against the nearest wall—one lined with
empty bookshelves.

"I warned you," he growled. "I warned you not
to push me. Now I'm going push back."

He braced his hands on the shelves, caging
her between his arms. One hard ridge caught her
along the back of the thighs. Another scored the
small of her back. The smell of wine was over-
powering.

He had her trapped, and her body responded
like any trapped creature's would. The hairs on
the back of her neck lifted. Her diaphragm worked
like a bellows, pushing air in and out of her lungs.
Her pulse accelerated to a mad, frantic thunder in
her chest.

"I'm s-sorry," she stammered. "So very sorry."

"Sorry for what? Sorry you read me that letter?
Sorry for my pain? Sorry that you had a hand in
destroying my life?"

Oh, Lord. So he *did* blame her.

"I'm sorry," she said carefully, "that Lady Emily
never understood the kind of man you are."

"Really." One of his hands moved to her waist.
His palm slid up and down over the liquid-smooth

silk, idly tracing the curves of her breast and hip. "And what kind of man is that?"

"A good one. One who's gruff some of the time, and off-puttingly arrogant a great deal of the rest. But loyal and protective when it counts. You went after her, Ransom. You rushed after her, when you could have let her go."

"Yes, I rushed after her. And if you think that made me the hero in her little story, you have it all wrong. Everything she wrote was the truth. I didn't love her. I never would have loved her. To her, I was always the villain."

I didn't love her.

The words should have made her relieved for his feelings. Instead, Izzy was selfishly relieved for her own.

"You have no idea." He leaned close. The heat of his breath rushed over her ear. "You have no idea how tempted I am to ruin you. Right here and now. The revenge would be so damned sweet. England's precious little innocent, spreading her thighs so wide for my cock."

At his carnal words, her knees went weak. She couldn't draw enough air. These wretchedly tight corset laces. With every shallow breath, her breasts pushed higher against the restrictive red silk. The exquisite friction chafed her nipples to hardened peaks.

"You wouldn't do that." She swallowed hard. "You're not the sort of man to take advantage."

"I don't need to be a man who takes advantage."

He sent one hand to burrow under her skirts. "Just one who takes an invitation."

He hooked a hand under her knee and lifted, drawing her leg to the side and propping her heel on the first shelf above the ground. Using the weight of his own knee, he pinned her in this lewd position.

Her heartbeat stalled as he pushed the folds of her petticoats and shift aside. She wasn't wearing anything but stockings beneath. But she couldn't bring herself to protest or shy away. His possessive touch excited her, and she found herself growing aroused even before his hand moved to cradle her sex.

She didn't want to scurry back to the dining room and continue pretending. She wanted to be here with him, raw and craving. Her flushed, breathless response to his touch . . . This was honest. The need gathering between her legs . . . It was real.

His thumb slipped over her crease, parting her gently for his explorations. Pleasure shuddered through her, and she gripped the nearest shelf for strength.

"Yes." He groaned. "I knew it would be like this. I knew you'd be so wet for me."

The crude words made her wild. He slid a finger inside her, and she bit her lip to keep from crying aloud.

Yes.

He knew just what she needed. He worked in and out, stroking a fraction deeper every time.

And still she craved more. She rocked her hips back and forth, trying to draw him deeper, deeper. She needed him. She needed him so deep inside.

"No one else has any idea, do they? What a naughty, wanton girl you are. No one else sees what I see. No other man makes you twist and pant and moan."

She arched off the shelves, gasping. "No."

"Only me." His fingers thrust deep. "Say it."

"Only you."

With a soft groan of approval, he bent his head to lavish kisses on her breasts. Using his teeth, he tugged her bodice downward. Before she could protest that the gown was borrowed and already stretched to its seams, she felt the small rip of fabric.

Her breasts spilled forward, and a dizzying rush of air flooded her lungs.

"Yes." He eased her breast from her stays and circled her nipple with his tongue. "I know what you need."

He slid both hands to her hips. In one swift motion, he lifted her six inches off the ground, setting her backside on the next shelf up. Nudging her skirts to her waist, he moved between her legs.

"If you don't want this, tell me." His voice was hoarse. "You don't have to scream. You don't have to push me away. You've only to say it."

Izzy didn't know what to say. Her body wanted his. That much was certain. But was this going to be her first—and possibly only—experience of lovemaking? A furtive, angry tupping against a dusty shelf? He wouldn't be making love to her. He'd be striking back at the very idea of love.

"I . . ." She worked for breath. "I'm not saying no."

He moaned and lifted her, so that she straddled his hips.

"But I'm saying, not like this. I want emotion. I want tenderness. I think you want those things, too."

His fingers dug into the flesh of her backside, and he ran his tongue across her chest. "Curse tenderness. To hell with emotion. I'm not the man to fulfill your heart's desires, but I can give you everything—*everything*—your body's craving."

"Just because . . ."

He sucked her nipple into his mouth, and she lost her voice to another wave of bliss.

She wove her fingers in his hair and tried again. "Just because she ran away, it doesn't mean a woman can't love you. Ransom, I . . . I know there's more to you than this."

"There's a great deal to me." He rocked his pelvis against hers, and the hard ridge of his erection stroked her core. "You could have it all. Just as long and hard and deep as you need it."

Oh. Oh, how she needed it.

He ground against her in a firm, delicious rhythm. The warmed, weathered buckskin teased over her thighs. Izzy whimpered and clung to the shelving, helpless to do anything but hang on for the ride.

With every roll of his hips, he was pushing her higher. Closer to release.

And he knew it.

"Come for me." He slid his hand between their bodies, and his fingers filled her deep again. As he worked them in and out, the heel of his hand rubbed against her pearl. "I need to feel it. I need to hear it."

A thin whimper of pleasure caught in her throat.

"My name." He stroked deeper. "Say my name. I want you to know it's me."

"*Ransom.*" Her grip tightened on the shelf.

And then suddenly—

Something gave way.

With a creak and a whoosh, her whole world turned on its axis. Plunging them both into the dark.

"Wh-?" She panted for breath. "What happened?"

Damned if Ransom could say. One moment, he was in paradise. Izzy gasping his name, all that tightness and heat surrounding his fingers . . . Victory, right in the palm of his hand.

A moment later, they were in hell. The entire section of wall, bookshelves included, had swung on its axis, depositing them here.

Wherever "here" was.

He couldn't tell. He just knew that everything

in it was close. And dank. The air smelled of rot and the mustiness of centuries.

"Is it some kind of secret passage?" Izzy asked, still breathing hard.

He withdrew his hand from her quivering flesh and lowered her skirts as much as he dared. However, he held her pinned against the shelving with his hips, keeping her feet well off the floor. God only knew what muck or misadventures lay at his boots.

With his free hand, Ransom felt around the space. "More like a secret closet. If this was ever a corridor, it's been closed off now."

"It must have been a priest hole. A hiding place. They built them in the sixteenth century when Catholicism was made illegal. There should be a way out of here. A lever, or—"

"Let me."

He scouted the shelves, pulling and pushing on each ledge. Nothing. He tried throwing his weight against one side of the panel in an attempt to make it rotate back the other direction. Nothing.

"Duncan and Miss Pelham are certain to come looking for us," he said. "When we hear footsteps, we'll shout for help."

She caught his coat. Her breathing was a labored rasp. "Just don't let go."

"What is it? Are you hurt?"

He felt her head shake no. Her hands found his coat lapels and curled in fists. "It's just . . . so dark, and I . . ."

"And you're not fond of the dark. I recall."

She ducked her head, burrowing into his shoulder.

Gods above. She hadn't been exaggerating. This was not merely fear but terror. He could feel it in the tremors that raced beneath her skin. He could hear it in the quickness of her breath. The same woman who stood defiant in the face of bats, rats, ghosts, and dukes was utterly petrified . . .

Of the dark.

Ransom couldn't bring himself to tease or gloat. All his angry lust had dissipated into the murky gloom. Sliding his arms around her back, he pulled her against his chest and clutched tight. Because he understood that fear, as well as he knew his own heart. He'd been that miserable soul, alone and terrified in the fresh hell of darkness.

"It's all right," he told her. "It's dark, but you're not alone. I'm here."

Her quaking continued. "It's s-so embarrassing and childish. It's been this way since I was nine."

"What happened when you were nine?"

That seemed rather late in life to develop an aversion to darkness. Maybe talking about it would banish the fear. At the least, it would fill the silence.

"I used to spend summers with my aunt in Essex. She had no daughters. Just a son, Martin. I might have mentioned him."

"The one who tossed you in a pond?"

"Yes." Her chest rose and fell with her accelerated breaths. Her story came in short bursts of words. "That's the one. Miserable, horrid boy. He was jealous, hated me. He wanted me gone. Whenever he caught me alone, he would strike me and call me cruel names. When his casual tormenting didn't work, he tried throwing me in the pond. And since that didn't get rid of me either, he caught me in the garden one day, dragged me into the root cellar, and locked me there. It was some thirty paces from the house, and, naturally, underground. No one heard my screams. A full day and night passed before they found me. And Martin got his wish. I cried so hysterically, Aunt Lilith sent me home. I've hated the dark ever since."

Things began to make sense to him. "That's why the bedtime stories began. Because you were afraid of the dark."

"Yes."

"And that's why you're always downstairs when I wake in the morning. Because you're still afraid of the dark."

She exhaled slowly. "Yes."

With a gruff curse, he ran his hands up and down her back. "That cousin of yours was a vile little bastard. I hope he got what he deserved."

"Not at all. He's a full-grown bastard now, and he reaped every reward for his vile behavior."

"How so?"

"My father's only will was older than I am,

drawn up when he reached his majority. I never even knew it existed, and he never revised it. But it left everything to his closest male heir, so . . ."

"Your cousin inherited everything."

She nodded. "When he came to claim the house and all our material possessions, I thought surely Martin would have matured over the years. Perhaps we might work out some arrangement. But no. He was still the same malicious, petty bully, and he only hated me more for my father's success. He took everything from me, down to the last pen nib. And he did it gleefully."

Ransom stayed completely still, not wanting to alarm her. Meanwhile, rage burned through him like a wildfire. He reconsidered the plan of waiting on Duncan and Miss Pelham to find them. He was angry enough to punch straight through the wall.

"You've gone very quiet," she said.

He inhaled and exhaled, trying to moderate his emotions. "I'm engaged in a creative-thinking exercise. Would I rather throw your cousin to a pack of famished jackals? Or watch him be picked apart by a teeming school of piranha?"

"That's a good one." She laughed a little. "I'll be sure to pose that question to Lord Peregrine."

All was quiet for a few moments.

"How do you bear it?" she asked. "How do you bear this all the time? The darkness."

"It wasn't easy at first." A grave understatement. "But with time, I've grown accustomed. The dark scares you because it seems boundless. But it isn't as vast as it seems. You can explore it, learn the shape of it, take its measure—just as you can see a room with your eyes. You have your hands, nose, ears."

"I have my mind," she whispered. "That's the worst part. It's my mind that fills the darkness with horrid things. I have too much imagination."

"Shut the door to it, then. No stories or wild tales. Concentrate only on the things you can sense. What's in front of you?"

Her hands flattened on the linen of his shirt, light and chilled. "You are."

"What's to either side of you?"

"Your arms."

"What's behind you?"

She inhaled slowly. "Your hands. Your hands are on my back."

He rubbed his hands up and down, warming her. "Then that's all you need to know. I have you. If there are beasties in the dark, they have to get through me."

After a few more moments, her trembling began to ease. Some knot of tension unraveled in his chest.

"You're so big and strong," she murmured.

He didn't answer.

"And you smell so comforting." Her forehead rested on his shoulder. "Like whisky and leather. And dog."

The description startled a laugh from him.

"You're learning the way of it. There's a great deal you can sense about people without seeing them at all. Scents, sounds, textures. It amazes me sometimes how little attention I paid such things before I was injured. If there's a boon in all this, it's that I notice things I would have overlooked."

The woman in his arms, for instance.

If he'd crossed paths with Izzy Goodnight at Court a few years back, Ransom was certain of one thing. He would not have given her a second look. She was dark, slightly built, and modestly dressed. Innocent, uncertain of her attractions. In sum, not his sort. His eyes had typically wandered to vivacious, fair-haired types.

In this case, his eyes would have done him a disservice.

Because this woman . . . she was a revelation. Every time he took her in his arms, he was astonished anew by her warmth and softness. The fresh, green scent of her hair and the wild-honey sweetness of her voice. Her instinctive passion.

And her tenderness. Her hands skimmed downward, and she slid her arms around his waist to hug him close.

Then she pressed her face to his shirtfront.

Nuzzling.

Well, she was back to herself again.

"So if noticing things you might have overlooked is the best part of being blinded, what's the worst?" she asked.

God. There were too many contenders for that honor. She could guess at many of them. Others, she could never fathom, and he would never share.

"Learning to hate surprise," he said, surprising himself with the confession. "I'm a creature of routine now. I have a mental chart of every room in this place, every tabletop. I have to put everything back precisely where I found it, or I'm lost. Makes me feel like an old curmudgeon, growling at anything unexpected."

"I was unexpected," she said.

"Yes. You were."

"And I've been altering your routine. Moving things about on your mental chart."

"Yes. You have."

She lifted her head from his chest. "I understand why you didn't want me in the castle. I was a surprise. You must have hated me."

He swept a touch to her face. "I didn't hate you."

"Well, if you didn't hate me at the first, you have reason now. Ransom, you must believe me. I'm just so sorry. For the letter, for the castle, for Lady Emily. For everything. You have every right to be—"

He shushed her. "Goodnight. We're trapped together in a small, dark space. For the moment, we're getting on as well as could possibly be expected. I don't think this is the time to remind me of my many valid reasons to resent your presence and despise everything you stand for."

"Right." She took a deep breath. "On second

thought, perhaps we shouldn't wait to be rescued. There must be a release latch somewhere."

"I'll find it."

"No, it has to be me." Izzy shifted her body. "Maybe if we re-create our position just before the panel turned. You were between my legs, and I had my hand on the shelf just about . . . here."

Ransom moved dutifully into place, lifting her by the hips and feeling like a jackass about it. Had he really held her like this? Spread wide and wrapped around him, while he pawed at her and made lewd demands, just so he could prove something to his wounded pride?

Yes. Evidently he had.

"Let's see," she said. "How did it go? Oh, yes. You had your fingers *inside* me, and you were pleading with me to say your name, and then . . ."

"Can we dispense with the details?"

Bloody hell. She was a penniless and homeless virgin who was just as much a victim of her father's charlatanry as anyone. And Ransom had never felt more disgusting. She had every reason to despise him, too.

"And then"—her body arced as she stretched high—"I think I pulled just here . . ."

Whoosh.

Chapter Seventeen

Izzy's world tilted once again.

The panel spun on its axis, spitting them back out into the library. But this time, the hidden door didn't make a complete rotation. It lurched and stopped halfway.

They both tumbled forward with the momentum.

"Oof."

Ransom twisted as they fell, catching her in his arms and taking the brunt of the fall.

She landed in his embrace, sprawled atop him and gasping for breath.

"Thank you," she said.

He released her. "Don't thank me. I was merely—"

"Oh, don't." Smiling, she pressed her fingers to his lips, shushing him. "Don't even bother."

Izzy refused to listen to yet another speech about his dastardly behavior and his life that was a scourge on decency and romance.

Everything was different now. He'd eased her trembling in the darkness. They'd shared their innermost thoughts and memories. He'd threatened her vile cousin with two imaginary, delightfully gory deaths.

They understood one another. At least, a little bit.

Most of all, Izzy knew, beyond a whisper of doubt, that all his talk of being a heartless villain was nothing more than that: talk.

Just to prove it . . . just to get back at him for all his crude, sensual games earlier . . . she bent over and pressed a tender kiss to his forehead.

And she held it, for two heartbeats more.

Take that, sweet man.

Then she pushed to her feet and did her best to cover herself with her displaced corset and the torn bodice. He remained exactly where he was, flat on the threadbare carpet.

"Are you hurt?" she asked.

He let his arms fall to the sides. "I'm slain."

Footsteps thundered down the corridor. Abigail and Duncan reeled around the corner and into the library.

"My God," Duncan said. He went straight to Ransom, surveying the dust and grime on his coat.

"There you are. We've been searching all over." Abigail ran to Izzy, taking in her ripped garments and disheveled hair. Then she glanced toward Ransom where he lay on the floor. "My goodness. What's happened?"

"We were . . . We were stuck." Unable to find the words to explain it, Izzy motioned toward the priest hole and hoped the rest would be obvious.

Abigail screamed.

"Well, it wasn't *that* bad," Izzy said. "We did get out. And I'm so sorry about your gown."

"It's not that," Abigail said weakly. She turned Izzy toward the priest hole. "Look."

Izzy looked. "Is that . . . ?" She cocked her head to the side, moving closer until there could be no doubt. Then she clapped a hand to her mouth. "Oh my God. It is."

There, tucked in the shadowed, dusty back corner of the priest hole, were bones.

An entire person's worth of bones.

They hadn't been alone in the dark at all.

The discovery brought a swift end to the dinner party. Centuries-old corpses had a way of doing that.

Ransom sent for both the magistrate and the vicar, and the two spent a full hour debating what was to be done with the bones. Whether reports needed to be filed; whether the remains could be buried on holy ground, and so forth. Even though he was found in a priest hole, he could have just as easily been a vagrant or a smuggler or a thief. There was no telling whether the dead man was even a Protestant or Catholic, so the men gratefully took Izzy's suggestion that the bones be interred in the castle's chapel.

They swept up the remains with as much dignity as could be mustered and laid them under a stone in the chapel floor. The vicar said a prayer.

And once the vicar had gone home, taking Miss Pelham and Izzy with him, Ransom was alone. He decided to honor the dead man in a different time-honored way. With heavy drinking.

He was on his second tumbler of whisky when he heard light footsteps traversing the hall.

"Is that a ghost?" he asked.

"I don't believe in ghosts, remember?"

Izzy.

She walked the length of the hall. "Abigail decided she'd rather sleep at the vicarage tonight. I can't say I blame her."

"I can't say I do, either." He'd assumed Izzy would be spending the night at the vicarage, too.

But she hadn't stayed at the vicarage. She'd come back to him.

His chest swelled with some unnameable, unthinkable emotion. He blamed the whisky.

She stopped by the hearth. "Why is the fire dying?"

"All the new servants left. No one wants to work in a haunted castle of horrors."

"Oh." She added wood to the hearth and gave it a stir with the poker. "What about Duncan?"

"Sent him down to the village pub," Ransom said. "He needed a drink, and he's not the sort to drink alone."

"But he wouldn't be alone. He'd be here with you."

"*I'm* the sort to drink alone." He tossed back another swallow. The earthy tang of whisky smoldered all the way down. "Why didn't you stay at the vicarage with Miss Pelham?"

"She invited me. But I declined."

"Not three hours ago, we found a dead man in the wall. And spent several minutes with him, in close company. You're not frightened to stay here tonight?"

"Of course I am," she said. "I'm always frightened, every night. You should know that now. But this is my house. I've waited too long for a proper home just to run away at the first—well, third or fourth—sign of unpleasantness."

She drew up a chair. "And if I'm honest, there's another reason I returned." Her voice softened. "I was worried. I didn't want you to be alone."

Good Lord. How was it that this woman saw the rest of the world through the gauzy filter of some fairy tale but had an eagle's keenness when it came to Ransom's shortcomings? No matter how small the weakness, now matter how he tried to hide it . . . she homed in on that vulnerability and latched onto it with talons.

She sat down next to him. "Finding that poor

man's remains . . ." He sensed her shudder. "Well, it shocked us all. But it seemed to truly unnerve you."

It had. It had unnerved him greatly. Because it could have *been* him.

He leaned forward, letting his head hang toward the floor. Two hundred years from now, that could have been him. A wasted, forgotten sack of bones in this castle.

"I'll have you know, Goodnight, you have been the ruination of all my plans."

"All of them?" she said. "Really? That sounds like an accomplishment."

"Don't be so smug. There weren't many plans left to ruin. There was exactly one plan remaining, in point of fact, which was to stay here until I rotted to dust." He sat tall again and pushed a hand through his hair. "Then you came along."

"Don't tell me you've found the desire to live again, and it's all to do with me." Fabric whispered as she slid farther into her chair. "I wouldn't recognize you."

"For God's sake. Don't do that."

"Don't do what?"

"Smile."

"How do you know I'm smiling?"

"I can hear it. Hell, I can *feel* it. It's all warm and sweet and . . ." He scowled. "Bah."

She made a little crooning noise. "Oh, Ransom."

"That's even worse." He lifted his shoulders, as if they could shield his ears. "See, this is why you've ruined everything. Just ask that fellow we found in the wall. For centuries now, a man couldn't find a better place than Gostley Castle to shrivel up and decay. Not anymore. Now there are draperies and dinner parties. It's insupportable."

"Maybe," she said gently, "this means you should return to London. Rejoin the world of the living."

He shook his head. Return for what? There was nothing for him there.

He had no true friends. He'd never wanted them. He was the Duke of Rothbury, one of the highest-ranked and wealthiest men in England. He didn't need to go courting acceptance, and anyone who tried to court *his* favor was a candidate for suspicion. They could only want something from him.

As for enemies . . . In his youth, he'd collected enemies like a boy collects shiny pebbles. If people hated him, at least he knew he came by that revulsion honestly. And it wasn't as though his enemies could hurt him. He was invulnerable.

Right up until the moment he wasn't.

Damn his eyes. Of all the injuries to incur. If he'd lost a hand, he could have done without. For that matter, he could have given a leg. Both of them. But unless he regained his sight, he could never manage his affairs unaided. Now he was a prisoner of his own youthful arrogance. Left alone, with no one he could trust.

Well, he revised grudgingly, that wasn't quite true tonight.

Right now, he was very much not alone. He couldn't remember ever being so aware of a woman in his life. The rawness of his senses was painful. Izzy was killing him in a hundred tiny ways.

The fire she'd stoked was sending waves of heat in his direction, and they were all scented of her. Smoky and herbal. He felt drugged by her nearness.

He could hear her removing the pins from her hair. One by one, those slender bits of metal hit the side table. Each tap concussed his eardrums like a powder blast.

Then she sighed. Just the faintest, softest release of breath. The sound swept through his chest like a hurricane, with the force to topple trees.

The irony didn't escape him.

They were alone. He was a little drunk, and she was more than a little vulnerable. This would have been the perfect time to continue with his ravishment scheme. He could lay siege to her virginal clothing. Ruthlessly dismantle her inhibitions. Steal an hour or two of fleeting pleasure before proving beyond a shadow of doubt: Romance is an exercise in willful delusion and nothing— *nothing*—ends happily. At least, not in this castle, and not with a man like him.

There was only one wrinkle in that scheme.

He liked her too much to go through with it.

"You need to retire for the night," he said darkly. "Now."

"Yes." She yawned. "I suppose I should."

But she didn't leave straightaway. She rose from her chair and did some moving about. At first, he assumed she was gathering a candle to light her way upstairs. But that couldn't possibly take her so long.

He listened to a solid minute's worth of andirons rattling and fabric rustling and furniture inching over slate before the truth sank in.

"Stop." He pushed to his feet. "Stop at once."

"Stop what?" Her voice carried an unmistakable note of guilt.

"Stop what you're doing."

"I don't know what you mean."

"Yes, you do." He rose to his feet and moved in her direction. "You just pushed that chair toward the table. And before that, you hung my coat on the peg."

"Very well, you caught me. Call the magistrate. Put me in the stocks for excessive tidiness."

"That's not tidiness, Goodnight. You know it's not."

She couldn't get away with this. He knew exactly what she was doing. She was putting the room to rights before she left for the evening. Making certain every chair and pillow and fireplace poker was in its place.

For him.

That wasn't mere tidiness. It was understanding and thoughtfulness. And considering his emotional state, tonight that behavior was dangerous. Any way she cared to spell it.

"I'll see you to your turret." He offered his arm before she could accuse him of chivalry or gallantry or anything else equally absurd. His motives were entirely disgusting.

He wanted to be close to her, shoulder to shoulder as they climbed the stairs to the next floor. He wanted to guide her down the corridor, sliding his hand across her waist and letting it settle just at the small of her back. He wanted to feel her unbound curls brushing against his exposed wrist.

He wanted . . .

God, he wanted her. All of her.

"Here we are." She stopped at the archway that led to her turret room. "Good night, Ransom."

He lingered, counting her steps as she climbed the stairs. *One, two, three, four . . .*

"Goodnight."

She stopped. Then came back down a few steps. *One, two . . .*

"Was that a dismissal or a summons?" she asked. " 'Goodnight, come here'? or 'Good night to you, now go away'?"

Hell, Ransom didn't even know. The word had just ripped from him. He suspected the sentiment behind it was something like, *Goodnight, take off all your clothing and wrap your limbs around me and never let go.*

"The fifteenth step," he said. "It's a bit more narrow than the rest."

"And you don't want me to fall and be hurt. How sweet."

"It's not sweet." He gritted his teeth. "I already swept up one pile of bones today. I'd rather not contend with another."

"Just the same." Her hand touched his face. "Thank you."

Her fingertips rested on his cheek, like a constellation of unexpected kindness. He encircled her wrist with his fingers, planning to wrench her touch away.

Instead, he brushed his thumb over the fluttering beat of her pulse. Her skin was so soft there. His mind's eye bloomed with petals. In every shade of pink. And since it seemed he'd already crossed the border into sentimental madness, and he couldn't possibly make it much worse—

He brought her wrist to his lips. And he kissed that tender, precious heartbeat, like a damn besotted fool.

Bless you.

He released her, squeezing his eyes shut. He was dangling by a thread already. If his eyesight miraculously returned to him at this moment, she would have no chance at all.

"Have mercy on a broken man. Just go to bed."

He stood at the bottom of the stairs, listening to her light steps spiraling up to the turret. Everything in him ached to follow. He leaned against the archway and gripped the stone, wrestling his desire.

As her last steps faded, he turned to walk away. He'd reached the end of the corridor and counted half the stairs back down to the great hall when he heard it.

"Ransom!"

He froze, one hand on the stone. A chill shot down his spine.

"Ransom, come at once."

And then, in the space of a second, he understood it. He understood the reason he'd walked this castle every night in the dark. Learning the length and breadth of every room, arch, corridor, and stair. It wasn't about regaining his strength, or mastering the space that was now his home and prison. He'd done it all for one purpose:

So he could get to her.

Now. As fast as his legs would carry him.

Chapter Eighteen

I zzy stood in the center of the room, frozen in shock. Ransom's steps came booming up the stairs.

He emerged into the room, breathless and red-faced. A storm of fury had gathered on his brow, and his scar forked from it like lightning. "Izzy, what is it? Speak to me. Are you hurt?"

"No." She felt horrible for alarming him. "It's not that."

"Tell me."

"It's this. You did this? You must have done this."

"Did what?"

"The candles. They're everywhere."

She turned a slow circle. At some point since she'd last been in this room, someone had placed a dozen sconces around the perimeter. Each one held a lit beeswax taper. In addition, there were two candelabras on her dressing table, and one on the table beside her bed. The sheer number was extravagant and ridiculous—they filled the space with enough light to rival a star, and their collective heat raised the temperature of the room by several degrees.

Izzy was overwhelmed.

They could only be Ransom's doing. She hadn't told anyone else.

She sniffed back a tear. "Downstairs, you berated me for pushing in a chair or hanging a coat. And then . . . this?" She swiped at her eyes. "Ransom, this is just unfair. Why would you go and do something so . . ."

"They're just candles."

She shook her head. He had to know these were not just candles. They were caring. He was caring about her, *for* her, and it was such an unfamiliar sensation, Izzy didn't know what to do with it.

In desperation, she fluttered her hands, as if she could shoo the emotion away. It didn't help.

"For God's sake." He moved toward her. "You're making too much of this. They're meant to keep you up here. In your room. Away from me. Every night, you've been stealing downstairs in the dark, waking me up before dawn. I couldn't understand what it was you were missing up here, but I tried everything. Blankets, brazier, writing desk."

She pressed a hand to her throat. "Those were all your doing, too? I thought Abigail . . ."

He shook his head. "No. I know what you're thinking, and I'm telling you, it's not that way. This isn't how it looks."

"You had better hope not." She swept another glance around the candlelit room. "Because this looks . . . sweet. It looks . . ." She swallowed hard. "Oh, Ransom, it's so romantic."

He pushed both hands through his hair in a gesture of frustration. "It's not."

"It *is*. This is romantic. *You* are being romantic."

"I didn't do it on purpose." His arms went around her. "I just . . . I just needed to keep you up here." He walked her backward until her knees met the edge of her bed, and they both tumbled onto the mattress. "In this bed."

He stroked her hair, fanning it out over the pillows, and framed her face in his hands. "But I couldn't discern what it was you needed to feel safe. I tried everything. Finally, tonight, you gave me the answer. Light. So now you have as many candles as you please. But now it's gone all wrong. Because you're here in this bed. But I'm here, too. And God help me, Izzy." His brow pressed to hers, and his weight settled over her, crushing and warm. "I don't know how to leave."

"I know how." She pushed on his shoulders. "I will make you."

He tensed. "You will?"

"I will. We can't do this. Every time we get close, something awful occurs. The weasel bites you, a rock falls on your head, we get trapped with a dead man in a darkened hole. If we do this . . . ? God knows what could happen. The whole turret might collapse."

He nodded slowly, as if giving it careful thought. "Izzy?"

"Yes?"

"Let it happen." His lips lowered to hers. "I don't damn well care."

Let it happen, Ransom thought, pushing her back against the bed. Let God and the devil do their worst.

The castle could crumble to the ground. The world could end. The entirety of the Moranglian Army could show up wearing jingling bells. All that mattered was this. Her, and him, and the light of two dozen candles. The both of them, tangled in this bed.

No darkness. No loneliness. No fear.

And he wanted to be sure she would have no regrets.

"Izzy, I want you. I feel the need to say it. Not to be crude or shocking, but just in case there's any ambiguity in this situation: Me, atop you, in your bed. You must know I want to . . ."

His mind skipped over all the possible words. *Bed you, tup you, fuck you, tumble you, make you my mistress . . .*

"I want to make love to you, Izzy. Very, very, *very* badly."

Ransom had never used those words before. She couldn't know that, but he did.

"I . . ." Her fingers went to his hair. "I want you, too. So much."

Her shyly voiced admission redoubled his heart rate.

It was after midnight, and he was tired. Normally, his vision would be shot at this hour. But with all these candles, and the extreme nature of their evening, he had enough sight remaining to him that he could make out the dark aura of her hair against the white linen. And most lovely of all, her wide, red smile.

"You're so beautiful."

He turned her onto her side and began tugging at the buttons down the back of her frock. She'd changed out of the soiled, torn red silk and into one of her everyday frocks. Even though the buttons were larger and the fabric easier to manage, his fingers didn't work too cleverly. It took him ages just to undo the first three or four buttons.

"Undressing you was easier when you were unconscious," he said.

She laughed. "It was probably easier when you weren't drunk."

Right. He supposed he could have blamed his trembling on the whisky. But in reality, Ransom knew better.

He was dashed nervous. Because this would be his first time in a long time, and it would be her first time ever.

And because this was Izzy, and he wanted it to be good.

With a curse, he gave up on buttons for the moment.

"Izzy." He cupped and kneaded her breasts through the linen of her frock. "I can't be patient. Not right now. Let me pleasure you."

He found the slit in her drawers and widened it with a swift, decisive rip of fabric. He pulled her to the edge of the mattress and knelt on the floor at her feet. Then he pushed her skirts and petticoat up, bunching them around her waist, and hooked an arm beneath one of her legs, spreading her wide.

There. Now he could touch all of her. Taste all of her.

"Ransom?" She struggled to sit up. "What are you do—?"

He laid his tongue to her core.

"Oh." She flopped back against the bed. "Oh."

God, she was sweet. Sweet and pink and musky and Izzy.

Izzy, Izzy. My own.

His cock throbbed vainly in his breeches. As he licked her, he freed it with one hand and began to stroke. Shameless, lewd. Bringing himself off right there on the floor while he pleasured her? But this was what she did to him. She reduced him to a panting, needing beast with no care for civility or etiquette. And she liked him crude and profane. She'd told him so.

On the bed, she writhed and wriggled. "Ransom. Ransom, are you certain this is—"

He raised his head just long enough to say: "Yes."

He worked his way over and around all her most sensitive places, taking time to accommodate and make adjustments.

She gasped his name and clutched at his hair, holding him fast to her core. God, he loved it when she touched his hair.

He increased his efforts, licking all along her folds, then sweeping back to the swollen bud at the crest of her sex and suckling hard, flicking his tongue back and forth.

She shuddered and moaned, arching off the bed and spasming under his tongue.

Yes. *Yes.*

Come for me. Me, and no other.

As her climax broke, he slid his tongue inside her, needing to be in her, in some way. To possess her. Her intimate muscles convulsed, pulling at him. Begging for more.

He hurried to rejoin her on the bed, fitting himself in the cradle of her splayed thighs. His cock brushed against the soft, dewy heat of her sex. He could be inside her in seconds.

But once he was inside her, there would be no taking it back.

He pressed his head to her shoulder and released a heavy sigh.

"Ransom?" She pushed up on one elbow. "What is it? Is something wrong?"

"I don't know," he said. "That's for you to decide."

Izzy stared at him, her vision hazy in the aftermath of that beautiful, beautiful pleasure. Surely he wasn't changing his mind *now*. The broad, smooth head of his erection lay against her thigh—hard and hot and eager.

He said, "I'm just drunk enough to think this is my most brilliant idea in ages. But I'm not too drunk to stop if you don't feel the same."

She was sober, and she knew very well that this might not be the most prudent idea. But something felt right about it, all the same. This wasn't impersonal lust. They understood each other. She was likely halfway in love with him, and he cared for her, too. He might never say it in those words, but this very room was ablaze with the proof.

Besides, a girl like Izzy didn't have the luxury of being choosy with her nights of wild passion.

This happened tonight, or never.

"I don't want to stop," she said.

"Thank God." He sounded relieved as he pulled at her buttons and laces. His fingers moved more easily now. "For a moment there, I thought the attempt at decency would come back and bite me. It usually does."

"Decency?" She slipped one arm free of its sleeve. "I should be terribly disappointed if you were decent. I'm expecting you to be wicked indeed."

He freed her breast and bent to suckle it. "I'll do my damnedest. It's been a while."

However long it had been, he hadn't forgotten how to make a woman twist and writhe.

He pressed a finger inside her. Then he added another finger to the first, stretching her with an exquisite fullness.

"Ransom . . . hurry. Don't you want—"

He pressed the heel of his hand against her mound, rubbing her in just the right place as he stroked his fingers in and out. Deeper, and deeper still. Before long, she was arching off the bed to meet his thrusts.

He bent to suck her nipple, and she moaned at the decadent heat of his mouth.

"Yes," he murmured, sounding triumphant. He swirled his tongue in ruthless circles, and the sweet tension began to build between her thighs again.

He withdrew his fingers and sat up on his knees. He pulled his shirt over his head and cast it aside, then worked to undo the remaining closures of his breeches. Izzy thought about asking if she could help, but he didn't seem to need assistance.

When he'd wrestled free of all his garments, he rejoined her on the bed. He dropped reverent kisses along her neck, her chest, her belly. She felt worshipped.

Then he moved between her legs, and his hips pushed her thighs wide.

"Wait." She stroked his shoulders and chest, exploring the firm, sculpted contours. "I . . ." She nearly lost her courage. "I want to see you. Touch you."

He sat back on his haunches in wordless invitation.

Izzy looked. There it was, in all its magnificence. Dusky, proud, alarmingly large. Jutting out from a thatch of dark hair and straining toward her.

She was entirely unaware of the protocol when becoming acquainted with a man's rampant sex organ. Did she reach out and give it a handshake? Touch one finger to the tip? Bid it a polite how-doyoudo?

In the end, she decided to ask for guidance. She put her hand in Ransom's. "Show me how to please you."

The words alone made him moan. He took her hand in his and curled her grip about the base of his erection. Then he guided her, teaching her to stroke him, up and down. She loved the feel of him in her hand. The soft skin sliding over rigid flesh beneath. Curious, she brushed her thumb over the tip and was delighted to find it silky and sensitive.

He squeezed her hand, preventing her from indulging in any further explorations.

"Did I do something wrong? Is there something else I should do?"

"Nothing wrong," he whispered, lacing his fingers with hers and pressing her hands back to the bed. "Nothing else. You're perfect. Just be there. Just be you. Lovely, lovely Izzy."

She felt the smooth, broad crown of his erection prodding at her entrance.

And then he was *inside* her.

She cried out. She couldn't help it.

"Am I hurting you?"

She bit her lip. "A little."

"Sorry." He pushed forward, sinking an inch deeper. "So sorry."

She struggled to breathe. He was just so foreign and . . . and just impossibly large inside her.

"I'm going to take this slowly." He dropped little kisses on her lips. She could taste the whisky in them. "Until I can't anymore, and then I'll probably take it hard and fast. I'll apologize now. Words might be beyond me then."

"It's all right," she whispered. "I understand."

She didn't, really, but she assumed she'd figure it out along the way. She was still struggling to adjust to the feeling of him inside her. The fullness, the stretching, the heat. He glided smoothly in and out, sinking a little deeper each time. Eventually, his body met hers, holding there a moment before retreating to do it all again.

Soon the pain of their joining receded, and she began to enjoy the friction of his hard, male body against hers. His legs, coarse with hair and dense with muscle, rubbing against her sensitive inner thighs. His chest pressing against her breasts.

This wasn't so bad anymore. It was rather nice.

He lifted up on his arms. His face twisted. "Izzy. God. I . . ."

Right. So this would be the "hard and fast" part now. She was glad that he'd warned her.

He shifted, and his hips spread her thighs to a new, wider angle, holding her open for his thrusts. He drilled deep, working in and out of her body at a furious pace. It hurt her. It excited her. It pushed her to the verge of . . . of something unknown.

She felt as though she were sprawled atop not a wool-batting mattress but a tense, brittle surface. A thin sheet of ice over black, fathomless longing. Each of his fierce thrusts put a crack in it. The unknown that lay beneath both thrilled and frightened her. She wanted to let go, to fall through it . . . but she was too afraid to let go.

He knew what she needed.

He reached between them and pressed his thumb to her pearl, working it in small, tight circles. The tension broke into a thousand facets of pleasure, and she clung to his neck as her world constricted to the thick, hard, stroking length of his cock. Her orgasm was weightless, helpless, endless. Like free-falling through clouds of bliss.

Above her, he cursed. Then groaned. Then cursed again.

Out of nowhere, she felt like laughing. He'd

been right. Words were beyond him now. It felt good to know she'd sent him to some other place.

One last frantic barrage of thrusts, and he slumped atop her. Heavy, panting, sweating, shuddering.

At last, he released her hands. His arms went about her middle, clutching tight. He laid his head on her breast.

Tentative, Izzy placed one hand flat on the slick surface of his back. With her other hand, she touched his hair.

He tensed for a moment. She did, too. And then he exhaled so deeply, she could believe he was expelling air from his lungs that had been there for months. Perhaps years. Everything went out of him—all the arrogance, pride, anger, fear, lust. Until he just existed in her arms.

She stroked his hair, teasing her fingers through the soft, heavy locks. Her heart swelled with an unbearable sweetness. It didn't matter what happened tomorrow. This tenderness was worth everything.

"Ransom," she whispered. "I've fallen just a little bit in love with you. You needn't be worried. I won't expect you to return the emotion, and I know that this can't last. But I've been waiting so long for somebody to care for, and I . . . I can't help it."

She waited, heart pounding in her chest, for his reaction.

And when it finally came, it was this:

A faint, reverberating snore.

Chapter Nineteen

*T*he strangest things woke Ransom the next morning. Sunlight, streaming warm on his face. A gentle breeze, scented of blossoms. The chirp of songbirds.

The tickle of hair against his neck.

"Ransom. *Ransom.*"

Someone was shaking the limp, dead weight of his arm.

Izzy.

He opened his eyes. He saw the halo of curls surrounding her pale face. Those dark eyebrows. Her red lips.

"Ransom, wake," she said, shaking him again. "What's wrong? Are you dead?"

"No." His voice was a rasp. "I'm not dead." Emotion burned at the corners of his eyes, like acid. He said it again, slowly. Gratefully. "I am not dead."

He was very much alive. Awakened, in a way he'd never felt before. His heart was like a new organ, pumping a fizzy, champagne-like joy through his veins. He felt like dashing to the window and bursting into song.

He hadn't been with a woman since . . .

Well, *since.*

For the first few months after his injury, he was simply in too much pain to contemplate it. And then . . . then, he'd feared it would be like entering an unfamiliar room. He'd be fumbling about, cursing. Making stupid mistakes as he learned the lay of the space. What if it was bad?

What if *he* was bad?

But it hadn't been bad. It had been good. So damned good for them both. Memories came back to him in bits and pieces. Her slick heat clenching around his fingers, making him wild to get inside her. The tight, willing welcome he'd found once their bodies joined. The sweet way she'd held him at the end.

Izzy, Izzy.

"Good," she said. "Now hurry and dress."

"What?" He blinked and sat up in bed.

She fluttered about the room, washing up and donning her clothing. Watching her was like watching a burlesque dancer. Water splashed and dripped as she dragged a sponge over her body. He watched, transfixed, as her white shift drifted down over her dark head, then the pale pink column of her nude body. She pulled her hair free, and it tumbled like a black cascade, transforming her silhouette once again. Light and dark tugging back and forth.

There was no doubt in his mind that she was the most alluring creature he'd ever beheld. Utterly, elementally sensual.

He moved to the edge of the bed, catching her by the waist and drawing her close. He pressed his forehead to her belly. "Izzy . . ."

She pulled away from his grasp. "We can't. Not now. I don't know where Duncan's gone, but he's sure to turn up soon. We can't let him find us like this."

Ransom rubbed his face. "Believe me, Duncan has seen far, far worse. And he knows better than to ask for explanations."

"I suppose this could be just another morning for the two of you. But it's a bit out of the usual for me." A wadded ball of fabric hit him in the chest. "Your clothing."

Stymied, he sorted out the tangle of garments. This wasn't "just another morning" for him, either.

He yanked the shirt over his head and punched his arms through the sleeves. Then he rose from the bed, pulling his breeches to his waist and fastening the closures.

He crossed to the dressing table, where she was hastily pinning up her hair. He dropped a kiss on her exposed neck. "Izzy, last night was . . ."

"I know."

"Really?" He caught a stray curl. "I don't think you do."

She nodded and turned to face him. "It's all right. You needn't be worried, Ransom. I understand. Last night was lovely, but . . ."

But?

Ransom couldn't believe he was hearing that word. Last night was so lovely, *but?*

No "but" belonged in that sentence. Only "and." Last night was so lovely *and* passionate *and* tender and erotic *and* . . .

"But it was like a dream," she went on briskly. "This morning, I'm clear-eyed and levelheaded. You needn't worry. I haven't formed any silly expectations of you."

Good God. He was shocked speechless.

These were words that any jaded rake would be thrilled to hear. Words that Ransom would have been thrilled to hear, from any other woman, on any prior occasion.

Coming from her, this morning? The words were gutting him.

"We'll get back to our work this morning," she said. "I can be very professional. I promise, it will be like nothing happened at all."

She slipped away from him, hastening down the stairs.

He let her go.

She had no expectations of him.

Truly, *none?*

Did she really think he would make love to her last night, and then want to go on today as if nothing had happened at all?

Well, of course she believed that. Why wouldn't she? She'd spent the past few weeks reading through abundant evidence of just such behavior. By now, she was intimately acquainted with his history, his temperament, all his vices and faults. He'd done nothing but underscore the impression with boorish behavior and the occasional groping. Add to everything the fact that he was a scarred, blinded wretch.

And then, last night, he'd taken her virtue—without so much as the mention of marriage, or even any promises beyond the one night's pleasure.

Naturally, she had no expectations.

He supposed that meant one thing.

If he wanted any chance of keeping her, Ransom would have to come up with some surprises.

Izzy needed the comfort of familiar tasks this morning. Too many aspects of her world had altered since yesterday. She was no longer a virgin. She was a bit sore between her legs. Her heart was raw and tender.

In sum, she ached all over.

What did last night mean to him? What did it mean to her?

She was afraid to ask those questions. She would rather linger in this giddy ignorance a while longer.

All these stretched and vulnerable parts of her needed some time to recover, that was all. And then Izzy could take a deep breath and a good, hard look at herself.

"You started without me?"

Then she looked up and saw *him.* The air vacated her lungs. Her grip tightened on her pen.

Snap, went the quill.

Thud, went her heart.

No man should be this handsome. It just wasn't fair. He entered the great hall, wearing a clean, open-necked shirt tucked into gray trousers. His hair was still damp at the temples, but the sunlight found the streaks of gold in his brown hair and teased her with them.

With effort, Izzy tore her gaze away and attempted to concentrate on the task at hand. It was rather like trying to work with a small, glowing sun in the room. Struggle as she might to avoid looking directly at him, she couldn't escape his intensity and heat. Much less her memories of last night. Perspiration beaded between her breasts.

"This morning," she said, clearing her throat, "we must settle down to business. No more going through every paper and sorting them into piles. I've read enough by now that I can tell Significant from Insignificant at a glance. We need to start making meaningful progress through this heap."

"Why the rush?" He didn't settle in his usual

place on the sofa. Instead, he came to stand at her shoulder. "You've been purposely delaying thus far. More days of work means more money for you."

Yes, but that was before. Before she'd realized something was amiss in these papers and before she cared enough about him to want it sorted out.

Something was wrong here.

"We need to find all the envelopes from your solicitors." She handed him an envelope, moving his thumb over the lumpy wax holding it closed. "They always use the same seal. You can find them by touch."

He cast the envelope aside. "I'd rather be touching you."

He moved behind her, putting his hands on her shoulders and kneading her tensed muscles.

"Relax," he murmured. "We don't have to do this right now."

"Yes. We truly do. I've been growing quite concerned."

"Don't be concerned." He kissed her just beneath the ear. "Izzy, I don't want you to worry about anything."

Her knees went to jelly again. She braced one palm flat on the table, leaning her weight on it for strength.

"Here's a letter from the solicitors. I should sit down and read it." She reached for her usual seat.

He slid his arm around her waist and kicked the chair away. "Not yet."

"It *is* possible to read standing, you know."

"It's possible to do a lot of things standing." He left a trail of kisses down the nape of her neck. His hands caressed her hips.

She laughed nervously. "I don't know what to make of you this morning. Where's the surly man who greets the dawn with a curse? What about 'Good grief, Goodnight'? Where are those charming maritime endearments?"

He pulled on a lock of her hair. "Octopus."

"Well, that's all wrong. You said it so fondly."

She made her voice chastening, but secretly, she was elated. Apparently, whatever it was between them, he wanted it to last longer than the one night.

She broke the envelope's seal and began to read. "It's dated three months ago. It begins, 'May it please Your Grace—'"

"What was that?" he murmured. "Repeat it for me. Just those last three words."

The last three words? Izzy consulted the paper. "Please Your Gra—" Oh, the shameless rogue. She gave in. "Please, Your Grace."

"With pleasure." He slipped one hand to cup her breast. The other delved under her skirts.

"Ransom," she chided. "Someone could come in at any moment."

"Yes. They could. That's what makes it so exciting."

Izzy couldn't deny it. It *was* exciting. Her nipples drew to tight points, and between her legs, she was already aching for him. "But you can't mean for us to . . ." She swallowed. "Really? Here?"

"Oh, I mean to do this everywhere. I plan to have you in every room of this castle. And why stop there? On the ramparts, beneath the stars. In the park, on a blanket spread amid waving grasses." He pushed her skirts to her waist. "But we start right here, right now. I've been dreaming of taking you on this table for weeks."

The lines started to blur together on the page. Her hand slipped forward, and papers spilled to the floor. There was nothing Significant anymore. Nothing except the wicked caress of his fingers, sweeping up her thigh.

"Hullo? Anyone about?"

The unfamiliar voice called up from the courtyard.

Izzy startled, sending a sheaf of papers to the ground. "Oh, heavens," she whispered. "Who's that?"

"Hullo!" The voice again. "Ho, there!"

"I don't care who he is. He needs to disappear." Ransom turned and called out the window. "For the love of God, man. I have England's sweetheart bent over the desk and panting for me. Go away and come back tomorrow."

Horrified, Izzy shoved him away. "*Ransom.*"

She hastened outside. Thankfully, the visitor wasn't anyone she knew. Just a messenger with an express post. Izzy gave him the postage and an extra coin for his troubles, apologizing for the duke's inappropriate sense of humor.

When she came back inside, she put off his attempts at returning to their interlude, putting a hand to his chest.

"Ransom, don't ever joke like that. I mean it. What if Duncan or Abigail had been about? Worse, what if that had been a Moranglian?"

"So what if it had been?" he asked. "Why do you care what those people think? Why are you so afraid of their knowing that you're not an innocent little girl anymore?"

"Because being that innocent little girl is how I've survived."

He couldn't possibly understand this. He was a wealthy, privileged duke, and he always had been. He didn't know what it was to be hungry and shivering alone in the dark.

"You recall how little I had to my name when I came here," she said. "If you succeed in taking this castle from me, I'll be left with nothing again. But my father's admirers support me, in their own . . . unique but well-meaning ways. I may not have money, but at least I have the goodwill of thousands."

He pulled a face. "You have a weasel. And sweetmeats."

"It's better than nothing." She broke the seal on the letter. "Yes, I might have to subsist on sweetmeats some days. Yes, the roof over my head might be that of my third host in as many weeks. But I *will* always have food. I *will* always have a bed. Just so long as I'm the girl they want me to be."

"So long as you're little Izzy Goodnight. Not Izzy Goodnight, scandalous mistress. Or Mrs. Izzy Something-Else-Entirely."

"Exactly. So please, Ransom. Don't ruin it. Don't ruin *me* with your thoughtless joking. Not unless you mean to promise me that I'll never spend another night of my life feeling cold, hungry, alone, or unloved."

He was quiet for a moment. "Love isn't something I know how to offer. I don't have the goodwill of thousands. You've read my letters. I don't have the goodwill of anyone. And not all of us spent our childhoods in starry bedchambers, tucked beneath coverlets with kisses and stories each night."

Her heart twisted in her chest. "How *did* you go to bed at night?"

"Wealthy."

The silence was distressing, so she turned her gaze to the letter as a diversion.

"I've never made pretensions of being a romantic hero. And now I'm scarred, blinded, scorned by the world. But it's not as though I couldn't provide for you. I am still a duke."

"Wait." She stared numbly at the paper in her hands, scanning its contents. "According to this letter, you might not be much longer."

"What?"

"This express that just arrived from your solicitors. It says they've arranged a mental-competency hearing. They're challenging your sanity and your ability to continue acting as the Duke of Rothbury." She lowered the paper. "They're coming here. Next week."

Chapter Twenty

For the rest of the morning, any visitor who interrupted them would have discovered nothing more scandalous than a harried secretary and her irate employer, both buried chest deep in paperwork.

They'd opened, read, and sorted through everything.

Everything.

Izzy's eyes were going crossed.

"Here it is, at last." She read the paper aloud. " 'May it please Your Grace, the business has been completed. Gostley Castle has been sold, at your request.' " She lowered the letter. "This was dated three months ago. So they *did* sell the castle to Lynforth."

"But I never made any such request. Nor

did I ask them to invest in mustard plantations or purchase an Arabian menagerie." Ransom flicked aside another pile of paper. "This explains the erratic record-keeping and purchases. They're *trying* to make me look unstable. I'm being set up."

"Set up?" Izzy echoed. "By the solicitors? Why would they do that?"

"They're working in concert with my heir, most likely. You're not the only one with a grasping cousin. Mine wouldn't dare throw me in a pond or lock me in a root cellar, but he'd happily take the title and control of my fortune, given the chance."

Izzy sifted through the pile of notices. "This is beyond my expertise. You need help. A new solicitor, perhaps."

He dismissed the idea. "I can't trust anyone."

"I know, and that's a problem. You need to start trusting people, Ransom. Start by letting them know you. Not just your strengths, but your weaknesses, too."

He paced back and forth on the stone floor. "Let them know the real me. All my weaknesses. Yes, I'll make plans to do that. Right on the heels of your announcement that Izzy Goodnight isn't a girl anymore but a twenty-six-year-old woman who likes her nipples pinched."

Izzy supposed his point was valid. They were both hiding parts of themselves. But the consequences weren't quite the same.

She tapped a stack of papers to tidy them. "I'm just saying that matters progressed to this stage because you were too ashamed—"

"Ashamed?"

"Yes. Ashamed." Izzy was tired of dancing around it. He was the one who'd insisted he didn't want coddling. "You're a duke, and your intended bride ran off with a lowly farmer. Then the farmer bested you in a duel, leaving you blinded. That had to have been humiliating."

"The farmer did not best me in anything, damn it." He stopped by the windows. "Do you know the only thing more dangerous than fencing against a master swordsman?"

"What?" she asked.

"Fencing against a love-drunk fool who hasn't a goddamn clue what he's doing. It's like defending both sides at once. He'd never even held a sword before. I had to try like hell not to run him through."

What was he saying? That he'd incurred his injury while trying *not* to win?

She rose from the table and moved toward him. "Ransom . . ."

"I couldn't kill him. What good would that have done anyone? I only chased after them because I feared she hadn't gone willingly. On that point, I was corrected."

Izzy ached for him. Now she regretted using the word ashamed. He shouldn't feel ashamed of his actions. He'd risked everything to protect that girl. He should wear that scar like a badge of pride.

"It was good of you." She said it firmly. Not as a placating gesture, but as a fact she wouldn't let him contradict. "You must have cared for her."

"I was planning to marry her," he said. "Of course I cared. As much as a man like me is able to care. No, we didn't share any grand passion or meeting of hearts and minds, but I thought she was . . . practical. Interested in becoming a duchess and spending my money, and patient enough to put up with my faults in exchange." He flexed one hand. "In the end, it seems I misjudged."

Izzy felt a powerful twinge of guilt, thinking of Lady Emily's letter. "She was so young. Probably just impressionable and frightened."

"No, no. I think it's the other way round. She was more perceptive than I gave her credit for." He turned back toward the pile of correspondence. "When I lose all control of my fortune, she will be able to celebrate her narrow escape."

If you lose all control of your fortune, what becomes of me?

Izzy chided herself for thinking it, but the fear was creeping in fast. It would seem the castle was legally hers, after all. But she'd never be able to keep the place—or find another home—without the wages he'd promised her.

"My goodness." Abigail and Duncan entered the room, surveying the drifts of paper. "What's happened here?"

Ransom rose to his feet. "Treachery. That's what's happened here."

"Was there another body in the walls?"

"No." Izzy lifted the letter that had come express. "We're expecting important visitors next week. Apparently, His Grace is to be the subject of a mental-competence hearing."

"A lunacy hearing? But that's absurd. The duke's not mad." She turned and whispered to Izzy, "He isn't mad, is he?"

Oh, Abigail. Izzy lifted her eyebrows and shook her head no.

The vicar's daughter continued in a not-quite-confidential murmur, "I mean, he did behave rather strangely last night."

Ransom cleared his throat. "Miss Pelham, I am standing right here. I am not deaf. And as it will be plain for the lawyers and doctors to discern, I am not mad."

But he *was* blind.

That was the true unspoken source of concern, and everyone was thinking it. Blind people were often put in asylums even if they were otherwise of sound mind. Considering the neglected state of his business affairs and his prolonged, dramatic absence from society, Ransom wasn't going to have an easy time of this. If his solicitors wanted him gone, the truth would be a heavy stroke against him.

"Christ." He pushed both hands through his hair. "I could lose everything."

"No, you won't," Izzy said. "We won't let it happen. Because if you lose everything, so do I. For that matter, so do Duncan and Abigail."

If Ransom wasn't the duke any longer, Duncan wouldn't have a post. If Izzy had to abandon the castle for lack of funds, Abigail would lose the support for the local parish.

They were all in this together now.

"Forget everything I said about honesty. If these solicitors have been lying to you, you can lie right back to them. They never have to know the extent of your injuries. When I arrived at this castle, it took me hours to realize you were blind."

"You were unconscious for most of them," he pointed out.

"Just the same. You know what I mean. You know this castle in the dark, and you can focus well enough that your eyes don't wander. All you have to do is bluff your way through this one interview. Once they're gone, you can sack Blaylock and Riggett and hire new solicitors."

"But the castle, Miss Goodnight." Duncan looked around. "It doesn't look like a ducal residence."

"Then we'll make it one." She squared her shoulders. "We have a week. The castle—the public parts of it, anyhow—need to be immaculate. But we mustn't change the arrangement of the rooms by even one inch. The duke will need a wardrobe. For that matter, I could use a new gown or two." Izzy twisted her fingers. "And we'll need servants. A great many servants. To clean, garden, serve at table . . ."

"Refreshing the duke's wardrobe will be a distinct pleasure," Duncan said.

"And Izzy, you know I'd love to help with yours. We're all ready for hard work. But that last bit—the servants—will be a challenge." Abigail looked regretful. "It was already difficult to convince the local people to come work at the castle . . . what with its bloody history, the ghostly rumors, and the duke's months of seclusion. But after the bones were found in the wall . . ." She shook her head. "In time, I'm certain I could convince them to come back. But this week?"

"Even if we did manage to hire them," Duncan said, "I don't know that I could train village folk to an acceptable standard in that time. Then there's the matter of uniforms and livery. It all seems rather hopeless."

"It can't be hopeless," Izzy said.

Abigail smiled. "You're right, Izzy. Would Cressida and Ulric just give up? Of course not. We'll pull through somehow. Doubt not."

And with that, all four of them fell silent.

Doubting.

But they couldn't waste much time with doubt. Not when there was so much to be done.

Over the next few days, everyone in Gostley Castle worked hard. And no one more so than Ransom.

A few days later, Izzy watched from the entryway as he scrawled a line of script across a blank page—once, then again and again. After ten repetitions, he lifted the paper and held it to the light, as if trying to judge the straightness of the lines.

Apparently dissatisfied, he cursed and crumpled the paper into the grate.

She held her breath and waited for all the evidence to be destroyed. Only when he drew out a fresh sheet of paper did Izzy gather the courage to approach.

"I'm busy, Goodnight."

He knew her footsteps too well.

"This won't take long," she assured him.

"Let it wait, then. Go sweep a cobweb from the rafters or polish a mirror. There must be some household task that needs attention."

"There is a task that needs attention. It's this one." She set her tray on the tabletop next to him. "You need to eat."

He ignored her.

She sliced a pear into wedges, then offered him one. "Your eyesight is better when you've eaten. And you need your eyesight because I have something important to show you."

"Fine." He reached out, catching her by the wrist. Then, using his teeth, he took the slice of pear straight from her fingers and devoured it. "There."

She offered him another slice. "More."

He ate more. Slice after slice until the pear was

gone. He finished by licking her palm and sucking the juice from each finger in turn. That wicked tongue of his swirled around her knuckles and teased the sensitive webs between her fingers.

At last, her littlest finger slid from his mouth with an audible *pop.*

"Now," he said. "What's this important thing you have to show me?"

Dashed if Izzy could remember after that sensual onslaught. She had to shake her head to clear it.

Oh, yes.

"Your new bedchamber."

His mouth tipped in that roguish half grin. "Perfect."

As she led him up the stairs and down the corridor, Izzy felt rather like a chicken leading a fox straight to his own den.

"Here it is," she said nervously. "The ducal bedchamber. We blocked out the bats with shutters, then cleaned the chimney. The bed hangings and tapestries are all new. The drapes, as well."

He strode to the center of the chamber, nodding thoughtfully. "I like what you've done with the place."

She laughed a little. "You don't have to contrive compliments. That wasn't my goal. I just wanted to give you a chance to map out the room, before the . . . Before the new servants arrive."

"It's not a contrived compliment. I can hear the difference." He took another measured step. "The whole room is softer. The echoes are muted, the hard edges are gone. It's cozy."

Izzy smiled, and her nerves lost their edges, too. He didn't need to praise their hard work, but it meant a great deal that he did.

"What about the bed?" he asked.

"It's . . . still there. Exactly where it was before."

"Show me."

She took the hand he offered and led him to the edge of the enormous four-poster bed. "Here. There's a new mattress, of course. And we re-strung the frame with new ropes."

He pushed up and down. "Hm."

Then he caught her in his arms and launched them both onto the bed. Izzy shrieked as they landed in a tangle in the center of the bed.

"What are you doing?"

"I'm testing something." He wrapped his legs over hers, then rolled them back and forth over the length of the bed. When he stopped in the center again, he said, "I was right. Large enough for a duke and six women besides."

"If you want six women, none of them will be me." She struggled to disentangle herself and sit up.

He pulled her back down. "What if I just want you? Six times."

"Six times in one night? Impossible."

"That sounded like a challenge." His hand slid to cup her breast. "I accept."

"Ransom . . ." Her words trailed off into a sigh

as he licked along the lacy edge of her bodice. "Ransom, we can't. Not now. There's too much to be done."

"You've done so much already." He shushed her, nudging her legs apart so he could reach between them. "You've been working so hard, Izzy. This room is proof of it. Just relax for a moment. Let me give you something in return."

It worried her that he couldn't seem to accept the smallest kindness—not even a sliced pear—without thinking he needed to repay her somehow. If not with wages, with pleasure.

Not that she minded the pleasure, of course. Izzy had scarcely slept in days. The soft, springy mattress cushioning their weight was so inviting, and his hard, wanting body atop hers felt so right. She'd missed him so much.

Still . . .

As he kissed her ear, she sighed and smiled. "Why can't you be cooperative, ever?"

He slid a hand under her skirt. "Where would the joy be in that?"

Joy.

The word surprised her.

Of all the words he could have used in that sentence. *Where would the sport be in that?* he could have said. Or, *Where would the fun be in that?*

But he hadn't spoken of "sport" or "fun." He'd spoken of joy. Was that truly what he felt with her?

She hoped so. She couldn't deny it any longer.

She wanted him to feel at home here. Here, in this castle—and here, with her.

If they managed to pull through this . . . inspection, of sorts . . . he wouldn't *need* to hide and brood in Gostley Castle anymore.

But might he possibly *want* to stay?

She touched his face, running her fingers over his cheek and reaching to stroke his hair. This impossible, flawed, wounded man who'd brought her in from the rain. Who'd eased her trembling in the dark. Who'd made her feel beautiful and cherished in his embrace.

He had so much more inside him if only she could find the way to reach it. Passion. Devotion. Love. Somewhere deep inside him was a true and constant heart, struggling to emerge from under all the scars and pride. Some part of her had known it from the first day, when he'd carried her in his arms.

"Ransom," she whispered. "Whatever happens, I hope—"

"Wait." He shushed her, frowning. "What the devil am I hearing?"

Ransom was listening to sounds he'd hoped never to hear again. The clop of hooves, the clack of wheels—and the ceaseless clanking of cut-rate armor.

Bloody hell. They're back.

"They're early," she said.

She'd known about this? "Izzy, you didn't."

"I did. Please don't be angry."

As if he could be angry with her. He rose from bed and went to the window, unwillingly and inexorably at once—as if drawn by the sight of a carriage wreck. That familiar silvery rainbow of people poured into the courtyard.

They'd been invaded by the Moranglians again.

Izzy joined him at the window. "I know. I know how you feel about them. But we're desperate for help. We can't be particular." She called down to the men filling the courtyard with their obnoxious clanking. "We are honored, Sir Wendell! How good you are to heed my summons in our hour of need."

From the courtyard, a voice floated up. "Doubt not, Miss Goodnight. We have returned from thither to offer our service anon."

Ransom wrested her away from the windows. "Izzy, no. No. I'm supposed to be displaying my sanity and competence in all things ducal. Having the castle overrun by delusionals with play swords and an unnatural fondness for the words 'thither' and 'anon' is not going to help."

"We don't have a choice. There's no time left to find, train, and outfit servants locally. These people want to help. They've drilled to act in unison, and . . . well, they do have matching attire."

"They are wearing breastplates from some blacksmith's scrap heap. It's hardly proper livery."

"I know it's unusual, but we'll play it off as my eccentricity," she said. "You know how everyone sees me. I'm a dreamy little girl, living in my father's storyland."

Damn it, he hated that she had to pretend that. He especially hated that she had to pretend one more moment of it for his sake.

"You're forgetting one more problem," he said. "Which is that all these people have me mistaken for their hero. They'll be calling me Ulric."

"No, no. You're the one who's mistaken. Everyone understands that stories are just stories. These people never believed you were Ulric. They just think . . . Well, they think you're one of them."

"One of *them*?"

"Yes. Ransom, they'd gladly be your friends if you'd let them."

Friends.

Friendship with these people was not what he needed. But the hard truth of it was, he did need servants. He couldn't appear to be moldering in a decrepit castle alone with his valet. Even though that's exactly what he had been doing up until a few weeks past.

"Just give them a chance," she whispered, kissing his cheek before she descended to greet her adoring throng. "Do it for me?"

Do it for me.

The woman had no idea the trials he would suffer for her. A great deal more than this foolishness.

He'd imprisoned himself in this castle to rot. He'd cut off all contact with the outside world.

And just when he thought he'd burned all his bridges, this woman—this impossible, sweet, foolish woman—arrived, determined to swim the moat. Breach his defenses. Make a home. Stay.

If not for her, this room would still be filled with rats and bats. If not for her, he'd be sitting unshaven and drunk in the great hall, morosely counting his steps to nowhere. And if not for her, he would have no reason to fight this battle at all.

Perhaps he would have no title or fortune to offer her, but he was determined to see her safe.

Everything he did, from this point forward . . .

It was all for her.

Chapter Twenty-one

*G*ather round, everyone. This will be our final time through the paces."

Izzy called down from the window of the ducal chamber, addressing the assembled knights, handmaidens, servants, and friends below.

Tomorrow, the solicitors arrived. This would be their last chance to practice.

She cleared her throat, and called, "Take your places, please."

The knights, cook, and servant-handmaidens disappeared inside, leaving only the Inquisitioners in the courtyard.

The "Inquisitioners" were Abigail and a few of the handmaidens who'd offered to pose as the visiting party. The girls had thrown themselves into the roles with enthusiasm, pulling their hair back into severe knots and donning dark, somber top-coats and beaver hats from the old vicar's wardrobe. They'd even taken bits of kohl and drawn sideburns and moustaches on their faces.

Except for the occasional burst of giggling, they made a fair approximation of a stern-faced party of solicitors and doctors.

"Now, when the visitors arrive, Duncan will welcome them to Gostley Castle."

Duncan opened the front door and bowed solemnly to the young ladies in costume. "Good afternoon, sirs. Welcome to Gostley Castle."

"Excellent. And then he'll show them into the—" Izzy turned to Ransom, who stood beside her in the upstairs room. "You're sure you prefer the great hall? We do have the salon now. It's a more manageable size."

He shook his head. "It has to be the great hall. I know how the space works, how the echoes sound."

"Then the great hall it is." She turned and called from the window again. "Duncan will show them into the great hall."

Duncan faced the "Inquisitioners" and tilted his head in invitation. "If the gentlemen would be so good as to follow me."

The tittering young women followed him inside.

Izzy stepped away from the window. "This is where we wait. Once Duncan has them settled in the great hall, he'll send one of the handmaidens up to knock."

They lapsed into silence, just waiting. Izzy studied her shoes. She had new ones for tomorrow, but for today her old nankeen half boots would have to do.

Ransom, of course, only looked more magnificent with each passing day. Duncan had dedicated many tireless hours to the task of brushing, laundering, pressing, and polishing every item of attire in the duke's wardrobe, and it showed.

His hair was still a touch overgrown, but she couldn't bring herself to suggest a trim. He wore that fall of golden brown hair like a shield over his wounded brow. She worried he would feel vulnerable without it.

"Don't be anxious about anything," she said. "We've planned every moment, made alternatives for any eventuality. And if all else goes wrong, there's a last resort. Plan E."

"Plan E? What's Plan E?"

"Snowdrop. If there's an unforeseen problem, one of the handmaidens will release the ermine into the room. It will be a diversion, at least."

His lips quirked to one side in that now-familiar manner.

She still didn't quite know how to read the expression, but she was coming to think of it as a smile.

A knock came at the door.

"Right," she said. "That's our cue."

She threaded her arm in his, and together they walked into the corridor and began heading downstairs to the great hall.

"I remember everything you told me," she said. "Blaylock has ginger hair and spectacles. Riggett is the portly one, with narrow-set eyes. When we enter the hall, I'll find them, and I'll tap out their position on your arm. The first count will be Blaylock. The second, Riggett. As for the newcomers, we'll have to rely on introductions. Duncan, should you need him, will always be just to the left of the entrance. Once you introduce me, I can take ov—"

He stopped in his paces. "Izzy."

"Yes? Did I forget something?"

"This." He bent his head and kissed her. Just a warm, lingering press of his lips against hers. "You seemed to need that."

She exhaled. "I think I did. Thank you."

All her drifting, scattered thoughts coalesced. His kiss was her anchor in the storm. So long as they could come away from this trial together, that was all that mattered.

When they entered the great hall, Izzy used their agreed-on system to point out the handmaidens designated as Blaylock and Riggett. Ransom acknowledged them with the slightest of nods in their general direction.

This was where his social rank worked in his favor. Ransom needn't bow to anyone. He certainly didn't shake hands. He needn't offer to serve his guests drinks. Unless his vision was particularly gray, he could distinguish a person well enough to focus on him when speaking. For a duke, that was enough.

They walked to the grouping of freshly re-upholstered furnishings near the hearth. Once again, Izzy used slight pressure against his arm to direct him toward an unoccupied chair.

Everyone was seated with a minimum of awkwardness.

"Excellent," she said, beginning to breathe easier. This really needn't be as difficult as it she'd feared it could be. "Once we're all seated, it's just a matter of chatting, drinking. Answering their questions."

"Wrong," Ransom said. "I'm going to be the one asking questions."

"That's all well and good, too. If the mood is amiable, I'll offer them a tour of the castle. I'll lead, of course, and you can bring up the rear. Once we've returned to the great hall, it will probably be time for dinner."

In an instant, Ransom's demeanor changed entirely.

Izzy's heart sank. She'd been hoping he would take this well. But it would seem she'd hoped in vain.

He frowned. "What do you mean, dinner?"

Damn it to hell. Ransom hadn't counted on this.

"Why does there need to be a dinner?"

"With any luck, there won't be a need," she said. "But we must be prepared for the possibility. The solicitors will have traveled all this way from London. They're going to be fatigued, hungry.

We'll probably have to offer them lodging for the night, too."

He cursed.

"Don't worry. I've planned everything, and we'll walk through it right now. Duncan will invite us in to dinner."

She motioned in Duncan's direction, and the valet-cum-butler did as she asked, intoning, "Dinner is served."

"Then you offer me your arm," Izzy said, taking the arm in question before he'd offered it at all, "and we'll lead the way to the dining room."

As they walked down the corridor to the dining room, Ransom felt as though he were walking toward the gallows. Every step he took was one step closer to doom.

Dinner. Of all the things. She couldn't have set him up for failure any better if she'd arranged for a target-shooting demonstration.

They reached the dining room. They must have been planning this out. On either side of the endless dining table stood an armored row of knights, waiting at attention in their role as footmen. He heard a wince-inducing creak as one of them shifted his weight from one foot to the other.

"I'll suggest seats for our visitors." She directed the costumed ladies in their oversized, dark coats to take various seats.

"You have to sit at the head of the table, of course." She nudged Ransom toward the appropriate chair. "As hostess, I'll need to be at the opposite end."

In other words, miles away.

He caught her arm and pulled it, keeping her close. "We're not doing this."

"Please don't panic."

He clenched his jaw. "I don't panic."

"It's fine," she whispered. "I promise. I've arranged for all the courses to be served *à la russe*. All the courses are plated in the kitchen and served individually. No carving, no serving. It's the newest style in France. We'll seem fashionable."

"I'm so glad you've thought this through," he said tightly. "However—"

"The first course is soup, of course. That's straightforward enough. For the meat course"— she motioned to one of the overgrown toy soldiers—"we have beefsteak."

A plate appeared on the table before him.

She pulled up a chair and sat next to him.

"I understand," she whispered. "Ransom, you can't think I haven't noticed that you never eat in front of us. You'll take a bit of bread, maybe, or a sandwich. But never a proper meal. So I tried eating a meal blindfolded, managing a knife and fork by touch. I made a hash of things before getting three bites in my mouth. I do understand."

Her voice was sweet. But she spoke to him like a damned infant. And bloody hell, she did *not* understand.

She took his hand and guided it around the plate. "I've made arrangements with Cook. Everything on your plate will be in bite-size pieces, save for the bread. Buttered roll at twelve o'clock, then beef from three to seven. Potatoes and broad beans from eight to twelve." She put a fork in his hand. "Go on, try."

"Izzy . . ."

She touched his shoulder. "Don't be discouraged. I know you can do this."

He inhaled and exhaled slowly, trying to remain calm. "I will eat when and where and how I wish. I don't need things cut in pieces for me. I'm not a child."

There it was, sitting on the table before him . . . All the frustrations of his life, dished up on one plate.

Here, Your Grace, have a serving of helplessness. With an accompaniment of bitter humiliation.

This—this, right here—was madness. He'd been a fool to agree to this plan. Within five minutes at the dinner table, his solicitors would see him for what he was: a blinded wretch. At best, he would be branded an invalid. At worst, he'd be institutionalized. He would lose his title, his fortune . . . possibly even his personal freedom.

And he would lose her. Any ability to protect her. Any chance to hold her tight and feel her sweet touch on his skin.

All because he couldn't cut beefsteak in the dark. The sheer stupidity of it gutted him.

Meanwhile, the handmaidens whispered and giggled. The knights clanked in their armor. The scrape of metal on metal felt like fingernails raking through his brain.

"I'm not hungry." He motioned toward the armored footman. "Take this away."

No one moved.

"Take it," he growled, "away."

The armored idiot stepped forward and retrieved the plate. Ransom winced with each creak and clank. At the base of his skull, he felt a headache looming. It was like knowing a villain stood poised behind him with an ice pick, ready to stab at any moment.

That settled it. He was done with this. He rose from the table.

Izzy followed, stopping him before he even reached the corridor.

"It's my fault," she said. "I should have known better than to surprise you. I know you must be exhausted. We're all exhausted. We can try again later. Perhaps for now, you should go upstairs and rest."

Now he needed a *nap*?

That was the final indignity.

He said, "We're done with this. All of this. Thank your Morphinians for their time, and then send them all away."

"Send them away?" She grabbed his sleeve, holding him in place. "We can practice for as long as it takes. But we can't give up. There's too much at stake for us both."

"You don't have to tell me what's at stake."

Her entire future hung in the balance. Ransom scarcely cared for himself anymore, but he had to make certain she'd be safe.

This plan of hers—passing himself as sighted, while dozens of fancy-dress dreamers looked on—simply wasn't going to work. He could stand here and argue the facts of it, but he knew Izzy. She wouldn't surrender that romantic optimism. Not with all her admirers standing about, hanging on her every word. She was too afraid of letting them down.

She was never going to choose Ransom over the goodwill and sweetmeats of a thousand strangers. Even if it was for the best.

So he would make the choice for her.

"I'm not giving up," he said. "I'm changing the plan."

"It's on to Plan E!" one of the knights called out. "Plan E, everyone! Who has the ermine?"

"Not *that* plan," Ransom said, gritting his teeth. To Izzy, he said, "There's no time to lose. Go upstairs and get your wrap."

"My wrap? Why? Where are we going?"

"To Scotland," he said. "We'll be married tonight."

Married?

Izzy was speechless for a moment. Her brain was awhirl. There were children's tops that spun slower than her thoughts were doing.

When at last she spoke, she did so carefully. And quietly, though there was no doubt that the assembled knights and handmaidens could hear everything.

"You want to be married? To me? Tonight?"

He pushed a hand through his hair. "I know. I don't like the idea either, but it's the only option. Get your things. We can reach the Scottish border in a few hours, at most."

"But . . ."

"The advantages should be plain." His voice was emotionless. "If we marry, that changes everything. At the very least, they'd wait to see if you're pregnant with my heir. During that time, I can make certain you get the money you're owed."

"Well, that sounds very . . . transactional. I hope you'll pardon the honesty, but this isn't quite the romantic proposal a girl hopes and dreams to hear."

"You're twenty-six years old," he said. "How many other proposals were you expecting?"

His cold words froze the breath in her lungs.

"Perhaps none," she said. "But that doesn't mean I have to rejoice in one so unfeeling."

"Grow up, Izzy. What are you waiting for? Some dashing hero? It's time to stop living in this"—he waved his arms at the knights and handmaidens—"fairy tale."

She stared at him, unable to believe the words coming from his lips.

"You're doing this on purpose," she said, slowly

understanding him. "You're pushing me away because you're afraid."

"I'm not pushing you away. I believe I just offered to marry you."

"In the most insulting, unappealing way possible."

Wendell clanked a few steps forward and called out to them. "Can I offer my lady some assistance?"

"She's not your lady," Ransom shot back. "She's Miss Goodnight. A grown woman. And it doesn't matter how many of your granny's tea trays you strap on your chest. They don't make you a knight."

Izzy crossed her arms. So, it wasn't enough for him to push her away. No, he wouldn't rest until he'd pushed away everyone.

"Your Grace, I am a knight," Wendell said. "I'm a Knight of Moranglia."

"And what makes you a Knight of Moranglia?"

"I swore an oath."

"Oh, you swore an oath. On what? A sword made of a vegetable marrow? You're not a knight. You're delusional. All of you." He lifted his voice. "Admit it. That's why you're here, styling yourselves as handmaidens and knights of honor. Because your own lives are too pitiful to face."

"You're jealous." She shook her head. "You've never known what it's like to be a part of something like this, and you're envious."

"Envious," he scoffed. "Of these men? I've ten

pounds that says Sir Wendell here still lives with his mother."

Wendell's face flushed bright red. "A great many bachelors live at home until they marry."

"Oh, yes," Ransom said. "And what marriage prospects are on your horizon? Do you have a sweetheart? An intended? At least tell me you've groped a tit or two."

Izzy stomped on his boot and ground her heel into his toe. "I said, that's enough. If your aim was to make a jackass of yourself and ruin everything we've been working toward, believe me, you've done more than enough."

But Ransom wouldn't let up. "Come along, 'Sir' Wendell. Admit it. You've never even kissed a girl, have you?"

Poor Wendell. His cheeks blazed an alarming shade of crimson.

Izzy couldn't see anything but red.

And then Abigail Pelham crossed the dining hall in determined steps, took a shocked Wendell Butterfield by the shoulders, and kissed him full on the lips.

"There," Abigail said. "He's kissed a girl now."

Inwardly, Izzy cheered. Good for Abigail.

With a desperate tug, she tried to draw Ransom aside. "Now that's enough. You're going to apologize. We need these people. And even if you are determined to destroy your own chances, *I* need these people. They're always here for me."

"They're not here for you. They are here for a

wide-eyed, precious little girl with emerald green eyes and sleek, amber hair. They were never here for you."

Oh, God.

The words came as such a blow to her, she actually fell back a step.

"*I* am here for you," he said, taking her by the waist. "Izzy, if we marry, it doesn't matter what they do to me. They can throw me in Bedlam and swallow the key. As long as my child is in your womb, you'll be protected." His hand slid to her belly. "We both know you could be carrying my heir already."

She lowered her voice to a horrified whisper. "I can't believe you just said that. Aloud, in front of everyone."

She couldn't even bring herself to look around for the handmaidens' reactions. Much less Abigail's. Unshed tears burned at the corners of her eyes.

All this effort. All this work. All this love in her heart. And it was nothing to him. He was throwing it away. She'd been hoping they could make it through tomorrow together—and they couldn't even make it through this afternoon.

And to make it worse, he'd just ruined her in front of the only friends she had left.

"You need to break free of this, Izzy." He tilted his head toward the shocked onlookers. "For that matter, so do they. You do them no favors by hiding the truth. Are you afraid they'll find out that fairy tales are a load of bollocks, all their 'oaths' and vows are worth precisely shite, and happy endings only exist in your father's storybooks? Good. I hope they do learn it. It might save some other man in my position a great deal of trouble."

She pulled away from him. "So that's it. This isn't about *The Goodnight Tales* or your solicitors. And it's not about me. This is about your pride, and Lady Emily Riverdale."

Duncan coughed, loudly and frantically.

"Lady Shemily Liverpail," she corrected. "Sorry. Either way. This is revenge for you. Is that it, Ransom? It wasn't enough to ruin England's precious sweetheart. Now you want to marry me, just to even the score."

He shook his head. "It's not about scores."

"You are the deluded one." She jabbed a finger in his chest. Poking right at that empty place where he ought to have a heart. "She didn't leave you because of my father's stories. She left you because you were cold and unfeeling toward her. The reason you find yourself alone and blinded and helpless is the fault of exactly one person in this room. You."

"Izzy . . ."

She swiped a scalding tear from her cheek. "And do you know what? She was right to run away. She deserved better. I deserve better, too."

Chapter Twenty-two

The men and women filling the dining hall were utterly silent as the last of Izzy's footsteps faded. Ransom could feel their collective condemnation.

The echoes of her words still rang in the ceiling vaults.

She deserved better. I deserve better, too.

Ransom tugged at his cravat, loosening the restrictive knot.

It came as a sick sort of relief to hear that sentiment voiced aloud, and to know everyone around him agreed. These past few days of amiable assistance and cheerful industry had made him feel like a stranger in his own house. Dozens of people organized to help him, for no wages or discernable reward? He scarcely recognized his life.

But this sense of empty, echoing isolation . . . ?

This was familiar. This was what he'd always known. What he'd been told, since before he could understand words. There could be no comfort for him. No kindness, no mercies. No one had ever loved him, and no one ever could.

You don't deserve that, boy.

Ransom wouldn't argue.

As he left the room and made his way to his dressing room, only Duncan followed.

"Duncan, draw me a bath, prepare my finest suit, and pack everything else. We're leaving to-night."

"For Scotland?"

"No. For Town."

Ransom crossed the room and began tugging loose his cuffs.

They would leave for London at once. Once there, he would go straight for the bank and empty his accounts. In the event his traitorous solicitors had already frozen his accounts, he'd go to the clubs—wherever he was still a member—and beg or borrow as much as he could.

Whatever funds he could manage to raise, it all went to Izzy. She didn't need to like him, much less love him—but he needed to know she was safe.

"Your Grace," Duncan began, "are you certain it's wise—"

Ransom cut him off. "No. Stop there. I don't want any sage advice. You're not my counselor, you're my valet."

"I thought I'd been promoted to butler."

"You've been demoted again. Draw a bath. Prepare my suit. Pack."

Ransom undressed while he listened to the sounds of kettles being put on to warm and the tub scraping across the floor toward the hearth.

When all sounded ready, he found the tub and lowered his body into it, anticipating the perfectly warmed bathwater to be poured over his shoulders.

What he got was a deluge of ice-cold, freezing shock. Dashed straight over his head.

He sputtered. "What the . . . ?"

"You can consider that my resignation, Your Grace."

"You can't quit."

"Certainly I can. My pension was settled and prepared years ago. I've only stayed on in the position for the stupidest of reasons. A promise I made long ago. But today, in the dining hall, you enlightened me. You made it perfectly clear that those oaths and allegiances are . . . Was it shite or bollocks? I can't recall."

Ransom pushed the freezing droplets from his face. "What are you going on about? You never swore an oath. There's no Valet's Promise, or Order of the Starched Cravat."

"Not to you. I swore an oath to her."

"To Miss Goodnight?"

"No. To your mother. I promised your dying mother that I would look after you. Absurd, isn't it? Like something from a soppy story."

Ransom inhaled slowly.

So, it wasn't enough that he'd been the instrument of his mother's death. He'd ruined Duncan's life, too. That was lovely to know.

Well, he could put an end to that torture quickly. "Consider yourself released from that promise."

"Oh, I do, Your Grace. I do."

Another barrage of ice-cold water crashed down over his head.

"You fool," Duncan said, in a seething tone that Ransom had never heard his valet use before. "I've seen you drunk, debauched, engaged in all manner of devilry. But I've never seen you behave so stupidly as you did today. If you let that girl get away, you are a true idiot."

Ransom shook himself. His teeth chattered. "It's b-better this way."

"Better?" Another dipper of freezing water splashed over his shoulders. "For whom?"

"For her." He pushed the water off his face. "For Izzy. You heard her. I d-don't deserve her."

"Of course you don't deserve her. No man *deserves* a woman like that. He mortgages his very soul to win her and spends his life paying off the debt."

"Soon I won't have a single asset to my name. I'm not going to take you and her and everyone else down with me."

Duncan was silent for a long moment. "She loved you, you know."

Loved. Funny, how that one little "d" took a miraculous sentence and made it heart-shredding. "You and Miss Goodnight have a great many chats."

"I'm not speaking of Miss Goodnight. I'm speaking of the late duchess."

Ransom steeled himself against the sharp pain of the mention. "Yet another woman who would have been better off if I'd never been born."

"I was just a young footman, hired on when you were in the womb. Everyone in the house walked on eggshells. There'd been a stillborn child the prior year, they told me. Rumor in the serving quarters was, the doctors had warned that the duchess might not survive another birth."

A stillborn child, the previous year?

Ransom had never known this.

"But she wanted to take the risk," Duncan continued. "She wanted you so much. Once the birthing was over, I was sent in to remove the doctor's case from the room. She reached out, and her hand caught my arm." The old valet cleared emotion from his throat. " 'Promise,' she said. 'Promise you'll show him love.' "

Ransom couldn't move.

"She was delirious," Duncan said. "Already slipping away. I knew she'd mistaken me for the duke. But I couldn't tell her so, and there wasn't time to summon him. The duke wouldn't have told her what she yearned to hear, anyway."

Damn right he wouldn't have. His father had

remained a cold, unforgiving bastard until the day he died.

"But I couldn't let the young duchess die uneasy. So I told her, *I* promise. I promise to show him love. And for thirty years, I've done my best to honor that."

Jesus. Where was another ewer of freezing water when he needed one, to mask all these other droplets on his face?

Sinking down into the tub, Ransom drew his knees to his chest and scrubbed his face with both hands. His nursemaids and tutors had been forbidden to show him kindness. But who had been there for him? Cleaned him up after every night of debauchery, stitched his wounds, slipped him into immaculate tailcoats made tighter than a mother's hug?

Who had stayed by him these seven months, as he crawled and fumbled his way back from the brink of death?

Duncan.

Duncan, all this time.

"Now," he scraped out. "You're just telling me this *now*."

"I never thought you were ready to hear it before. And I was right."

"But . . . why? There's no pension in the world worth thirty years of serving me. It's not as though I gave you any reason for devotion."

"Of course you didn't. I kept that promise for thirty years because it gave my work meaning. It gave me honor. A small, domestic kind of honor, but honor nonetheless.

"But apparently, in your view, I've wasted my whole life. Just another of those shite-filled vows and bollocks oaths. Now that you've released me from it . . ." The valet heaved a deep breath. "I believe I'll retire to a little seaside cottage in Ireland. I'm rather looking forward to that."

Ransom groped about for a towel or his clothing. Nothing.

"Where's my shirt?"

"I wouldn't know, Your Grace. That's not my job anymore. But if I might offer you one bit of parting advice . . . You're not in a position to be selective. If someone offers you love or friendship, take it. Even if it comes dressed in a tea tray. Also, stay away from stripes. Unflattering."

Ransom was left blind, naked, wet, and shivering. And completely alone, just as the day he was born.

There was nothing to do but start over.

And try to get everything back.

Izzy paced her bedchamber by the light of a single candle.

She checked the clock again. Half past two in the morning. Only nine minutes since the last time she'd checked.

Where on earth could Ransom have gone? In the dark of night, on his own? At her insistence, Duncan had gone out searching for him. They should have returned hours ago. Now, Izzy was worried for them both.

She alternated between anger at his desertion and the fear that something horrid had happened. He was a grown man, she told herself. Magnus was a faithful guide. But none of that was a guarantee against accidents or injury. What if he'd gotten lost? What if he'd fallen in the stream?

What if he'd gone to Scotland with one of the handmaidens instead? She didn't know that she would blame him, after some of the angry things she'd said.

Lord. The uncertainty was killing her. Maybe she should venture out herself. She could take a lamp and rouse Snowdrop from her bed of wood shavings.

That was it. Izzy reached for her cloak and boots. She couldn't just sit here and do nothing.

Her fingers trembled as she worked at unknotting the laces of her boots. Why she never unlaced them when she took her boots off at the end of the day, Izzy didn't know. It was a lazy habit, and she'd never regretted it more than she did this moment.

Now that she'd made the decision to go out in search of him, her anxiety had intensified. And unlike her usual heart-pounding terror in the dark, this fear had a defined shape and edges she could grasp on to.

Because this wasn't imagined fear. Not anymore. This was genuine terror for the safety of someone she cared about. Someone she *loved*. She loved him, and it didn't matter that he'd sabotaged all their hard work and future happiness today. If he was out there somewhere, hurting in the dark, she had to help.

And then—just as she'd finally worked loose the knot on her second boot—she heard noises in the courtyard. She ran to the window.

Oh, thank heaven.

He was home.

He was home, his arm slung over Duncan's shoulder, and he was . . . laughing.

Laughing?

Her fear was gone. In its place, she knew a rush of pure fury.

Izzy stormed down the staircase and into the great hall, just in time to greet the returning men.

She wrapped her arms about herself to stop her trembling. "Ransom. I've been worried sick. Where have you been?"

Duncan seemed to know his cue to clear out. "I have some . . ." He gestured vaguely toward the ceiling. Then turned his head to look over his shoulder. "The laundry. Need to . . ."

"Just go," Izzy pleaded.

He went, and gratefully.

"My thanks," Ransom called after him. "For all of it."

Duncan paused and bowed. "It was my honor."

"So?" She hugged herself tight. "Where have you been?"

"I've been . . ." He gestured expansively. "Making friends."

Making friends? She couldn't have been more astonished if he'd answered, Chasing unicorns.

"Where?" she asked. "And with whom?"

"Well, I started at the vicarage. Wendell Butterfield was there for dinner with the Pelham family. Then, after a few hours, I went to the village inn. When their public room closed for the night, I moved on to the seedy tavern. The Musky Boar, I think it's called. Charming, sticky little place, filled with interesting types. At least one or two of them could read."

"Read."

"Yes," Ransom said. "You see, that's what I've been doing. Moving from place to place all evening. I needed something read aloud to me, and I couldn't ask you. Something important."

"Oh? And what was that?"

"The Goodnight Tales."

She felt his answer like a blow to the knees. "Oh, no."

"Oh, yes. It became clear to me today, if I had any hope of ever understanding you, deserving you, much less winning you back—I needed to know what was in those stories. And now, thanks to Abigail and Mr. Butterfield, and the kindly patrons of the local drinking spots, I've been through the entire saga. Start to finish. Not that the tale is finished, of course. I've some questions for you about that."

No. *No.*

Not him. Not Ransom. The one man who didn't treat her like some insipid little girl in a fairy tale but as a full-grown woman. A beautiful temptress of a woman, with interesting ideas and sensual wit.

Now that he'd read all those stories, he'd be just like Lord Archer and Abigail and everyone else.

Izzy reeled away from him before he could do something soul-destroying. Like pat her on the head. Or offer her a sweetmeat.

He sang out, "Put out the light, my darling Izzy, and I'll tell you such a tale."

She choked back a sob. "How could you?"

"How could *I*?" he asked. "How could *you*? That's what I want to know. I must say, I have some sympathy for those people who write you so many letters. No wonder they're deranged. Ulric's been left hanging for more than a year now, and Cressida's still stuck in that tower . . . You must tell me who the Shadow Knight is. I need that much, at least. I have my theories, but—"

She buried her face in her hands. "This is terrible. Not you, too."

"Yes, me, too. I'm a full-blooded Moranglian. A convert to the wondrous enchantment that is *The Goodnight Tales*." He stretched out on the sofa, folding his arms beneath his head and facing the ceiling. "You warned me the first few years were rubbish. I'll give you, you were right on that score. Juvenile and predictable, for the most part."

"Predictable?" Against all logic, Izzy was a bit miffed.

He went on talking. "But then, somewhere into Cressida's second kidnapping, the story started to change. Like a good whisky aging in a barrel. There were deeper layers, more shadings of emotion. And the words painted such vivid pictures. I could see it all happening in my mind. So clearly, as if it were taking place before me, but the story kept taking me by surprise. By the time we reached the end—or the *Not* The End—I was riveted to my barstool. The tavern didn't even exist. I found myself wishing I were half the man Ulric is. I don't mind saying, I'm rather taken with Cressida."

She whimpered with despair.

"But the biggest shock of all had nothing to do with the characters or the storyline." He sat up, facing her. His dark eyes seemed to focus on hers. "It had to do with you."

Her heart quivered in her chest.

Oh, God. He knew.

"Yes," he said, confirming her fears. "I know the truth."

That was it, then. Her charade of thirteen years was up. He knew everything.

Which left Izzy with only one possible response.

Run.

Chapter Twenty-three

With a painful gasp, Izzy broke the icy veneer of her panic. She tore from the great hall and dashed up the spiraling staircase.

"Izzy."

She rushed on.

He chased after her. "Izzy, stop. Don't run from me, damn it. Don't ever run from me."

She stumbled to a halt in the corridor, putting one hand to the wall for strength.

He was right. Lady Emily Riverdale had run from him. She'd done it because of Izzy's stories, and in doing so, the girl had ruined Ransom's life.

If Izzy could give him nothing else, she owed him this. The chance to confront her, face-to-face.

So she stopped running. And turned to face the truth.

"Ransom, I . . . I can't imagine how you must be feeling right now."

"Oh," he said, "I think you can."

He caught her by the waist and steered her into the nearest room—which happened to be the newly refurnished, never yet used ducal chamber.

He kicked the door shut behind them.

"You did dream up all those outlandish stories, after all. So it's clear that you can imagine quite a lot of things." As he spoke, he backed her toward the bed. "So perhaps you can put yourself in my place, as I sat there—first in the vicarage, then the inn, then that sticky tavern—slowly coming to the certain realization that the author of these tales was not Sir Henry Goodnight. It was, and always had been, you."

The edge of the mattress hit her in the back of the knees, and she fell backward onto the bed. He fell with her, caging her with his limbs and using his weight to pin her to the mattress.

"So, tell me." His voice was as dark and hollow as a cave. "*Can* you possibly imagine how I felt? *Can* you put a name to that intense emotion that filled my chest so completely, it pained my ribs?"

"Anger," she guessed, feeling faint.

He shook his head. "Wrong."

"Rage? Betrayal?"

"Wrong, and wrong again." He touched her lips, tracing their shape with his thumb. "It was pride. Oh, my Izzy. I was so damned proud of you, I thought my heart would burst."

Her heart stopped beating altogether.

"Proud of . . ." She cleared a lump from her throat. "What do you mean? How could you be proud of me?"

"Stop that nonsense. Don't pretend anymore, not with me." He swiped away her tear. "I was proud because you wrote it. You wrote all of it."

"Yes, and that means it's all my fault. My work is to blame for Lady Emily's elopement. Your injuries and blindness. The fact that you're now on the brink of losing everything. It's *my* fault, all of it."

"Then all I can say is . . ." He inhaled and exhaled slowly. "Bless you. Thank you."

"You can't mean those things."

"But I do. If you had not taught that silly, flighty Emily Riverdale to dream of love, I would have had no chance of believing in it, myself. I would not have come here. I would not have met you. Even if I had, I would have been too arrogant and hardheaded to ever let you close."

He dropped his head, burying his face in her neck. "Izzy, I owe you everything. You are my heart. My very life. If you leave me . . . "

His voice broke. Her heart swelled.

She slid her arms around his neck and hugged him tight. "If you'll only let me hold you, I won't ever let you go."

They kissed deeply, sweetly. And slowly. As though now they had all the time in the world.

"I'm so sorry for earlier," he said. "The stupid things I said. I was a bastard."

"I won't argue."

"I ruined all your work. Worse, I destroyed all the plans I'd been making."

Her brow wrinkled. "What plans had you been making?"

"Well, to begin with . . ." He rose up on his elbows. "I'd been planning to seduce you in this bed tonight."

Izzy swallowed. "Has that plan altered?"

Please say no. Please say no.

"Yes, it has." He rose up and straddled her waist. "I don't think seduction is called for. I think you're overdue for a ravishing."

A thrill shot through her.

Yes.

This was just what part of her craved—for him to take control. Just this once. She'd been the responsible person in the Goodnight household since the age of ten. All those years of feverishly scribbling stories, working to keep bread on the table and oil in the lamps. Then the constant tension of keeping the truth to herself—always counting her statements in any conversation, clenching her fists and holding her tongue. Making sure no one got close enough to guess. Because she needed to guard not only their family income but the dreams and hopes of thousands.

And all the while, she'd been yearning for someone to take care of *her*. She'd dreamed of this.

A man strong enough to protect her, bold enough to see her for who she truly was. Willing to claim her for his own.

She was long overdue for a ravishing. A lifetime overdue.

But it couldn't happen tonight.

When he laced his hands with hers and pushed her back against the bed, she protested. "No."

He frowned. "No?"

"Not like this. I can't let you ravish me."

She took advantage of his surprise, turning and flipping their positions on the bed so that she lay sprawled atop him.

"Tonight," she vowed, "I'm going to ravish *you*."

Ravish *him*?

Ransom made a halfhearted attempt at demurring. He muttered a few incoherent words of protest. But his body betrayed him.

"I know you want it," she whispered, hiking her skirts to straddle his hips.

And he did. He wanted this badly indeed.

She couldn't know what it meant to him, to be pushed back against the bed, divested of all his clothing, and then . . . just touched. Caressed. And best of all, kissed. Kissed everywhere. With no reciprocation or compensation expected. Nothing up for barter or exchange. Just the outpouring of her sweetness, her passion. Her beautiful heart.

She kissed him everywhere. Everywhere.

He found it adorable, some of the places she chose to grace with her lips. The inside of his elbow. His knobby chin. His hairy, muscled calves. And all the while, her soft, sensual hair dragged over his skin, like a thousand caressing fingers.

She kissed his lips, of course, sliding her tongue deep to twine with his. She kissed his cheeks and temples both the unmarked and the scarred. She kissed the tender place just beneath his ear, and she ran her tongue down the center of his chest and . . .

And stopped at his navel.

Damn.

He didn't want to press her for it. But by this point, she'd put her mouth on him just about everywhere else, and his cock was getting ideas of its own. Straining for her touch, aching for her kiss. Even leaping, like a tethered beast.

"Izzy."

At last, she took his erection in hand. She pressed her lips to the crown. Encouraged by his moan of helpless pleasure, she did it again. And again, this time sweeping gently with her tongue.

"Show me," she whispered. "Show me what to do."

He couldn't resist that invitation. He fisted his hand in her hair, guiding her to take him in her hot, wet, lovely mouth and stroke him up and down. She didn't need a great deal of instruction. Once she had the rhythm, he released his grip and let his head fall back against the pillow, reveling in the bliss.

She took him deep in her mouth one last time, and then released him, sliding her tongue along the sensitive underside. He groaned in a wordless plea for mercy.

"Are you ready to be ravished?" she asked, in a sultry, honeyed tone.

"Yes," he said through clenched teeth. "Very much so."

She climbed his body, straddling his pelvis and rubbing her heat up and down his rigid length. Then she froze, poised above him. Holding the tip of his cock lodged just where it wanted so desperately to go.

Dear God. She would kill him.

"Izzy." The unspent lust had his voice in a stranglehold. "Now. Do it now. I'm begging you."

"You know the word I'm waiting to hear."

Did he know?

Ah. Yes, he supposed he did. The little minx.

"Please." He reached for her, tangling one hand in that long, wild, curling hair, and said it again. *"Please."*

"That's more like it."

She sank down on him, slowly and smoothly, taking him all the way to the root.

Yes.

For as long as he could bear it, he allowed her to set the pace. She rode him in a slow, gentle, rolling rhythm that teased his patience to the brink.

And when he couldn't be patient anymore, he grasped her hips in his hands and guided her to move faster. Harder. He planted his feet on the bed and pushed upward with his hips, meeting her halfway with his thrusts.

She fell forward, and the soft, bouncing heat of her breasts met his chest. He held her, wrapping her in his arms so tight, treasuring her every tiny gasp and sigh of pleasure. He held himself back as long as he could, driving into her again and again—pushing her higher and higher, until she shuddered and came apart in his arms.

And when she came, he came, too. It was oneness, and it was glorious, and it was perfect, and it was her. All her.

God, he loved her.

Gathering her close, he rolled onto his side and tucked her head to his chest. She nuzzled sweetly, curling in his embrace.

He rested his chin on her head. "I'm going to ask you a question, Izzy. I've never asked this of a woman before. And it's taking me a great deal of courage to even broach the subject, so please—I beg you, consider your answer carefully."

"What is it?"

"Izzy, my heart . . ." He tenderly stroked her hair where it fanned across the pillow. "In the morning, will you make me a pancake?"

Chapter Twenty-four

As soon as the dawn came streaming through the windows, Izzy shook her sleeping lover awake. It pained her to do it. He was so beautiful there, his bronzed limbs tangled amid crisp white sheets and downy pillows.

He looked at peace.

But today was going to be an interesting day, to say the least. He couldn't sleep through any more of it.

"Ransom." She nudged his shoulder.

He startled. "What? What is it?"

"Wake and dress. The solicitors are coming today. I don't know where Duncan is, but he's sure to turn up soon."

"Izzy, for God's sake. Curse the solicitors.

Duncan resigned. And I thought we'd moved past this. I'm not going to hide what we have any longer."

"I'm not hiding it." She plopped down beside him on the bed and ruffled his hair. "I'm just hurrying you along. If you want your pancake, it has to be now."

"Oh. Well, then."

A few minutes later, wearing rumpled clothes and a rare smile, Ransom followed her down the stairs and into the kitchen just off the great hall.

She stoked the fire and began pulling bowls and spoons from the cupboard. "So, how did you guess the truth?"

"How did I *know*, do you mean? I've had my suspicions for some time now. You describe sunsets as dying warriors, you read in voices, and you write me silly lines of dialogue. Once I finally heard the stories, it was obvious. I knew because I know you. Izzy, you shouldn't deny or pretend any longer."

Very well. She wouldn't pretend any longer. Not with him.

The rest of the world could never know the truth, but she couldn't deny how much it meant to know this one man had discerned it. He'd looked beyond the expectations and the public perceptions, and he'd seen her. The real Izzy.

"You truly liked them?" she asked. It was the silliest question, and he chided her for it accordingly.

He tugged on her hair. " 'Liked' isn't the word."

But what is *the word?* she wondered.

Admired? Adored? Cherished?

Loved?

She didn't need him to say that word, she told herself. But secretly, she couldn't help wishing he would.

"Why didn't you tell me?" he asked. "For that matter, why don't you tell the world? If I'd written England's most popular book, I'd never stop crowing about it."

Was he mad? "Of course I could never tell anyone. Not without ruining everyone's enjoyment and making my father out to be a fraud."

"Your father *was* a fraud. He was a cowardly, shameless fraud, taking all the glory for your hard work."

She shook her head, reaching into the cupboard for eggs. "At the outset, he was the one protecting me. I was so young. The publishers wouldn't have even looked at the *Tales* if they thought I'd written them. I didn't want the attention, the admirers. The public adoration made my father happy. It was the writing that gave me joy."

"Until he died, and you lost everything. Don't you miss it now?"

"Of course I miss it. Terribly." Even now, more than a year later, she carried a sense of aching loss that never quite went away. "But how could I continue? If I tried to pass the work off as my father's, it would legally belong to Martin. If I sent it under my own name, the publisher would only send it back. Unread, most likely. "

"How will you know if you don't try?"

"You don't understand this, Ransom. You can't see."

His head jerked in affront. "I don't know what my blindness has to do with it."

"Everything." She sighed.

His blindness had everything to do with it.

No man had ever—*ever*—treated her the way he did. She was small and plain and insignificant. But on the page, her words could be so much more. They could be influential, admired. Even powerful.

But only if they weren't *hers*.

She'd come to accept that this was how it would always be. She was at her best when she was invisible. That's why she'd written herself with emerald green eyes and sleek amber hair. The real Izzy wasn't good enough.

Until now. The real Izzy was good enough for Ransom. He would never know how much that meant. But she would endeavor to show him.

She squeezed his arm. "Let me make your pancake."

He looked on as she gathered eggs and began cracking them in a bowl.

"Who taught you to make pancakes?" he asked. "Your family's cook?"

She laughed a little. "We had no cook. My father's only income came from a handful of pupils he tutored. Until the stories became successful, we never had the money for servants." She poured milk in the bowl, sifted in a measure of flour, and began to beat the mixture with a spoon. "No cook, no maid, no governess. It was always just me and Papa. I taught myself to make a fair number of things, but pancakes were a favorite."

"So. You spent your childhood acting as your own cook, maid, *and* governess. Then you became the family provider at the age of thirteen." His hands framed her waist. "I'm tempted to take that spoon from your hands and send it sailing out the nearest window. You should never make another pancake again."

She smiled and kissed his cheek. "This is different. It's my pleasure to make one for you."

He slid his arms about her waist and hugged her as she added a sprinkle of salt and sugar to the bowl.

And she decided—right here in this kitchen—there was something else she'd like to share with him, too.

"Would you like to know how it continues? The true identity of the Shadow Knight?"

"Are you joking?" His arm cinched tight about her waist. "I would trade almost anything to know that. Anything but pancakes. Pancakes are not for up negotiation."

"So Ulric was dangling from that parapet." She found the butter in its crock. "And just beginning to pull himself up, when the Shadow Knight unsheathed his sword and severed one of his hands in a single blow."

Ransom winced. "Good Lord. You do have a bloodthirsty imagination."

"Now he's dangling by only one hand. With the rain falling, the wind whipping about the parapets. He has not only the weight of his body but the weight of his armor. It's too much. He's starting to lose his grip. It's over, and both Ulric and the Shadow Knight know it."

She set the bowl of pancake batter aside, offering him her sugary fingers to lick.

She went on with her tale. " 'Tell me,' Ulric says, as he slips from three fingers to two. 'Before you send me to my death, tell me who you are.' At last, the Shadow Knight lifts the visor of his helmet, revealing an all-too-familiar face, and says"—she lowered her voice, giving it an ominous cast—" 'Ulric. I am your brother.' "

He let her fingertip slide from his mouth. "No."

"Yes."

"*No.*"

"*Yes,*" she replied. "It's truly not that much of a twist. The motif runs through most chivalric literature. Knights-errant are always having to face down a nemesis who is revealed to be their father, brother, or a long-lost son."

She put a pat of butter in the heated pan and followed it with a generous spoonful of batter.

"But I thought Ulric's brother died in the Crusades," Ransom said.

"Ulric thought so, too. He *thought* Godric died on the battlefield, but he survived. It took him years to make his way back to England, and with every step, he dreamed of vengeance on the brother who had left him for dead."

He shook his head. "Next you'll tell me Cressida's truly their sister."

"Cressida, their *sister*? Lord, no. What on earth would make you think of such a thing?"

"It would be a good surprise," he said. "You have to admit."

She made a sound of disgust as she flipped the pancake. "They can't be siblings. They've *kissed*."

"Not very deeply."

"It's still a *kiss*. They are not brother and sister." She laughed. "What a suggestion."

She slid the finished pancake on a waiting plate. Just then, the door to the kitchen creaked open, and Izzy looked up just in time to see a familiar figure, capped with a shimmering knot of blond hair.

"Izzy, there you are."

Abigail.

Izzy bit her lip, uncertain what the vicar's daughter would think of her now. Ransom's declarations yesterday had left little room for ambiguity, and here they were in rumpled half dress, making early-morning pancakes in the kitchen. The fact that they were lovers must be obvious.

And just in case it wasn't apparent enough, Ransom slid his arm about her shoulders, drawing her close.

"Abigail," she said. "Good morning. I was just—I mean, we were . . ."

"It's all right, Izzy." Abigail moved into the room, drawing Izzy aside. "I won't tell a soul. In fact, I'm here to ask you for a favor. If anyone asks you, I stayed here at the castle last night."

"Oh?" Understanding dawned. "Oh. Of course you did."

"I most definitely did not spend the night at the Moranglian Army encampment," Abigail went on in a low whisper, "allowing Mr. Butterfield some mildly unchivalrous liberties." A wash of pink touched her cheeks.

Izzy smiled. "Of course you didn't."

"Thank you."

"Not at all. What are friends for?"

Abigail gave her a squeezing hug and heaved a sigh of relief. "Now," she said brightly, "what's to be done about these solicitors? How do we prove that the duke's not an incompetent lunatic? Surely we haven't given up."

Izzy looked to Ransom. "We haven't given up. Have we?"

"No, we haven't," he said. "Let them come. No more charades. No more pretense. I will answer their questions, honestly. If, at the end of it, they mean to challenge my fitness as duke, I will see them in the Lord Chancellor's court."

"I like that plan," she said. "Abigail, can we still count on your help?"

"Of course."

"Duncan has resigned," Ransom said, scratching his unshaven jaw. "But I think I can convince him to stay. As a friend. We'll still need footmen." He looked to Abigail. "You said the Moranglian Army is still camped nearby? Perhaps I can persuade them to come back."

Izzy wasn't sure that was a wise idea.

"Ransom, you were so hurtful to them yesterday. Lord knows what they're thinking of me. Whatever you say to them . . . I suggest you consider beginning with a sincere apology. And concluding with the word 'please.'"

He chewed a bite of his pancake and shrugged. "They're reasonable men. I'm certain with a bit of conversation, we can reach an understanding."

Evidently, an understanding wouldn't be so easily reached.

Not two hours later, Ransom found himself in the Moranglian encampment. Surrounded, hooded, and held at sword point, with both hands bound behind his back.

And now they were taking him into the woods.

He tried to make himself heard through the clanking of armor and the sacking thrown over his head. "Good sirs, truly. I know yesterday I said hurtful things. But today, I've come in peace. I wish to join your ranks."

A pointed object jabbed him in the kidneys. "One does not simply *join* the Knights of Moranglia. It's not that easy. There's a ceremony and an oath."

"And a trial," another said.

"Very well. I will submit to your trials. But really, is the hood necessary? I am already blind."

He took another jab to the kidneys. "Kneel."

He knelt. Someone removed his hood.

Ransom took a greedy gulp of fresh air. "So what do I do? What do I need to say?" He cleared his throat. "Anon I pledge mine fealty thither . . ."

They put the hood back over his head.

"Prithee," he protested, "if thou wouldst waiteth a goddamned second—"

"Brother Wendell, he's not taking this seriously," one of the knights said. "Our order is a sacred trust. We're here because we're united by a higher purpose."

Another chimed in. "If we admit him to our ranks, we must treat him as one of our own. As a brother. Do you think he's going to treat us the same way?"

Ransom bowed his head and managed to shake his hood loose. Unburdened, he lifted his eyes and spoke to the faceless men surrounding him.

"Listen," he said. "I know. I'm not your friend. I'm the bastard who thrashed you and took your pocket money at school. But right now, I'm on the ground. In the woods. Kneeling in something highly unfortunate, on the day after my valet quit his post. I am serious about this. I am seriously apologetic for what I said. And I seriously need your help."

That was the first time Ransom could recall

ever saying those words: *I need your help.* And look, he hadn't even collapsed of humiliation.

The first knight spoke again. "Don't allow it, brother. He's not a true Moranglian."

"But I am now," Ransom insisted. "And Sir Wendell should know it. He was there at the vicarage for dinner when we read through the first part."

"Then prove your worth," the second knight said. "In installment seventeen, what three ingredients did Ulric fetch for the Witch of Graymere's potion?"

Bloody hell. That was very specific. Ransom searched his memories of the previous night. He'd been paying attention to the story—he'd been lost in it, truly—but he hadn't taken sodding *notes*. "Toe of troll, hair of newt, and . . . and unicorn piss? Damn it, I don't know."

"Do you see?" the knight said. "He's not sincere. I bet he doesn't even know the Doubt Nots."

"Wait," Ransom said, perking up. "Those, I know."

He remembered this part. It was a good part, with Ulric taking his leave of Cressida before departing on his quest to slay the Beast of Cumbernoth. He'd made quite a speech.

"Doubt not, my lady," he recited. "Doubt not. I shall return. Doubt not my blade."

"It's steel," someone corrected, adding a corrective thump to the back. "Doubt not my steel."

"Right, right." He concentrated on the muddy

ground. "Doubt not my steel. Doubt not my strength. And there's something more, and something else about the king, and then 'you remain queen of my heart' and it ends with, 'For my lady, and for Moranglia.'" He lifted his head. "There, is that good enough?"

"No." He recognized Wendell Butterfield's voice. "That was pathetic."

"He's just using us," the first knight said again. "Once he gets what he wants, he'll forget us. Cut us in the street. Make sport of our rituals at his fancy gentlemen's clubs. He doesn't understand how we are."

Ransom shook his head. "No, no. No one likes *me* at those clubs, either. Believe me, I know what it's like to be reviled. I was gravely injured seven months ago, and guess how many visitors and well-wishers I've had? Exactly none. I'm an outcast, too."

"A wealthy, highly ranked outcast with a half dozen estates," Wendell pointed out.

"At the moment, yes. But if my solicitors and heir have their way, I could lose everything. Make no mistake, I'm not asking your help for me. I need to protect Miss Goodnight. If this hearing doesn't go well, she will be forced to sell the home of her dreams. Allow me to join your ranks, and I swear to you: We *will* be united in a higher purpose. Her."

There was a prolonged silence.

Ransom didn't know what more he could say.

"I'll take that as your solemn oath." Sir Wendell

laid a blunted sword to his shoulder. "I dub thee Sir Ransom, a brother in the Order of the Poppy and a true knight of Moranglia."

Thank God.

"Order of the Poppy," Ransom mused, as his hands were cut loose. He rubbed his chafed wrists. "Does this mean we get to smoke opium now?"

"No," Wendell said. But to his compatriot, he added, "Pass him the mead."

A flask of sweet, sticky wine was offered to him. Ransom drank from it. "Not bad. You have my thanks, Sir Wendell."

"Brother Wendell," he corrected. "You're one of us now."

Really. He was one of them now.

How unexpected. There, kneeling in the forest, surrounded by men who represented the odd pegs and loose ends of English public schools, Ransom was seized by the strangest, most unfamiliar sensation.

Acceptance.

"And when we're not on guard," Wendell went on, "it's Mr. Wendell Butterfield, Esquire."

"Esquire?" Ransom repeated. "But . . . you can't mean you're a barrister?"

"Oh, yes. I am."

"I didn't know they allowed barristers to spend their free time tromping the forest in makeshift armor."

Wendell answered, "Why not? We spend our

work days wearing long black robes and powdered wigs."

Ransom supposed that was true.

"And I may be useless when it comes to performing a footman's table service, but I can get your legal matters sorted. If you'll accept the help, that is."

Wendell stuck something blurry and flesh-colored in Ransom's face.

His hand.

A last pang of bruised pride knocked about his chest, heaving in its death throes. He didn't need help rising to his feet, that pride insisted. He wasn't an invalid or a child.

But he was human. Hopelessly in love, for the first time in his life. And in danger of losing everything. As Duncan had said, he needed all the friendly help he could get.

He swallowed back his instinctive refusal and accepted the man's hand.

Once Ransom had gained his feet, Wendell called for the knights to circle close. Their hands clapped on his shoulders and back.

"All knights salute!"

Fists thumped armor. "For my lady, and for Moranglia!"

Chapter Twenty-five

"Izzy, you're not going to believe this." Abigail pulled her toward the turret window.

"What is it? Oh, please tell me it's not the solicitors. We're not ready at all. I'm not dressed. Ransom isn't even here."

"It's not the solicitors. Look."

Izzy poked her head out the narrow window. There in the distance, winding down the road to the castle's barbican, was the familiar, gaily colored sight of the West Yorkshire Riding Knights of Moranglia. Accompanied by their sister chapter of Cressida's Handmaidens. Their banners waved briskly in the breeze, and sunlight glinted off armor.

"The duke did it," Abigail said, clutching Izzy's arm. "He convinced them to come back."

"I suspect you had something to do with it, too," Izzy said. "Sir Wendell obviously has his own reasons for returning. But it doesn't matter why they came. It just matters that they're here."

A silly tear came to her eye. Even after everything yesterday, they hadn't abandoned her. They were still here, still her friends. They still believed.

Doubt not.

The next few hours were a flurry of activity. Cook and the handmaidens were busy in the kitchen. The knights had another course in table service. Duncan whisked Ransom off for a bath, shave, fitted coat, and gleaming boots. Abigail expended nearly three-quarters of an hour and a great deal of patience on a quest to tame Izzy's hair.

When the carriage wheels sounded in the drive, Izzy couldn't even bring herself to look. Abigail had to do it.

"Yes," she said. "It's them. Now they're here."

"How many?"

"Two coaches. Three . . . No, four men in all."

Four of them? Oh, dear. Only two would be the solicitors. The others must be . . . doctors, witnesses, assistants to the Lord Chancellor, perhaps?

She paced back and forth, just hoping everything was going well downstairs. Duncan would be greeting them, seeing them into the hall, and then it would be time for . . .

A knock sounded at the door.

Ransom.

"Are you ready?" He offered her his arm, and together they made their way down the corridor. "Don't worry about anything. Just stay close to me."

"Won't they find it strange if I'm plastered to your side the whole time?"

His mouth tugged to one side. "Believe me. None of my solicitors will be surprised to find a beautiful woman plastered to my side. It will only bolster the impression that I'm my old self."

His reputation wasn't the source of her concern. She strongly doubted his solicitors were used to seeing him with women like her.

"Wait." Izzy held him back.

"What is it?"

"I . . . I have to tell you something."

"Hm. Right. That would be lovely, but perhaps it can wait until after this crucial meeting we've been preparing for all week?"

"It can't wait," she said, pulling on his sleeve. "There's something you need to know. Urgently."

Now that she had his attention, she almost lost her nerve. She forced herself to blurt it out. "I'm not beautiful. At all."

His brow furrowed, and lips pursed as if he would ask a question, but the question seemed to just . . . get stuck there.

"I should have told you ages ago. You can't know how it's been weighing on me. It's just . . . No one's ever called me beautiful. No one's ever made me *feel* beautiful. And I couldn't resist enjoying it, even though it was all a misunderstanding. But you need to know it now. If we go into that room together, me draped on your arm . . . There will be no clearer evidence that you've gone blind. They won't know what in the world you're doing with me."

"Izzy." His hand swept up her arm.

She pulled away. "I'm not fishing for compliments. Truly. It's important that you believe and understand this. I'm not beautiful, Ransom. Not pretty. Not comely. Not even passably fair. I'm exceedingly plain. I always have been. No man has ever paid me the slightest attention."

"All right, then. So you're not beautiful."

"No."

"Of all your layers and revelations . . ." His hands settled on her shoulders. "*This* is the deepest secret you've been keeping from me."

"Yes." She tried to reach for him.

His grip firmed, forbidding her to move. "Don't."

As he backed her up against the wall, words just kept spilling out of her. Useless, foolish words.

"It seemed harmless enough at the start. I never dreamed it would cause any trouble, and I told myself there wasn't any reason you needed to know the truth. Except now . . . now there are other people here. And you want to pass me off as your lover, and—"

"I'm not passing you off," he said. "You *are* my lover."

She pressed her hands to her face. Curse her ridiculous vanity. Now his whole future was at risk.

He said, "I can't believe this is happening. This . . . *this* . . . is your great, shameful confession. You tell me you're not beautiful." He laughed. "It's just absurd."

"It is?"

"Yes. That's nothing. Do you want to hear a truly ugly secret, Izzy? Here's mine. I killed my mother."

Ransom could feel her recoil at his words, palpably shocked.

He didn't blame her. They were ugly words. Never, ever pleasant to hear. They'd taken a toll on him, too.

"My mother labored for thirty-odd hours to bring me into the world, and died less than one hour afterward," he said. "I killed her. That's precisely what my father told me, in those exact words, from the time I was old enough to understand them."

The memories were still so clear. Every time he'd cried, every time he'd shivered, every time he'd stumbled and wanted a bit of cosseting. His father would haul him by the collar, heels dragging along the marble floors, and push him to the floor before the floor-length portrait of his mother.

Stop that sniveling, boy. She can't wipe your tears now, can she? You killed her.

God, she was beautiful in that portrait. Golden

hair, blue eyes, pale blue gown. An angel. He used to pray to her. Little blasphemous petitions for miracles, forgiveness, playthings . . . any signs that she could hear.

But she didn't hear. She was gone.

He'd never prayed to anything since.

"All the servants," he said, "nursemaids, house-keeper, tutors . . . they were sternly instructed to show me no affection. No hugs, no kisses, no nurturing or comfort. Because those were things my mother would have given me, and I didn't deserve them. He blamed me for her death."

He felt the breath sigh out of her. "Ransom, that's just terrible."

"It is," he agreed.

"It was so wrong of him to treat you that way."

"It was. He was a cruel, disgusting bastard. Let's just say, there weren't many bedtime stories."

"I . . . It's meaningless to say it, but I'm so very sorry."

He pressed his brow to hers. "It's not meaningless at all. It means everything. And if later, you want to take me to bed and stroke my hair for days, I'll take it gladly." He pulled back, putting distance between them. "But that's later. Right now, we're discussing you. Not-beautiful you.

"I know women, Izzy. I've known far too many women." He'd spent years searching for that physical comfort he'd been denied, always shying away from any deeper connection. "And I've known, ever since that first afternoon, that you were unlike anyone who'd come before. I'm glad of it. And if men never paid you attention, I'm glad of that, too, selfish cad that I am. Otherwise, you'd be with some other man instead of here with me.

"But no matter how tightly I hold you, no matter how deeply I sink inside you—I've felt there's always some small part of you I can't reach. Something you've been holding back. Your heart, I assumed. Oh, I wanted it. I want all of you. But I couldn't bring myself to ask for something I so clearly didn't deserve."

He felt her draw breath to object, but he cut her off before she could try.

"And it's nothing to do with my birth or my childhood. I'm old enough now to recognize my father's treatment for the senseless cruelty it was. But it's everything since. You think a few features scattered on your face make you plain? I am ugly to the core. All England knows it. And after reading through my papers, you must know it. You sifted through a mountain of my misdeeds. Of course you'd build a wall around your heart. You're a clever girl. How could you love this? How could anyone?"

"Ransom." Her voice wavered.

"And now I learn that this . . . *this* . . . is what you've been guarding. This is the reason for that reluctance. You don't feel pretty enough. For a blind man. Christ, Izzy. And I thought *I* was shallow."

The words came out more harshly than he intended. So he followed them with kisses. Tender, soothing kisses to her cheek, her neck, the pale, arousing curve of her shoulder . . .

Bless this woman and her silly, all-too-human vanity. He might never know how to be the man she deserved, but this?

This, he knew how to remedy.

"Izzy," he moaned, pressing his body to hers, "you make me wild with wanting you. You can't imagine." He started pulling up her skirts.

She gasped. "What are you doing?"

"Just what it seems like."

"We can't. The solicitors. They're just downstairs, waiting."

"This is more important."

"Tupping me in the corridor is more important than saving your title?"

He held very still. Then he kissed her lips. "Yes."

He said the word simply, solemnly. Because he meant it, with everything he had left to him. Body and soul. The solicitors and dukedom could go hang. There was nothing worth defending in his life if he couldn't make her see this.

"I can't judge how beauty looks anymore," he said. "But I know the sound of it. It sounds like a flowing river of wild, sweet honey. Beauty smells like rosemary, and it tastes of nectar. Beauty sneezes like a flea."

She smiled. That beautiful smile. How could she ever doubt her effect on him?

"This is how plain you are." He caressed her breast with one hand, while with the other he undid the closures of his breeches placket. "This is how unattractive I find you."

There wasn't time for foreplay or finesse. Only joining.

He fought his way through the petticoats, found her to be every bit as ready as he was—and put both hands on her backside, lifting her off the ground and against the wall. She clung tight to his neck, wrapping her legs about his waist.

And then he thrust.

"I love you."

Saying those words—the words he'd been denied so long, until he denied that they meant anything— damn, it felt good. And saying the words while sliding deep inside her? It felt amazing.

"I love you, Izzy." He thrust deep and true, sliding further home with every dig of his hips. "I love you. *You*. Beautiful . . . tempting . . . clever . . . lovely . . . you."

He paused inside her, sheathed to the hilt. Holding her pinned to the wall, the both of them fighting for breath. Her thighs quivered against his. There wasn't any way to get closer. He'd pushed into her just as far as he possibly could, thrust as deeply as he could ever reach.

But was it enough? Could he manage to touch her heart?

He had to know.

He closed his eyes and pressed his brow to her

sweet, powdered skin. That old, insidious voice thundered in his blood. *You don't deserve this. You don't deserve her.*

But he had to ask anyway.

He spoke the words that were most difficult of all.

"Love me."

Chapter Twenty-six

*L*ove me."

The words were a hoarse, faint whisper. But Izzy knew how much they'd cost him.

"I do." She hugged his neck tight, lest she be swept away by this flood of tender emotion. She kissed his brow, his cheek. "Oh, Ransom. I love you. I do."

On a shaky gasp, he pulled almost all the way out, then thrust home once more. "Again."

"I love you. I love you."

She could have said it a hundred times. She could have held him deep inside her for just as long as he could wish. But they didn't have that kind of time. He worked hard and fast, bringing them both to a stunning, silent crisis. She sank her teeth into her wrist to keep from crying out.

Then he withdrew from her body, setting her feet back down on the floor. He held her for a few moments longer. Just breathing.

"I needed that," he said. "You don't know how much."

She smiled. "I think we both did."

She lowered her skirts and smoothed out the worst of the wrinkles while he refastened the buttons of his breeches.

"Izzy, here is what I can say with confidence, as a man who would know." He straightened his waistcoat with a tug, then each sleeve in turn. "You're a wildly attractive, palpably sensual woman. Perhaps suitors kept their distance because of the *Tales*. Perhaps your father held them at bay because he feared losing you. I don't know why men never pursued you in the past. I can only tell you why they won't pursue you in the future."

"Why's that?"

He gave her an *isn't-it-obvious* shrug. "Because I won't let them."

"Oh." Izzy melted against the wall.

He spread his arms for her appraisal. "Am I put back together? Will I do?"

"You're devastating." Still reeling, she touched a hand to her coiffure. Or what remained of it. "My hair. You go ahead. I'll just run upstairs and—"

"Leave it." He took her arm and pulled it through his. "And don't be worried about appearances. Stay close to me, every moment. There won't be any doubt in those solicitors' minds about what

I'm doing with you." He paused. "Unless you're worried what your friends will think, in which case—"

"I'm not," she told him, hugging his arm tight. "I'm not worried about that at all."

And with that, Ransom went to face the Inquisitioners.

When he entered the great hall, everyone stood. He saw a group of four gray figures, adrift in a sea of gray mist. Brilliant. He couldn't tell them one from the other. Had no idea who the others might be, once Blaylock and Riggett were accounted for.

These four ominous shadows had come to pass judgment on his life.

But he had Izzy on his arm. The subtle creaking of the knights around him was an unexpected source of reassurance.

And he had a new lawyer. A good one. One he could trust.

He was among friends.

One of the visitors approached him. Ransom could feel the man taking in his appearance, scrutinizing his scars. "Your Grace, it's a relief to see you in such good health."

A relief? Ransom snorted. Somehow he doubted relief was what the man felt right now. Despicable, grasping swindler.

Izzy pressed her fingertips against his wrist, letting him know the solicitor's identity.

"Blaylock," he said. "This is Miss Isolde Goodnight. The new owner of Gostley Castle. Lynforth willed the place to her."

Izzy curtsied. "How do you do?"

"We've brought along with us Mr. Havers," the man went on, "from the office of the Lord Chancellor."

Havers came forward. "A pleasure, Miss Goodnight. The Lord Chancellor sends his regards. His son is a great admirer of your father's stories."

Blaylock completed the introductions. "You'll remember my colleague, Mr. Riggett. And this kind gentleman is Dr. Mills, from the Holyfield Sanitarium for the Mentally Dispossessed."

Ransom acknowledged their vague forms with a curt nod. "If your introductions are concluded, I'll proceed with mine. This is Mr. Wendell Butterfield, esquire. My new legal counsel. And before we proceed any further this afternoon, we will make one thing clear. I will answer any questions. About how I ended here seven months ago, and why. About what I've been doing since. About my injuries, my blindness"—he waited for them to absorb this news—"and my mental state. I will submit to your examinations. But first . . ." He snapped his fingers, and Wendell put the papers in his hand. "You will sign this."

"What is it?"

"It creates an irrevocable trust for Miss Goodnight in the amount of twenty thousand pounds."

His solicitor balked. "What? Twenty thou—"

"Your neglectful management meant she inherited this castle from her godfather and arrived to find it in a shameful state of disrepair. The least we can do is provide her the funds to restore it."

"Your Grace, we cannot authorize—"

"It is my fortune. I am the duke. Until a court decides otherwise, I do the authorizing." He thrust the papers in the solicitor's hand. "I will sign. You will witness. Then, and only then, will I be at your disposal. If you refuse . . . ? I swear to you this. I will fight you, every step of the way, and I will see you brought up on charges of fraud."

The solicitors conferred.

Izzy's arm tightened on his. "What are you doing?" she murmured.

"I'm ensuring your future here in this castle. Everything else is secondary."

"Your fate's not secondary," she whispered. "Not to me."

Ransom acknowledged her sweet words with a squeeze of his fingers. But he didn't withdraw his demand. Twenty thousand was a significant sum, but it was only a small portion of what they'd control if they succeeded in wresting his fortune away. He was relying on their greed to carry the day.

"Well?" he prodded. "Perhaps I should rescind the offer and press straight for the charges of fraud."

"That won't be necessary," Blaylock said. "In the interests of Miss Goodnight, we will sign."

"Good." Once he'd scrawled his name at the

bottom of the papers, and the solicitors had done likewise, Ransom could breathe easier. Izzy was safe.

Now, to make her a duchess.

The doctor approached him. "These fraud remarks concern me. Do you often see conspiracies surrounding you, Your Grace?"

Here it came. The interrogation.

Ransom dropped onto the sofa and settled in. He answered query after query. What year it was, the current ruling monarch, the color of the sky. They asked questions about his injury, poked at his scar.

He mined every reserve of patience he possessed. He could tell they were waiting to pounce on the slightest error or irregularity. With this many witnesses, they couldn't fabricate a lunacy charge. If it came to a formal trial, Ransom knew he'd prevail. But it would be so much easier to be done with this today.

After an hour or so of their questioning, he couldn't be patient any longer. A headache threatened at the base of his skull. "Someone get me a drink. Whisky."

The doctor made a note. "Devoted . . . to . . . whisky."

"That's hardly a new development," Ransom said.

"I must admit," Mr. Havers remarked, "I find your house staff's attire to be . . . fascinating."

"Oh, that's my whimsy," Izzy said, adopting

that girlish, treacly voice he despised. "You know how devoted I am to my father's wonderful stories. And now, with the backdrop of this magnificent castle, I just can't resist bringing a bit of *The Goodnight Tales* to life. I'm so lucky to have the handmaidens and knights here with me. Do you have any sweetmeats?"

The doctor leaned forward. "How do you feel about this atmosphere, Your Grace? Do you enjoy living in a fairy tale, too?"

One of the knights—Sir Alfred, Ransom thought he was called—creaked and clanked forward. He placed a tumbler of whisky in Ransom's hand. The glass jostled in the exchange, and spirits splashed them both.

"Apologies, my brother," Alfred said.

"Brother?"

Damn it. Ransom knew that sound. That was the sound of a pounce.

Blaylock's voice sharpened. "Did that footman just address you as brother?"

"Are you testing my hearing now?" Ransom tried to sound bored. "I believe he did."

"Surely you don't permit the footmen to address you in that familiar manner, Your Grace. Or have you forgotten yourself?"

"I haven't forgotten myself."

"You, there." Riggett called to the young knight, who had clanked his way back to the side of the room. "Why did you just address his grace as 'brother'?"

"B-because we are both members of the same brotherhood," the youth answered. "The Order of the Poppy."

When Ransom heard the resulting laughter, there was no gray in his vision any longer.

Only red.

"The Order of the Poppy?" Blaylock was like a greedy boy with a bowl of trifle and two spoons. "Do tell us more."

"It's the Moranglian order of knighthood, sir. We have banners, tournaments. Badges, and an oath."

"And the duke is a willing part of this?"

"I . . . I don't know, sir." Alfred hesitated.

Of course he hesitated. Ransom recognized the youth's voice now. He was the one of the knights who'd been arguing against Ransom's inclusion. And perhaps for good reason. Alfred had known this moment would come even if he hadn't guessed it would be so soon.

He'd known Ransom would be put to the test.

So, here it was. He could have his fortune, title, and authority restored today—but only if he denounced Izzy's hard work and everything her friends stood for.

Yesterday, he'd had no difficulty doing just that. He'd mocked and belittled every person standing on the fringes of this room.

And today, they'd come back. For Izzy, and for him. Was he supposed to abuse them all over again?

"Do you believe me now?" Riggett was eager to seal the matter. "He's addled, clearly. His blow to the head has left him hopelessly confused. A lunacy trial is our only course."

The doctor leaned close. "Your Grace. Do you know who you are?"

"Yes." Ransom rose to his feet. "I know precisely who I am. I'm Ransom William Dacre Vane, the eleventh Duke of Rothbury. I'm also the Marquess of Youngham, Earl of Priorwood, Lord Thackeray. And . . ."

"And?" the doctor prompted. "And you believe you're someone else, as well?"

He heard Izzy's small hiss of warning. But damn it, he'd sworn an oath. On her name. He couldn't deny it now.

"I'm a Knight of Moranglia."

Izzy clapped a hand to her mouth.

Oh, no. He'd done it now.

Ransom thumped his chest, and all the knights saluted in return.

Half of Izzy wanted to cheer, and half of her wanted to weep. It was a sweet, valiant gesture on his part—but at what cost?

The solicitors moved into action at once.

"You see, Havers? We have no choice." Riggett pointed at the duke. "He needs to stand for a lunacy trial. He's delusional. Probably dangerous."

The doctor agreed. "In my professional opinion, he should be taken into custody, held for examination in London."

"Please," Izzy said. "Please wait a moment. Let's discuss this further. Surely an asylum isn't necessary."

But her pleas were lost in the din. Other objections drowned them out.

All around the great hall, the knights and handmaidens were rousing themselves to Ransom's defense.

One of the knights drew his saber—a saber that didn't look sharp enough to cut sponge cake—and thrust it into the air. "You can't take him!"

"This is a brotherhood," another cried out.

"I *knew* all this training would be for something."

"We stand as one. We will fight to the death."

Even Magnus began to growl and bark.

A shout lifted over all: "Release the ermine!"

"Stop!" Izzy ran to the end of the hall, clambered up on the table, and cupped her hands around her mouth. "Stop!" she cried, putting the force of her full body into it. "Stop, all of you! Stop!"

They stopped. And turned to her.

When she had the room's attention, she took a deep breath. She made her hands flat in front of her, as if she could use them to physically smooth the tension in the room.

"No battles will be necessary. No examinations, either. This is all a misunderstanding. The duke is perfectly sane. Mr. Blaylock, Mr. Riggett, Mr. Havers, Dr. Mills. You must believe me. I have been sharing this castle with the Duke of Rothbury for weeks now, and I know him to be perfectly sound of mind. The knights, the hand-maidens, the romantic stories . . . he doesn't believe in all this. He *shouldn't* believe in this."

"You see . . ." Her eyes flitted over the knights and handmaidens. *"The Goodnight Tales* were . . . Well, they were a lie. I was never that innocent little girl with sleek amber hair. Sir Henry wasn't a doting father though he tried his best. I didn't want a weasel for a pet, and I didn't ask for this." She indicated the castle. "Cressida might be brave, but I'm terrified of the dark. Ulric can say, 'Doubt not,' but I have doubts all the time. I've doubted the truth of happy endings. I've doubted the existence of lasting love. Most of all, I've doubted myself."

To the solicitors, she said, "The duke is humor-ing me. But he knows this is just pretense. Shite and bollocks, I believe he called it yesterday." She looked around the room. "Didn't he? You all were there."

A murmur of reluctant confirmation swept the room.

She turned to Ransom. "So tell them. It's all right. I don't need to pretend any longer, and you don't need to protect me. Just tell them everything you've been saying to me for weeks. You're per-fectly sane. Romance is the delusion." She pressed her hand to her belly. "It's all right. Truly."

Ransom considered. She watched his chest expand with a deep breath. He scratched his neck as he stared at the floor.

Blaylock moved forward. "Well, Your Grace?"

Do it, she silently willed him, trying to send the message all the way across the hall to where he stood. *Disclaim all of this. Save yourself.*

Just tell the truth.

"I will say only this." When Ransom lifted his head, a sly smile played about his lips. "Doubt not."

Her heart flipped over in her chest. "No. No, Ransom, don't."

"Doubt not, my lady. I shall return."

"Not this," she pleaded. "Not now."

He began to walk in her direction, continuing the recitation. "Doubt not my steel. Chains, arrows, blades, stones. I shall never know their sting."

Not Ulric's speech. Anything but this.

"Doubt not my strength." His voice was getting stronger, too. "No storm . . . No storm . . ."

He paused.

Good. Izzy knew what came next, but she wasn't about to help him.

He looked to the knights for a cue.

One of them whispered, "No storm-churned seas."

"Right, right." He took a step in retreat and began that bit again. "Doubt not my strength. No storm-churned seas, no windblown sands. Nor mountain tall could bar me from you."

"See?" Blaylock prodded the doctor. "He's gone raving mad. He thinks he's a character in some fairy story."

Ransom paid them no attention. He didn't acknowledge anyone in the hall but Izzy. His progress toward her was slow, but unswerving.

On the edges of the great hall, the handmaidens looked ready to swoon.

"Doubt not my heart." He was declaiming loudly now, and with feeling. His deep, resonant voice was made for this role. "Time may pile into months and years. It cannot sway the eternal."

"Ransom, please," she whispered. "They think you're mad. I'm starting to wonder, too."

The solicitors and doctor moved toward him, as though he needed to be restrained.

And they could try to hold him back. But Izzy knew he'd just keep coming.

In fact, he kicked aside a chair and forged on with the next part:

"Doubt not my love."

By this point, all the knights and handmaidens were joining in. Of course, they all knew the words, better than Izzy knew them herself.

But Ransom was the only one who knew the words were hers. That they'd always been hers. And now he was giving them back to her. In a gesture of love and faith, and . . .

And sheer insanity.

She pressed a hand to her heart. Her hero.

A dozen handmaidens rushed to her side, lifting her down from the table and sweeping her forward to meet him in the center of the hall.

"Doubt not my love," he repeated, with a chorus of knights to bolster him. "If men would seek to part us, death itself would be a veil too thin. For lo, though I wander the earth for my king, you remain—now and ever—queen of my heart."

He went down on one knee and kissed her hand.

"Don't be angry," he murmured, coming to his feet. "It's your life's work, and they're our friends. I couldn't do it."

"Of course I'm not angry." She took his face in her hands. "You can't know how much I love you right now."

"Then say you'll marry me. I'll go to London, sort out this legal business. And then I'll come back with a ring. Diamonds or sapphires?"

"I don't need a ring at all. I just want you."

There was time to steal a quick, heartfelt kiss.

And then they tried to take him into custody.

"Your Grace, remain calm." The solicitors flanked him. "We'll be taking you to London now. There are some very fine doctors we wish you to see."

He shrugged off their hands. "I'll take myself to London. No custody required. But yes, you had better believe I'll be seeing you in court."

"Actually," Mr. Havers interjected, "I don't believe there will be any proceedings. Not a lunacy hearing, anyhow."

"What?" Blaylock said. He waved at the scene. "But you witnessed that . . . display just now."

"I did. And I assure you, the Lord Chancellor will be wholly uninterested in hearing the matter." Havers turned to Izzy. "As I told Miss Goodnight, his son is a great admirer of these tales. The young man fell from a horse in his childhood, and he's been confined to his bed ever since. The stories have been a boon to him."

"Confined to his bed?" A suspicion formed in Izzy's mind. "But you can't be speaking of Lord Peregrine?"

"The very one," Havers said. "The Lord Chancellor will have no desire to hear this matter. Lock away Izzy Goodnight's intended groom for lunacy? He'd never hear the end of it at family dinners. For that matter, all England would be grumbling."

Riggett gestured wildly. "But the knights. The armor. The Order of the Poppy."

"For God's sake, man. They're just stories. The rest of us here understand that." Mr. Havers gestured at Ransom. "Look at him. The man's not delusional. He's in love."

Ransom's lips quirked in that familiar half smile. "Well, that's one charge I can't argue."

It wasn't a typical wedding. Rather a quiet affair.

The ceremony took place early on a Tuesday morning. The bride wore red, so the groom could see her in a crowd. The narrow pews of the village chapel were crushed with knights in makeshift armor and handmaidens in medieval gowns.

And, after a wedding breakfast at the village inn, the happy couple eschewed the waiting carriage in favor of a long, leisurely stroll back to their castle, walking arm-in-arm.

As they approached the barbican, Izzy stared up at the ancient stone fortress. The new glass panes in the windows acted like facets of a diamond, sparkling in the morning sun. So much had changed since that first rainy, gloomy afternoon, when she'd been deposited here with nothing more to her name than a weasel, a letter, and her last shred of hope.

Ransom stopped her in the courtyard. "Wait."

She glanced up at him. And then she spent the next few moments collecting her scattered wits. The castle might have changed in her perception, but this man hadn't. That wild, untamed masculine beauty made her knees weak every time.

"What's wrong?" she asked. "Did we leave something behind at the inn?"

"Nothing's wrong. I've just been wanting to do this again."

He bent at the waist, and in one swift move, he scooped her into his arms, tucking her close to his chest.

And this time, Izzy managed not to swoon.

Just barely.

Epilogue

Several months later

The candle was nearly guttered in its holder when Ransom reached the thirty-fourth stair. "Izzy, it's late. You should come to bed."

"I know." Izzy replaced her quill in the inkwell and propped her elbows on the desk. With a sigh of fatigue, she closed her eyes and rubbed her temples.

He came to stand behind her. His strong hands settled heavily on her shoulders. "You're working much too hard these last few weeks."

"I know that, too." She picked up the quill and began to write again. "I'm sorry. It's only that I'm desperate to have a few months' worth of install-ments completed before the baby arrives. The work's going more slowly than I'd like. Add to that, I'm drowning in correspondence to answer."

His thumbs kneaded the muscles at the back of her neck, coaxing a deep sigh from her chest.

"What can I do?" he asked.

"That massage is a lovely start." She sorted through the pile of envelopes. "Maybe you can help me answer this letter from Lord Peregrine?"

"What conundrum has he posed this time?"

"It's my turn to pose the conundrum, actually, and I'm stumped for one." She tapped her quill on the blotter. "Aha. I have it." She dipped her pen and began to write. "'Would you rather find a weasel in your bed or an octopus?'" She scribbled the letter's closing and set it aside.

"That's unfair. He gets to *choose*? I don't get to choose."

"No, you don't. You're stuck with both." Smiling, Izzy pulled a magazine from her pile of correspondence. "Now *here's* something from the post you'll find amusing. There's a letter to the editor of the *Gentleman's Review*. And it's about me."

"Read it, then."

Izzy opened the magazine to a marked page and read aloud in a lofty, affected baritone. "'Like so many devoted readers of your publication, I was pleased to see that England's beloved daughter, little Izzy Goodnight, newly the Duchess of Rothbury, has taken up her pen and decided to continue writing in the marvelous world Sir Henry gave to her, and to us. I read the first installments with great anticipation and much interest, but I am sorry to say they did not impress.'"

Ransom scowled. "Impertinent jackass."

"He's entitled to his opinion. Let's see . . . Here we are." She lowered her voice again. "'Though she has swiftly ascended to a higher social rank than her late father enjoyed, these first chapters make it sadly clear that Her Grace will never be his literary equal. Her writing pales beside the richness of Sir Henry's prose though I am pained to say it."

"I'll pain him to say it," Ransom grumbled.

"Oh, but it gets better," she told him, skimming ahead. "He goes on, '*The Shadow Knight's Journey* isn't without its faint glimmers of promise, however. With maturity and time to hone her craft, perhaps the duchess can aspire to be half the writer her father was—and that in itself would be a genuine accomplishment for any writer so young, and so female.' And it's signed, The Right Honorable Edmund Creeley, of Chatton, Kent."

She set aside the magazine, laughing helplessly.

Ransom didn't laugh. He didn't say anything.

"Well?" she prodded. "Aren't you amused? Have you no response?"

"Oh, I have a response. The Right Honorable Edmund Creeley can take his quill and—"

The profanity that followed had Izzy clapping her hands to her belly, as if she could cover her unborn child's tender ears. The babe, however, merrily kicked and cartwheeled in her womb.

Oh, goodness. It seemed this child would take after Ransom.

She didn't mind that one bit.

"We will have the last laugh," she reminded him. "Mr. Creeley will be forced to eat his words, if not . . . those other things you listed. He'll learn the truth in time. As will everyone."

Ransom had given her a fairy-tale ending, and Izzy had vowed not to squander it. She was going to claim her work, and continue the stories she—and so many others—loved. But she wanted to go about it cautiously, with respect for Cressida and Ulric, and for her father's memory and that purple counterpane—and most especially, for the readers who'd made *The Goodnight Tales* not quite "true" but truly meaningful.

So rather than pick up where the original tales left off, she'd begun a new story: *The Shadow Knight's Journey.*

No doubt many readers, those more perceptive than Edmund Creeley, would begin to guess the truth. A few had already written her with their suspicions. But for now, Izzy was playing coy.

She meant to follow the Shadow Knight through his side of the adventures, right up until that climactic scene at the parapet. And then, once the two tales were intertwined, he would lift the visor, revealing his true identity—

And Izzy's.

When the truth came out, there was bound to be a bit of scandal. Izzy worried more about how

Ransom would cope than she worried for her own feelings. She hoped reading him Mr. Creeley's letter might work as an inoculation of sorts.

"You'd better prepare yourself, Ransom. When that installment is published in a few years, no one will be patting me on the head. I'm sure to receive more unpleasant letters."

He was silent for a moment. "Good."

"Good?"

"Yes, good. Because I've decided that the proper response to any unpleasant letter is kisses, and I like having excuses to kiss you."

"I think this particular unpleasant letter merits more than one kiss. Something like ten or twelve."

"I won't stop until you count one hundred," he said wickedly. "Later."

She pouted. "Later?"

"Right now, I want to show you something. It's a surprise."

Izzy was undeniably intrigued as she followed him down the spiraling stairs. She went slowly, cautiously. Her center of balance was changing by the day.

"What surprise could be better than a hundred kisses?" she asked, following Ransom down the corridor.

"This one, I hope."

He stopped before a particular bedchamber. The one they'd designated as a nursery. He pushed open the door.

She clapped her hands together. "Is it finished?"

Izzy had been strictly forbidden from involvement in the major renovations—too much dust and danger, Ransom said. She hadn't argued. She was happy to focus on the writing for now. And it warmed her heart to see his growing investment in the castle that had been his ancestral home.

The castle that was now *their* home.

"It's done, as of today. The laborers finished painting this afternoon." He waved her toward the open door. "Have a look."

With a smile, Izzy rushed through the entryway.

And then she froze in place, awestruck.

"Oh," she breathed. "Oh, Ransom."

"Now, don't start complaining about girlish treatment. I know you're too old to be given a purple room with golden stars. But I also know it was a dream of yours, once. I thought you might want to give it to our children instead."

Izzy pressed a hand to her chest, overwhelmed. The room was beautiful. A cradle with purple quilted bedding, draped with clouds of tulle. A plush carpet of twining vines and lush blooms. Rows and rows of bookshelves. And on the ceiling were painted silver moons and golden stars. Even a comet or two.

On closer look, a few of those celestial objects appeared a bit less precise than the others— uneven and smudged in places. Hardly in line with the exacting standards Ransom imposed on all their workmen.

But in her heart, Izzy knew the explanation for those less-than-perfect stars.

Those must be the ones he'd painted himself.

He shuffled his feet. "You're not saying anything."

"I'm overwhelmed. There are times when even a writer can run out of words." She sniffed back a tear and hugged him as tight as her swelling belly would allow. "Thank you. I love you. This is the best gift I can imagine."

In fact, it was the gift she'd been imagining all her life. Now it was real. They would give their children this magical room, set in their very own castle. But more important than that, they would give their children love. And security.

And stories. Night after night of stories.

This was the true fairy-tale ending. He'd given her the "happily" part the day they'd agreed to marry. This room was the "ever after."

And the best part of all?

So many years stood between them and "The End."

NEW YORK TIMES BESTSELLING AUTHOR

Cathy Maxwell

Lyon's Bride
The Chattan Curse
978-0-06-207022-7

Lord Lyon hopes that by marrying—and having a son—without love, perhaps he can break the chains of his family curse forever.

The Scottish Witch
The Chattan Curse
978-0-06-207023-4

Harry Chattan is taking the battle against the family curse to Scotland, where he will fight not only for his family's honor, but also for Portia Maclean, the woman he's grown to love.

The Devil's Heart
The Chattan Curse
978-0-06-207024-1

Determined to save her brothers' lives, Lady Margaret Chattan arrives on Heath Macnachtan's doorstep with a mythical quest . . . one that just might help him discover who murdered his own brother.

Don't miss these passionate novels by #1 *New York Times* bestselling author

STEPHANIE LAURENS

Viscount Breckenridge to the Rescue

978-0-06-206860-6

Determined to hunt down her very own hero, Heather
Cynster steps out of her safe world and boldly attends
a racy soiree. But her promising hunt is ruined by the
supremely interfering Viscount Breckenridge, who
whisks her out of scandal—and into danger.

In Pursuit of Eliza Cynster

978-0-06-206861-3

Brazenly kidnapped from her sister's engagement ball,
Eliza Cynster is spirited north to Edinburgh. Determined
to escape, she seizes upon the first unlikely champion
who happens along—Jeremy Carling, who will not
abandon a damsel in distress.

The Capture of the Earl of Glencrae

978-0-06-206862-0

Angelica Cynster is certain she'll recognize her fated
husband at first sight. And when her eyes meet those of the
Earl of Glencrae across a candlelit ballroom, she knows
that he's the one. But her heart is soon pounding for an
entirely different reason—when her hero abducts her!

At Avon Books, we know your passion for romance—once you finish one of our novels, you find yourself wanting more.

May we tempt you with . . .

- **Excerpts** from our upcoming releases.

- Entertaining **extras**, including authors' personal photo albums and book lists.

- Behind-the-scenes **scoop** on your favorite characters and series.

- **Sweepstakes** for the chance to win free books, romantic getaways, and other fun prizes.

- Writing **tips** from our authors and editors.

- **Blog** with our authors and find out why they love to write romance.

- **Exclusive content** that's not contained within the pages of our novels.

Join us at
www.avonbooks.com

An Imprint of HarperCollins*Publishers*
www.avonromance.com